JUL 11 138169

NOV 10

D1564226

DATE DUE

Jayes			MM
NN E.P.			D M
BA			
Cann			
warren			
Coutts			
CC 8/200			

The Patient in Room 18

Also by Mignon G. Eberhart
in Thorndike Large Print ®

The White Cockatoo
Two Little Rich Girls
Another Woman's House
Three Days for Emeralds
Casa Madrone
Fighting Chance
Alpine Condo Crossfire
Next of Kin

The Patient in Room 18

Mignon G. Eberhart

Thorndike Press • Thorndike, Maine

Published in 1994 by arrangement with Brandt & Brandt
Literary Agency, Inc.

Thorndike Large Print ® Basic Series.

The tree indicium is a trademark of Thorndike Press.

The text of this Large Print edition is unabridged.
Other aspects of the book may vary from the original edition.

Set in 16 pt. News Plantin by Carleen Stearns.

Printed in the United States on acid-free, high opacity paper. ∞

Library of Congress Cataloging in Publication Data

Eberhart, Mignon Good, 1899–
    The patient in room 18 / by M.G. Eberhart.
        p.   cm.
    ISBN 0-7862-0086-3 (alk. paper : lg. print)
    1. Large type books. I. Title. II. Title: Patient in room
eighteen.
[PS3509.B453P33   1994]
813'.52—dc20
                                                        93-44784

To
WILLIAM AND MARGARET GOOD

CONTENTS

1

An Unpleasant Dinner Party

St. Ann's is an old hospital, sprawling in a great heap of weather-stained red brick and green ivy on the side of Thatcher Hill, a little east and south of the city of B—. The building, though remodelled and added on to here and there, still retains the great, solid walls, the gumwood and walnut woodwork, the large, old-fashioned rooms, and the general air of magnificence and dignity that characterized what was known, in the grandiloquent nineties, as the Thatcher mansion.

Time has made changes; quantities of windows, low and wide, modern plumbing, electricity, a telephone to every floor, and added wings whose brick walls have been carefully weather-stained to match the original walls are some of them. On the west is the main entrance, an imposing affair of massive doors and great travertine pillars and curving driveway. But on the south, at the extreme end of the south wing, is another and less imposing entrance, a small, semi-circular, colonial porch and a glass-paned door that leads from the hushed hospital corridor directly upon a narrow strip of grass and then shrubbery and apple orchard and willows and thickets of firs. From this door, too, is a path leading up and around the hill, and, considerably below and beyond the thickets of trees and brush, winds a road, dusty and seldom used.

The south wing is the most recently rebuilt wing of St. Ann's, and time was when Room 18 was the brightest and sunniest room of the whole wing. I say, time was. Room 18 is now cleaned and dusted regularly twice a week by two student nurses. Occasionally Miss Jones the office superintendent, tries to enter a patient in Room 18, but patients from the city remember too well the newspaper headlines — such as ROOM 18 CLAIMS ITS THIRD VICTIM — and refuse at the first hint of that significant numeral. Patients from out of town present a no less serious problem in that, even though they take the room assigned to them without demur, they invariably demand removal to another room after only a few hours' residence in Room 18. Once we tried giving the whole wing a new set of numbers but it made no difference. Room 18 was Room 18 and the patients placed there, with one exception, have never remained past midnight.

I do not know whether this situation is due to the patients mysteriously getting wind of

Room 18's history, in spite of the nurses being forbidden to speak of the unfortunate affair, or to the undoubtedly sinister aspect the room has managed to acquire. This latter has puzzled me more than a little. The room has the same hygienic and utilitarian furniture it always had, the same southeast corner location, the same outlook of close-encircling orchard and dense green shrubbery, though, of course, the shades are drawn to a decorous length, and the same rubberized floor covering. It is true that the last item may somewhat induce the atmosphere of the repellent that Eighteen's very walls seem to exude, because it holds, despite the efforts of various scrubwomen, a certain darkish stain there at the foot of the narrow bed.

It is a fact that five minutes in that too-still room bring chills up the small of my back, clammy moisture to the palms of my hands, and a singular and pressing desire to escape. And I have a good stomach, no nerves, and little imagination.

And in the long, dark hours of the second watch, between midnight and early morning, I still avoid the closed, mysterious door of Room 18!

The night it began, Corole Letheny had a dinner party up at the doctor's cottage on the hillside, at the end of the path from the south door. She telephoned hastily, late in the afternoon, for Maida Day and me. She was giving the dinner, it appeared, for a young civil engineer, a friend of Dr. Letheny's, who had dropped in unexpectedly on his way from a bridge in Uruguay to another bridge in Russia. Ordinarily I do not care for Corole's dinners, which are apt to acquire an exotic tinge that is distasteful to me, but a travel tale and an engineer allure me equally and since I did not go on duty that night until midnight I promised to come. Maida was a little harder to get, seeming, indeed, to be unusually reluctant, and her voice, as I heard it, standing beside her at the telephone, was anything but cordial.

"Never mind," I said as she hung up the receiver and Corole's warm, husky tones ceased. "Never mind. It may be quite diverting. And this is cold roast beef night here at St. Ann's."

Maida laughed.

"Corole's dinners often are — diverting," she said rather cruelly. "I shouldn't have gone but she really is in a mess. The man just arrived this afternoon and he is leaving in the morning. Corole knew, too, that we both had second watch this two weeks and that we could be away from the hospital until twelve."

"I think," I said reflectively as we strolled from the office, whither we had been called

12

to the telephone, back along the narrow corridor that leads to the south wing, "I think I shall wear my silver tissue."

Maida nodded, giving me the straight look from her intensely blue eyes that I had so grown to like in the three years that she had been a graduate nurse at St. Ann's.

"Do so, by all means," she agreed. "And put your hair up high on your head."

Maida professes to a great admiration for my hair, and I daresay it is well enough in its way; that is, if you like red hair and plenty of it. I have never cut it; no woman of my years, especially one with a high-bridged nose and inclined to embonpoint, freckles, and ground-grippers, should cut her hair.

Later, gowned in the silver tissue, and with a dark silk coat over my finery, for the June night had turned cloudy, I slipped into the south wing for a last look to be sure that everything was going well. Having been superintendent of the wing for more years than I care to mention, I feel a natural sense of responsibility. Dinner I found to be well over, seven o'clock temperatures taken, the typhoid convalescent in Eleven a bit less feverish, and the new cast on Six a little more comfortable.

Six caught at a fold of my dress admiringly.

"All dressed up?" he said. He was a nice boy, who had a tubercular hip bone and had

13

spent the last six months in a cast.

"Isn't she fine?" said Maida from the doorway. I saw the boy's eyes widen before I turned toward her.

I had grown accustomed to Maida in her stern white uniform. Now her black hair and the sword-blue of her eyes and the vivid pink that flared into her cheeks and lips at the least touch of excitement — all this, above a wispy, clinging dinner gown of midnight-blue that was somehow barely frosted in crystal beads, affected me much as it did the boy.

"Gee!" he breathed finally.

Maida laughed a little tremulously; the compliment in his eyes was pathetically genuine.

"Don't be silly, Sonny," she said, but her blue eyes shone. "How is the new cast?"

"Oh — all right," said Sonny gamely.

"I'll come in and tell you about the party when we get back," promised Maida (knowing that in the agony of a ten-hour-old cast he would still be awake.)

"Gee," sad Sonny again, "will you, Miss Day?"

"Yes," said Maida with that grave sincerity that was one of her charms. "Ready, Sarah?"

I followed Maida from the room and along the corridor south to the end of the wing. Once through the door and across the small porch we reached the path that wound through the orchard, over a small bridge, and across a field of sweet-smelling alfalfa to the Letheny cottage.

The path is not wide enough for two abreast, so Maida preceded me and I found myself studying her slim shoulders and gracefully alert carriage. Maida always seemed to me to be poised on the crest of a wave; as if she were continually victorious and yet not arrogant. She is that rare thing, a born nurse. She can deal successfully with the most difficult hypochondriacs and yet I have seen her in furious, desperate tears over a case like Sonny's. It is not my intention to rhapsodize over Maida. I suppose I admired her because she was so gloriously what I might have been in my younger days had things been a little different. Though, of course, I am not and never was the beauty that Maida was.

Well, we found Corole waiting for us and the other guests already having cocktails. Dr. Letheny greeted me as meticulously as if we had not operated together that very morning. He was a tall man, dark and thin, with an extraordinarily precise manner, and was almost too correct as to dress. He lingered a little over taking Maida's wrap and said something in a low voice that I did not understand, though Maida replied briefly and turned away, her slim black eyebrows reg-

15

istering annoyance.

Dr. Balman, Dr. Letheny's assistant, was there; a lanky man of medium height, with a thin, pale face, a high benevolent forehead, thoughtful eyes that were usually detached and rather dreamy, and a thin pointed beard that was awry now, as always, owing to a habit he had of worrying it with his slender, acid-stained fingers. His scant, light hair was ruffled and needed to be trimmed, his cravat uneven, and his dress clothes formal and old-fashioned.

There was Dr. Fred Hajek, too, pronounced "Hiyek" and referred to flippantly among the student nurses as "Hijack." He was the interne who lived at the hospital, answered the telephone nights, took care of dressings and emergencies, and generally made himself useful. He was considerably younger than the other two doctors, though one wouldn't have guessed it from his matured, well-built figure. He had a squarish head, a ruddy face with more than a hint of the foreign in it, a hint that was augmented by his small, black moustache, and dark eyes whose somewhat slanted lids looked too small for the eyes and thus gave a curious impression of tightness and restraint. He had a pleasant manner, however, and a fresh, vigorous appearance that was not unattractive.

Then my eyes were caught by a blond young

16

giant who advanced as Corole spoke.

"Jim Gainsay," she murmured casually over her creamy brown shoulder as she offered Maida a cocktail.

He said something or other to me politely but I saw his keen eyes go to Maida and linger there as if unable to take themselves away, while I quite deliberately took stock of this tall young fellow with bronzed hands and face who built bridges here and there over the world and looked as if he hadn't more than got out of university. In fact, a fraternity crest gleamed on the surface of the thin, white-gold cigarette case that he held open in one hand as if the sight of Maida had frozen him in the very act of drawing out a cigarette. On closer observation, however, I was obliged to revise my hasty estimate. There were wrinkles about his eyes; his sun-tanned eyebrows were a straight, inscrutable line almost meeting over his nose; his jaw was lean and rather ruthless; his smooth-fitting Tuxedo disclosed lines that were muscular, without an ounce of super-fluous flesh. Here was a man accustomed to dealing with other men; yes, and of shaping them to suit his own ends, or I was no judge of character.

And just then Huldah, Corole's one maid, announced dinner somewhat breathlessly as if she must fly back to the kitchen, and we all took our places around the long, candle-lit table.

The soup was bad and the fish poorly seasoned, but the Virginia-baked ham was delicious and I found myself warming to the soft, wavering lights, the gleam of silver and glass and flowers, the white and black contrasts presented by the men setting off Maida's red-and-white beauty and Corole's rather blatant charm. Corole had charm, in spite of my questionable adjective — charm of a sort rather flagrant and too warm, but still it was difficult not to fall a little under its sway. She sat at the foot of the table with Jim Gainsay on one side and Dr. Hajek on the other. Her hair was arranged in flat, metallic, gold waves and she wore a strange gown of gold sequins with gleams of green showing through. It clung smoothly to her and was extremely low in the back, showing Corole's brownish skin almost to the waist, and I could not help speculating on the probable reaction of our board of directors to such a gown worn by our head doctor's housekeeper. Corole was a cousin of Dr. Letheny's and had kept house for him since the death of old Madame Letheny. We knew little of her history and I should have liked to know more, though I am not inquisitive. I often wondered what circumstances produced the brown-skinned, gold-haired

Corole we knew. She was a great deal like a luxuriant Persian cat; she even had topaz eyes and a peculiarly lazy grace.

The conversation during the dinner was rather languid. Corole did not seem much concerned about the dinner, but she was a little abstracted, though automatically, if one-sidedly, flirting with Jim Gainsay, who had eyes for no one but Maida. That was very clear to me, though none of the others seemed to notice it — with the possible exception of Dr. Letheny, who saw everything through the perpetual cloud of cigarette smoke that almost obscured his narrow, dark eyes. Dr. Balman was frankly absorbed in dinner and admitted that he had been interested in a laboratory experiment and had not eaten during the day.

"But you left it to come to my dinner," smiled Corole.

"Oh, no," said Dr. Balman flatly, without looking up from his salad. "I had finished anyhow."

"Oh," said Corole, and Dr. Letheny's thin mouth curved the least bit.

"So you have been bridge-building in Uruguay?" I addressed Jim Gainsay. He turned his keen eyes steadily toward me.

"Yes."

"I suppose Uruguay is now prosperous, European, and civilized?" I went on, hoping to get him started telling of some of the adventures that must have befallen him. I have an explorer's instincts and stay-at-home habits, so have to get my travels by proxy.

"Yes. Though the remoter portions are still, in some respects, the Banda Oriental."

"The Banda Oriental?" said Corole blankly.

"The Purple Land that England lost," said Maida softly, and Gainsay's eyes met hers with quick interest — interest and something more.

Corole's eyelids flickered.

"Serve coffee in the Doctor's study, Huldah," she said. "And open the windows."

The night had turned unbelievably sultry while we sat at the table, so hot that the very breath of the tapers seemed unbearable and we all felt relieved, I think, to leave the table and dispose ourselves comfortably in the great, cushioned chairs and divans in Dr. Letheny's study. The one lamp on the table was enough, though it left the room for the most part in shadow — rather uncanny green shadow, for the lamp was shaded with green silk and fringe. The windows had been flung to the top but there was not a breeze stirring, even here on the windward side of the hill, and it was so quiet that we could hear the katydids and crickets down in the orchard, and the faint strains of radio music from the open windows of the hospital, whose lights gleamed dully through the trees.

"Radio in a hospital?" queried Jim Gainsay amusedly.

"Lord, yes!" Dr. Letheny's voice was edgy. "You have been out of the world a long time, Jim, not to know that a fashionable hospital must have all the latest fancies, including the best radio set to be had, with specially made loud-speakers connecting with it in every room. The money that is wasted," he added bitterly, "on such notions could be employed to a good deal better advantage in other ways. How can we make much headway in research if all our money must be thrown away on — on lawns and flowers —" he waved impatiently toward the hospital — "on expensive apparatus that we seldom if ever use, on eight-thousand-dollar ambulances, on weather-staining bricks, on —"

"On radios," suggested Gainsay blandly.

Dr. Letheny smiled faintly but the hand that lit a fresh cigarette seemed a little unsteady.

"On radios," he agreed.

"You are right though, Dr. Letheny." Dr. Balman, who had apparently been engaged in digesting his dinner, spoke so suddenly that I jumped. He lounged toward the window and stood with his hands in his pockets looking down at St. Ann's lights.

"You are right," he repeated. "If I had one-half the money that is thrown away down there the experiment that failed for me this afternoon might have succeeded." The bitterness in his voice was so grim that I think we all felt a little startled and uncomfortable. All, that is, except Corole, whose feelings are not easily accessible and who was manipulating the coffee machine over by the lamp. Its light brought the flat, gold waves of her hair into relief.

"Here is the coffee," she said huskily. "As coffee should be: black as night, hot as hell, and sweet as love." She offered the tiny cup to Gainsay.

Well, the rest of us had heard her say that before and Gainsay did not appear to hear her now. I could see that she was hesitating on the verge of repetition, but she was too wise for that.

"Can't you stop needless expenditure?" asked Gainsay.

"Stop it?" Dr. Letheny laughed acidly. "Stop it when the hospital is privately endowed and the board of directors a bunch of ignorant, conceited asses! Look at this matter of radium. Nothing must do but that we buy a whole gram of radium. They had heard of radium. Other hospitals had it. Radium we must have and radium we bought. But try to talk to them of research, of discovering a new remedy for an old need, of the necessity for laboratories, for equipment, for study. You might as well try to stop the thunder storm that is coming as to ask them to see anything that is not squarely in front of their fat stomachs."

"But radium," said Gainsay mildly, "is a good thing for a hospital to have, isn't it? I thought it a great discovery."

"Of course, of course!" broke in Dr. Balman. "But we don't need that much. Half a gram, a fourth of it — even a sixth of it would have served our purpose. But no! We must spend sixty-five thousand dollars for one tiny gram of radium. Sixty-five thousand dollars! And to my plea for half of that — only half of that money — they laughed. Laughed at study! At research! At laboratories and equipment! And called me a visionary. God! A visionary!"

It must have been that the increasing sultriness of the night and the tension of the approaching storm made us all a little nervous and easily stirred. A curious hush followed Franz Balman's outbreak, during which I became aware of the heavy breathing of Dr. Hajek near me. I stirred impatiently and moved away. I had never either liked or disliked Fred Hajek, but that night I felt suddenly a sharp distaste for him. The atmosphere in the room seemed unbearably heavy and I shivered a little despite the heat and wondered if my dinner was not going to agree with me.

Gainsay got up, moved to get an ash tray, and sat down again in another chair. I noted that the move brought him nearer Maida, whose fine white profile was visible in the shadow near the window. She did not smoke — not, I believe, from any fastidious prejudice, but merely from distaste — and her hands, delicate yet strong, lay passively on the carved arms of the chair. She was the kind of person whose silences seem thoughtful and neither flat nor detached; a most companionable person to have around.

Corole noted the move, too, for she took my seat next to Hajek and murmured something under her breath to him.

"Are you both experimenting in the same field?" asked Gainsay, his ordinary, easy tone making my disquiet seem uncalled-for and silly.

"No," said Dr. Letheny shortly.

"No," said Dr. Balman. He turned abruptly away from the window and sat down at the shadowy end of the davenport; his shirt front thrust itself up in an ungainly hump but he did not appear to care.

"Well," said Corole, "if I were a millionaire I should give you both the money to work to your heart's content."

"Indeed." Dr. Letheny spoke so satirically that I feared an outburst from our hostess, whose temper was never of the best.

But she surprised me.

"No!" she retracted with disarming frankness. From habit Corole could lie like a trooper, but when she was inclined toward truth-telling she was quite candidly honest. "No," she went on, "if I had a million dollars I should spend it — oh, *how* I should spend it! Silks and furs and jewels and servants and cars and cities and —"

"By that time it would be gone," observed Dr. Letheny drily.

"Maybe," Corole laughed huskily. "But how gloriously gone."

"I suppose," began Fred Hajek, with a little of the awkwardness that assails one who has remained silent a long time while others of the group are talking, "I suppose that idea is a sort of unacknowledged fairy dream hidden in everyone's mind."

"Of course." Dr. Letheny's voice grated to my ears. "Everybody wants money. Usually for reasons such as Corole has so charmingly admitted."

"Not always," disagreed Gainsay. "You and — er — Dr. Balman have just agreed that you both needed it for research."

"A selfish reason, though," replied Dr. Letheny. "We get the same pleasurable reaction out of study and science that Corole does out of clothes and jewels and — cream in general. Miss Keate, over there," he nodded toward me, "gets the same kick out of hard work and a smooth-running hospital routine. Only her — demands — are not so expensive."

His tone irritated me. It may be true that I am considered something of a martinet, especially among the student nurses, but somebody has to see to things.

"Nonsense," I spoke sharply. "I want money just as much as anybody."

I suppose my words rang sincere, for Dr. Letheny sat up.

"What is your repressed desire, Sarah Keate?" he demanded with just the shade of amusement in his voice that always riled me. "Come on, out with it! Do you long for the gay night life? Or have you secret urges to become a front-page sensation?"

And I must say that, in the light of what was to occur, it was remarkable that he said just that.

"She might make a splendid aviatrix," said Jim Gainsay, smiling into the dusk.

After that I was not going to tell them that above all things I longed to travel and that everybody knows travel costs money. I said curtly:

"Everybody wants money."

"How about you, Maida?" broke in Corole rather maliciously.

Maida is, as a rule, almost too perfect at the art of concealing her emotions. It may have been that the semi-darkness of the room concealed an intended air of frivolousness, or it may have been that the threat of the approaching storm plucked at her nerves and pierced her habitual armour of reserve. At any rate her answer was unexpected.

"Money!" she said. "Money! I think I would give my very soul for money!"

Of course, I knew she didn't mean that. But Dr. Letheny shot her a glance that fairly pierced the dusk, Corole laughed a little metallic ripple, and Jim Gainsay turned straightway around in his chair to face Maida's shadowed eyes.

"I haven't any money," he said directly and quite as if Maida had asked him a question, though I think the others were too preoccupied to observe this. "I haven't any money at all."

"And are you happy without it, Jim?" asked Corole, her warm voice caressing.

"Well . . ." Jim Gainsay paused. "I was, until lately."

He was still speaking to Maida. I believe Dr. Letheny understood that somewhat singular fact, also, for he spoke so quietly that there was a suggestion of deliberate restraint about his words.

"And what do you intend to do in the face of this sudden realization?"

"Make some money," replied Jim Gainsay simply.

Dr. Letheny laughed — not pleasantly.

"But my dear fellow, is it so simple as that?"

"It should not be difficult." Gainsay did not appear to be disturbed by the perceptible edge of irony in Dr. Letheny's questions.

"Owing to the fact that several billions of people over the face of the earth are engaged in profitless efforts in that direction, will you tell us just how you propose to accomplish it with such expedition?"

"Certainly not. If I can manage to lay my hands on — say — fifty thousand I can make — oh, as much money as I want. I can do it. And I will." He was grave and yet quite casual. A mere matter of information for Maida. If she wanted money he would see that she got it and that was that! It seemed so clear to me that I felt something very like embarrassment, though neither Maida nor Jim Gainsay seemed disturbed.

"Fifty thousand dollars," mused Dr.

Letheny softly. "That is quite a lot of money. Many a man has failed for its — inaccessibility."

"I'll get it all right," said Jim Gainsay.

"And when you get it what are you going to do with it? How are you going to make it grow into as much money as you want?"

"Contracting." There was an undercurrent in the short reply that warned Dr. Letheny off.

Corole laughed again.

"Funny!" she said. "Every single one of us has confessed to a fervent desire for money. That is, all but Franz and Dr. Hajek. And we all know that Franz would give his very eyes — no, he needs them for experiment — ten years of his life, then, for money to carry on those same precious experiments."

"It is a good thing we are all law-abiding citizens," I remarked drily.

"I think I shall be on the safe side, though, and lock up my jewels to-night!" said Corole.

"Don't be a fool," observed Dr. Letheny.

Corole's topaz eyes caught a glint of angry green light.

"Why, really, Louis, being what one can't help is better, at any rate, than longing for what one can't get."

Her somewhat stupid reply did not, to my mind, warrant its effect. Dr. Letheny moved suddenly upright in his chair, his thin lips drawn tight over his teeth.

"Until later, dear cousin." The words had a sharp edge of fury. "Until later. We have guests at present."

I could only suppose that the stifling atmosphere had disturbed Dr. Letheny's always hair-trigger nerves. Otherwise he had not been so needlessly vulgar. He was a brilliant man with a cutting tongue, but gossip had whispered that what Corole lacked in the way of brains she more than made up for in feline cunning of attack. This was the first time, however, that I had heard the two ill-assorted housemates come to open and bad-mannered warfare.

Dr. Hajek relieved the strained silence that naturally followed the little contretemps.

"I hear that you used the radium to-day." He had a peculiarly inflectionless manner of speech that made him seem heavy and dull.

"Yes." Dr. Letheny rose and pulled the curtain still farther from the window. "Torrid night, isn't it? Yes, we are trying it for old Mr. Jackson." He paused. "I don't know that it will do any good," he added callously. "But we may as well try it. By the way, Miss Keate, I shall be in shortly after midnight to see how the patient is getting on. You might leave the south door unlocked for me. Let me see —

he is in Room 18, isn't he?"

"Yes, Doctor."

"So you are going to Russia on another bridge project, Jim?" Dr. Letheny was again master of himself.

"What — oh, yes! Yes." Jim Gainsay started a little as if Dr. Letheny had recalled him to a forgotten fact.

"Will it be a long stay?"

"Why, yes, probably. It should take about two or three years. It will be an interesting job. The preliminaries are rather sketchy, but it looks as though there might be some problems involved."

He spoke in an oddly detached way, as if he were not much interested in the subject, and it was not surprising that the conversation flattened out again. Presently Corole suggested bridge and even made up a table, but Dr. Balman definitely refused to play and Jim Gainsay, being engaged in watching Maida's eyelashes, did not appear to hear Corole's suggestion that he make a fourth, so Dr. Letheny made a reluctant partner for me against Corole and Dr. Hajek. However, we played only a few desultory hands until Maida and Gainsay drifted over to the window and fell into a low-voiced conversation, when Dr. Letheny, who had been darting quick glances in that direction, trumped my ace, flung down his cards, said it was too rotten hot to play and, paying no attention to Corole's protests, went to the piano.

Dr. Letheny was a discriminative musician of far more than amateur skill, and the great, jarring, Moscow bells of the C Sharp Minor Prelude presently surged over the room. I am a practical, matter-of-fact woman and I have never been able to account for the strange disquietude that crept over me as I listened. It was the strangest thing in a strange and unreal evening. The couple at the window turned and moved closer together. Corole's flat eyes caught the light like a cat's. Dr. Balman stared at nothing from the shadows and worried his beard. Only Dr. Hajek was unmoved by that passionate sweep of sound.

All at once the room was intolerable to me. I twisted about in my chair and fought down a childish desire to run from its heat and breathlessness. And then the keys under Dr. Letheny's white fingers slipped into the higher notes of the second movement and a hot, fetid breath of air from the hushed night billowed the curtain a little and touched my hot face and heightened the nightmare that had taken possession of me.

By the time the climax had carried us all along with it in its torrent, and the Doctor had sat, in the hush that followed the last note, for a long moment before he turned to us again, — by that time little beads of perspiration shone all along the backs of my hands and my heart was pumping as if I had been running a race.

I rose.

"I must go," I said, my voice breaking harshly into the silence. "I must go. It is nearly twelve."

"Yes," said Maida. "Yes. We must go."

Somehow we got away. I remember being vaguely surprised when Jim Gainsay merely took Maida's hand for a conventional instant, although I'm sure I don't know what I had expected.

Maida and I walked slowly, feeling our way through the great, black velvet curtain that was the night. The hospital was now darkened and the path twisted unexpectedly. The air was as heavy with the presage of storm, there under the trees, as it had been in Corole's lamp-lit house. The sky was thick and black with not the glimmer of a star showing through. The katydids and crickets were all hushed as if waiting. The path was hot under our thin-soled slippers, the alfalfa sickeningly sweet in its warm breath, the shadows of the thickets were dense and not a leaf stirred. I know that orchard and those clusters of trees and elderberries and sumac as well as I know

33

the twists and turns of the old hospital corridors, and never until that night did I catch my breath when my hand brushed against a leaf, or take a long sigh of relief when we emerged from those suddenly unfriendly thickets into the silence of the long, night-lighted corridor of the south wing.

Up in the everyday surroundings of the nurses' dormitory I still failed to shake off the sense of the unreal that had come over me. Together we changed into our crisp, white uniforms. I remember we talked of silly, inconsequential things — such as the sogginess of the bread pudding we had had for lunch, and the new cufflinks that Maida was inserting into her cuffs. They were small squares of lapis-lazuli edged in engraved whitegold. Lovely though they were, they yet contrived to be simple and dignified at the same time.

"I like lapis," said Maida without much interest. "I like things that are real." She was adjusting her proud, white cap as she spoke. In spite of the business-like white linen that became her so well, she was still the flushed and vivid Maida of the blue and crystal-frosted dinner gown, whose eyes had grown starry under Jim Gainsay's regard. I sighed as I pinned on my own cap. I had always felt that if love came to Maida it would be swift and compelling.

I thrust in the pin too forcefully and withdrew my scratched thumb with an irritated exclamation. I had read somewhere that thin old maids were pathetic and fat old maids gross and all old maids sentimental, and had resolved to be none of the three, myself.

So, I was not in the best of moods as I wound my watch, took my way to the south wing, and stopped at the desk for a glance at the charts. If only the storm would break and give us a breath of fresh, cool air.

The two nurses going off duty were very evidently glad to be relieved.

"It is a queer night," said one of them, Olma Flynn. "Makes me feel creepy."

"H'm," I spoke brusquely. "Likely you have been eating green apples again." And she flounced indignantly away.

2

In Room 18

That night began much the same as other nights and with no suggestion of the events it was to unfold. There was the usual twelve-o'clock stir of drinks and temperatures and pulses and hot pillows to be turned and electric fans to be brought. The only unusual thing, and that was natural enough, was that the sick patients had turned restless under the heat and the breathless hint of storm and were fretful and somewhat peevish. We were very busy for some time, but I remembered to leave the south door unlocked for Dr. Letheny's call.

It happened that I was in the corridor when he came in about twelve-thirty. The gleaming white and black of his pearl-studded shirt front and smooth-fitting dinner jacket were incongruous in the bare, night-lighted hall, with its long length of white walls, shadowy now in the darkness that was relieved only by the shaded light over the chart desk at the far end, and the tiny red signal lights that glowed here and there over sick-room doors. A hospital is never a cheerful place, especially at night, and its long, dark corridors with black voids for doors, and its faint odours of ether and antiseptics and sickness are not, to say the least, conducive to good spirits.

Dr. Letheny was still nervous and irritable. He gave Mr. Jackson a rather cursory glance, felt his pulse for a moment, and examined the dressing. The trouble he was trying to cure with radium was in the patient's left breast and the radium itself, placed as is usual in a sort of box that is especially made for the purpose, was arranged in such a manner that its rays would penetrate the afflicted area. It was held in place by means of wide straps of adhesive, and would have been, to the layman, a strange-appearing affair. All was well and the patient seemingly reacting as favourably as might be expected, so Dr. Letheny did not linger. After rearranging the pillows and turning out the light over the bed, I followed the Doctor into the corridor. He paused for a few moments, asking me unimportant questions as to various patients in the wing, and smoking rapidly, regardless of the rules which he himself had made against smoking in the hospital. More than once I caught his gaze travelling past me down the corridor toward the diet kitchen and drug room, and finally he asked me outright if Miss Day was on duty.

"Yes," I said. "She is about — somewhere in the wing," thinking, as I replied, that I had not seen Maida for a few moments. Doubtless, however, she was busy with some patient, or paying her promised visit to Sonny.

He lingered for a little after that, but presently strolled to the south door and disappeared. I did not follow him and lock the door according to custom; it was breathlessly hot, as I have said, and we needed every atom of air that we could get. Later, when the rain came, I should close it.

An errand took me to the diet kitchen; as I passed down the length of the darkened corridor I glanced into the open doors along the way but did not catch a glimpse of Maida's white uniform. The place was very hot and very still and the vases of flowers along the walls, on the floor outside various doors, sent up a hot, sickening breath. I snapped on the light in the diet kitchen, wishing as I did so that there were more lights in the corridor outside. I had to search for and open a fresh bottle of beef extract, so it took me some time to prepare the beef tea, but at length I started into the corridor with the cup in hand. As I reached the door I glanced down the hall toward the south door just in time to see a white uniform gleam against the blackness of the night as it entered from the porch outside.

It was Maida, of that I was sure, for her movements were unmistakable, and just as the thought ran through my mind that she had been outside trying to get a breath of fresh air, I also realized that I had no spoon to accompany the beef tea and turned back into the diet kitchen. Someone had cleaned the silver drawer that day, and it took me a moment or two to find a spoon, and when I entered the corridor again I met Maida face to face.

In the dim light it seemed to me that she was very white, but in that night-lighted corridor nothing retains its normal colour, so I thought nothing of it.

"I was wondering where you had gone to," I said carelessly as I passed her.

She regarded my casual remark as an inquiry.

"I — I've been with Sonny," she said. Her voice was unsteady.

"Poor boy, he is having a hard time," I murmured and went on. It was not until I was standing beside Eleven watching him drink the beef tea that I recalled with a little start that she had not been with Sonny, that I had seen her with my own eyes coming into the corridor from the porch.

Beef tea and Eleven did not go well together; in fact, a few moments after drinking it he was violently sick and for about a quarter of an hour I was fully occupied with him. I had closed the door into the corridor at first symptoms of his unhappy reaction, so that the disturbance should not arouse patients in near-by rooms. I stayed with him until he was back on his pillows again, quiet and exhausted, then I turned out the light, opened the door into the corridor, and left him. The hall was silent and dark and not a signal light gleamed in the whole length.

I felt a little ill myself from the heat and stifling air, and judging it to be a good time, I slipped quietly to the south door and let myself out onto the little colonial porch. The air was a shade less fetid there and I remember standing for a moment or two at the curved railing. The dim light coming from the door back of me made a little circle on the porch, faintly lighter than the surrounding night, and beyond that stretched thick blackness. Far below me toward the west twinkled vaguely the lights of the city and above on the hillside I caught the barest glimpse of green light through the trees; it was shining from Dr. Letheny's study. All else was impenetrable darkness.

I could not have stood there for more than five minutes when without any warning an inexplicable thing occurred.

There was a sudden, sharp little whisper

of motion from somewhere back of me, something flew past my shoulder, caught for a fleeting second the reflection of a light from the corridor back of me, and was gone into the dense shadows of the shrubbery, beyond the railing.

The thing was gone before I could realize that it had actually happened.

I started, drew in my breath sharply, and stifled the exclamation that rose to my lips. I stared in the direction the thing, whatever it was, had taken and strained my eyes to see into the thick black void that surrounded the porch. It was exactly as if an arrow, small and sharp and gleaming, had been shot from somewhere behind me into the shrubbery. But no one shoots arrows from hospitals in the dead of night.

I rubbed my eyes angrily and, but for the sharp little whisper of sound the thing made as it passed me, would have doubted their evidence. But that sound, coupled with the flash of light, was conclusive. Someone had deliberately thrown some small article with all the force at his command across the porch and into the shrubbery that extends downward into the orchard. It had come from one of the windows at either side of the door or from the door itself. Hastily in my thoughts I ran over the patients then in the wing. Not one of them was able to walk. Maida was the only person in the wing who could have been about, and what on earth was Maida throwing out into the night!

Feeling this to be a curious circumstance that should be investigated I took a few steps toward the path that leads from the east corner of the little porch. It was very dark there, and without pausing to reflect that in the night I could never find the thing that so puzzled me and that was now hidden somewhere in the orchard, I groped for the iron railing and made my way cautiously down the two or three steps. I paused at the path, my ear caught by the sound of footsteps. And at the very instant, the sudden little rush of sound came closer swiftly and someone running at top speed along the outside wall of the hospital collided with me, gasped, swore, caught me in mid-air and set me on my feet again and was gone, leaving me trying to get my breath and dazedly righting my cap. I could hear his footsteps still running along the little path toward the bridge.

"Well —" I said. "Well —" and found myself both angry and frightened. People have no right to run around hospitals at night, knocking middle-aged nurses about and swearing and what not. Who was this midnight prowler?

Evidently the man was up to no good purpose and as evidently he was in a hurry to get away. My heart began to beat rapidly as I walked along the hospital north in the direction the man had come from. But the windows above me all seemed dark and undisturbed. Built on the slope of the hill as St. Ann's is, the windows are at varying heights from the ground, some of them not more than three or four feet above it, but I doubted if an intruder could have made his way into that silent wing without arousing it. I walked as far as the lighted window of the diet kitchen. It, too, was open and I could see the top of Maida's white cap as she stood at the farther end of the small room.

All seemed quiet and I dismissed the half-formed notion of rousing Higgins, the janitor and so-called night-watchman, and demanding a thorough search of the premises. I was still uneasy, however, as I retraced my steps, and I drew back into the shadow of the orchard in order to see into the windows of the wing without, possibly, myself being seen.

It was just as I passed the thick clump of elderberry bushes about midway of the long wing that my foot struck something in the grass that gave a dully metallic sound. I reached over to fumble in the grass and picked up a small, flat object, smooth and hard. I turned it rapidly over in my hands. It was pitchy dark there in the shadows and the air was extraordinarily close. I slipped the object I held into my pocket for future examination and as I did so I sniffed. There was something in the air — some familiar odour — but something entirely out of place in an apple orchard. It was — a swift vision of the operating room rose before me and I realized that my nostrils had caught a faint but unmistakable odour of ether.

Ether in an apple orchard! And in the middle of the night! Why, it was impossible! Something in the heated air, some mingling of alfalfa and sweet clover and growing things had combined to deceive me. I shrugged, tried to laugh, and feeling all at once that absurd fear that something is about to clutch at your heels, I hurried through the dense shadows toward the little porch. It was still deserted.

I recall glancing up at the impenetrable sky and catching, away off toward the south, a faint gleam of lightning. Surely the storm would break soon and I would be relieved of this feeling of oppression that was strangely mingled with something very like fear.

The corridor, too, was still deserted. Maida was not in sight, and as I looked a red signal light down toward the chart desk clicked. I went to answer it, my starched skirts whispering along the hushed hall.

It was Three, begging for a bromide, and it took me a few moments to convince her of the fact that she didn't in the least need it.

Then I sat down at the desk, which is at the north end of the corridor, opposite the south door, with all the shadowy length of gray-white walls and dark doors of the corridor intervening. A shaded light over this desk is the sole illumination and a person seated at the desk faces the chart rack and has her back turned to the corridor. It remained hot and very still and I wondered if the wind that accompanies our western thunder storms would not soon rise.

I had not more than entered Three's pulse and the time — one-thirty — when a sudden sound, dull and heavy, brought me standing, facing the corridor and unaccountably startled. Only the bare walls met my eyes. Perhaps the south door had blown shut. It had sounded like the muffled bang of a door — or possibly like a window that had dropped to the sill. The chart in my hand, I walked quickly through the corridor to the south door. It was still open and I felt no breeze.

As near as I could tell the sound that had aroused me had come from this end of the wing. The door of Room 17 was open and a glance assured me that the window was still open for I could see the dim shadow of the sash. The door of Eighteen was closed, however, so I opened it cautiously in order not to wake Mr. Jackson. I did not enter the room; I stood there only for a moment, holding the door half open and peering through the dim light from the corridor. The patient was lying quiet and the window seemed to be open, so I closed the door as gently as I had opened it and took my way down the corridor again.

And when I reached the chart desk I found that my knees were trembling and there was a little damp beading under my cap.

"It is the night," I assured myself. "It is a nerve-racking night. I shall suffocate if I don't get some air."

But nevertheless I felt nervous and ill at ease. I forced myself to study the charts, and in the middle of Eleven's temperature chart I recalled the small flat object I had found in the orchard. I was in the very act of drawing it from my pocket when, with a swoop of wind through the corridor, a blinding flash of lightning and a crash of thunder, the storm broke.

I ran the whole length of the corridor. The wind was sweeping along it with such fury that my skirts were pulled back tight around me, my cap slipped back on my head, and several top-heavy vases of flowers must have blown over for we found them so later. With some difficulty I closed the door. As I fastened it, leaving the key in the lock in my haste, I could see through the panes of glass the first great spatters of rain, and down below the hospital on the little back road shone the lights of a hurrying automobile. Then they were gone and another flash of lightning nearly blinded me and there was a sharp crackle and sputter. Simultaneously the light went out as if by black magic, leaving me alone in the dark with eighteen windows to get down and eighteen patients to reassure.

I knew in an instant what had occurred; the power line from the city had been struck and the fuses burnt out or some such matter. Where was Maida? The rain was coming in torrents by the time I had felt my way into Room 17 and closed the window. Occasional lightning aided me as I groped my way to Room 18, crossed it and pulled down that window. As I turned toward the door again a bright flash of lightning lit up the whole room and in the brief second I saw that the patient had not roused in spite of the tumult of the storm. He lay still. Too still.

Then the light was gone and, scarcely knowing what I did, I reached the bed and put my hand on his face and sought his pulse.

A seasoned nurse knows when death has

come. Even in the gibbering darkness with the storm outside crashing against the window I knew at once that our patient was dead.

Standing there for what seemed an eternity, but what was actually not more than a moment or two, my mind raced over the situation and strove to comprehend it. There was no reason for his death of which I knew. Barring the affliction for which he was being treated and which in its present stage had not been critical, our patient had been in good health only an hour or so ago. What had caused this? It could not have been heart failure for his heart had been sound.

I must have a light. I must call Dr. Letheny. I must — There was the sound of windows being lowered. I found my way to the door. If I could make Maida hear me — but, of course, I couldn't through the confusion of patients calling out from fright as they found the lights failing to go on, and the constant roll of thunder and crashing of rain. The flashes of lightning were frequent and I caught a fleeting glimpse of Maida crossing the corridor farther down the hall.

It would be of no use to call her; furthermore, she was busy. I disliked leaving Eighteen with no one in the room, but I must have a light. I ran down the length of the corridor — it seemed long and unfamiliar — groped in a drawer of the cupboard in the diet kitchen, found the burnt end of a candle and some matches, and flew back to Room 18. At the door I met Maida. Our faces gleamed eerily in the lightning and then vanished into darkness.

"Isn't this awful!" she cried. "Where were you! Every window in the wing was open. And the lights have gone out! What — what in the world are you doing?"

She was at my elbow in Room 18. My fingers shook so that I could scarcely light the candle, and when I did succeed it made only a feeble little flicker that did not dispel the shadows.

She followed me to the bed.

"Why, Sarah! Is he —" She reached over to place her hand on his face as I had done. *"He is dead!"*

Setting the candle on the table, I pushed aside the covers to find his heart. If there were the least flicker of life, something could yet be done. But there was not.

It was as I drew back that I made the astounding discovery.

The box that held the radium was gone! Adhesive and all had been stripped clean!

"Look —" I tried to cry out but a roll of thunder that shook the very foundations drowned my voice. I pointed with a finger

49

that shook and held the futile little flame nearer, while Maida searched frantically among the sheets.

It was a useless search. That I knew even in the moment of lowering my candle to look under the bed. The dead man had not torn from himself that box with the wide strips of adhesive.

Arising from my knees I stared across the narrow bed into Maida's panic-stricken eyes.

The very storm outside quieted for a second as if to give my words significance.

"He is dead," I whispered. "And the radium is gone!"

She nodded, her hands at her throat, her face as white as her cap.

The tiny flame wavered and jumped and threatened to go out, the shadows in the room crept nearer, the gusts of wind and rain beat upon the black window pane with renewed fervour.

"We must telephone to Dr. Letheny. Then get lights and see to the wing. Will you go down to the office and telephone to the Doctor? I shall stay — with this."

Maida's eyes widened and she flung out her hands with an odd gesture of panic.

"No," she stammered. "No. I — I *can't* call Dr. Letheny!"

Not knowing what to say I stared at her.

50

Suddenly she straightened her shoulders and mastered her agitation.

"Yes," she said. "Yes. I'll call him immediately."

I was too disturbed to worry over Maida's aversion to telephoning to Dr. Letheny, although it was to recur to me later. I set the candle down again, wishing that the lights would come on and that my knees would not shake.

It was clear to me, even in those first terrifying moments, that the radium had been stolen. And a hideous conjecture was slowly settling upon me. It did not seem possible that my patient had died a natural death!

What had caused his death?

It is strange how one's hair prickles at the roots when one is frightened. My hair stirred and I peered fearfully about the room. A curious sense of something evil and loathsome near at hand was creeping over me. The room, however, was as bare as any hospital room. I even took the candle in my hand, and holding my teeth tight together to restrain a disposition toward chattering, I made a circuit of the room, holding the candle into the corners. Of course, there was nothing there. Indeed, there was scarcely any place to hide in the whole room. There were the usual shallow closets, two of them, barely large enough for

51

a patient's travelling bag and clothes. I opened one closet which held a bag and a light over-coat. The other one was locked and the key gone, probably lost by some student nurse.

The candle was dripping hot wax on my hand so I placed it again on a saucer on the table.

Maida had been gone for some time, surely time enough to rouse the whole hospital staff. A thousand fears crossed my mind while I stood there waiting; my eyes kept travelling from one corner of the room to the other, and the feeling of a presence near me other than that of the dead man on the bed became stronger with the dragging seconds.

I was beginning to think that I could remain no longer in that fear-haunted room, with only the ghastly flickering of the candle-light for company, when there was a quick rush of foot-steps and Maida was in the room, panting, her eyes black and frightened.

"Dr. Letheny is out," she cried. "Corole didn't know where he was. She said he wasn't anywhere in the house. She thought he had gone for a walk in the orchard and got caught in the storm."

"A fine time to go for a walk," I cried, fright making me irritable.

"So then I telephoned to Dr. Balman," went on Maida hurriedly. "It was so dark I couldn't see the directory, so I had to ask Information for the number. He finally answered and said he would be right out. It's as dark as a black cat all over the building."

"Did you call Dr. Hajek?"

"Yes. That is, I knocked at his door and called him several times but couldn't wake him. Girls from other wings are running around in the dark, there near the general office. Nobody has lights and the bell that connects with the basement is out of order. At least, they can't rouse Higgins."

I thought rapidly. Such a situation! No lights, a storm, frightened patients — it only needed the news of the radium theft and this strange death to complete our demoralization.

"We can't both leave this room," I thought aloud. "We must not leave him alone. His death is so strange — so —"

Maida must have been struck with something in my manner for she gripped my arm.

"What do you mean?"

"I mean," I replied with difficulty, speaking through oddly stiff lips, "I mean that — I'm afraid this is — is murder."

She shrank back, her face as white as the dishevelled sheets.

"Not — that!"

"You see, he was in good condition. And combined with the theft of the radium — Oh!

53

I know it is a fearful thing to suspect. But what explanation is there?"

"Who could have done it? How —"

"I don't know." With an effort I pulled myself together, forced myself to think. "We have no time to think of that now. We must keep things going — get a doctor." I paused, eyeing her dubiously. "Could you stay here with — with it — while I go to the office, rouse Dr. Hajek and the janitor, and get some sort of lights?"

She glanced from the bed, where her horrified eyes had fastened themselves, to the feeble ray of the candle.

"The candle is almost burnt out," she whispered.

"I know," I said. "I'll hurry."

Her lips tightened to a thin white line.

"Hurry."

Once groping my way through that dark corridor I was vaguely surprised to find my hands like ice and my face damp. My mind was whirling but one thought was predominant: I must not leave Maida alone for long in that terrifying room with what it held, I must hurry.

As I turned into the corridor running east and west, that connects the south wing with the main portion of the hospital, the storm burst upon the place with renewed savagery.

At another time the fury of the thunder and lightning and wind and rain would have appalled me, but then it seemed all in a piece with what I feared had happened.

I have only a chaotic memory of colliding with various other nurses, of ringing for the janitor, of calling the Electric Power Company only to hear a pert-voiced operator tell me that the wires must be down in our direction, of being afraid that the matches the nurses were lighting would set fire to the whole place, and of bruising my knuckles on Dr. Hajek's door. He finally opened it, and I was so unstrung by that time that at the sound of his slow voice I clutched into the darkness with both hands. My touch encountered his coat, which was damp.

"Go to Room 18," I stammered, half-sobbing from fear. "Hurry, Doctor. Room 18 in the south wing."

"It is dark. Can't you turn on the lights?" he said stupidly.

"The lights have gone out. The storm — Hurry!" I believe I pushed him toward the door. Somebody had found a lamp and the hall was full of weird, wavering shadows.

"What is it? What has happened?" asked some nurse at my elbow.

I have never known what I replied; I remember only her frightened, pale face. But somehow I restored things to a semblance of order, mercifully thought of some lamps and candles that were in the storeroom, unearthed a couple of flashlights and sent someone to wake Olma Flynn to help out in the south wing. Then, taking the flashlights, I hurried back to the wing.

At the door of Room 18 I paused.

Maida was standing beside a table, staring downward, her face paper-white; her sleeves had been rolled up and a wisp of dark hair across her cheek gave her a curiously dishevelled appearance. Dr. Hajek was standing at the foot of the bed; he was gripping the footrail with such force that the knuckles on his small hands showed white. Dr. Balman had arrived; he was sitting at the other side of the bed and I did not see him until I stepped into the room. His stethoscope dangled from his hands, his gleaming raincoat dripped moisture steadily on the floor. He, too, was staring downward.

No one moved as I approached the bed. It was as if some evil spell held us all staring at the dead man. And through that brooding silence, broken only by the hurling rain and wind outside, I knew as well as I shall ever know anything that I was right. That the man there on the bed had been murdered!

My throat was very dry. I had to make several efforts and finally achieved a single word:

"How —"

Dr. Balman glanced at me, apparently noting my presence for the first time.

"Overdose of morphine," he said.

"Morphine!" I was shocked out of the numbness that had enveloped me. "Morphine. But he was not to have morphine. How do you know?"

With a laconic gesture he showed me the tiny hypodermic scar on the patient's arm.

"That — and look here — the pupils of his eyes," Dr. Balman drew the lids upward gently. "As well as his general condition. You know —"

I nodded slowly. Morphine!

It was then that a strange thing happened. We were all staring at the small wound, else we should not have seen the little pin-prick of red that crept slowly from it. It was not a drop by any means, it was barely enough to be visible, but it brought to our minds the old superstition: a corpse bleeds when its murderer is near. A cold shiver crept up my back as I looked, and Dr. Balman sprang to his feet with a hoarse word or two, and Maida cried out, gasping, and started back, and even phlegmatic Dr. Hajek muttered something under his breath and drew his hand across his eyes.

With an effort I controlled myself. This sort of thing would turn us all into gibbering idiots and there was much to be done.

"Dr. Balman," I said, my voice sounding strange to my own ears, "Dr. Letheny is caught out in the storm somewhere and we have not yet been able to find him. Mr. Jackson was not to have morphine: it was not ordered and moreover at twelve-thirty he was all right. He has evidently been — killed — so that someone could steal the radium. There will be — confusion. Someone must take charge from now on — and since Dr. Letheny is gone —"

"Leave things to us, Miss Keate," said Dr. Balman at once. "See to your wing as usual and Dr. Hajek and I will do what is necessary."

"Do you intend to call the coroner?" I asked.

"Certainly. I shall telephone at once. It means police — detectives — all that, but this is a terrible thing. Steps must be taken immediately. A delay in such a matter —"

"Here I am, Miss Keate," said Olma Flynn from the doorway. "I hurried to get dressed. What —" her pale eyes travelled past me to the bed. "Why — why what is it? He is — *dead!*" Her voice rose. I suppose our very attitudes and gray faces told her the truth, for suddenly she began to scream. I seized her by the arm none too gently, clapped my other hand over her mouth and pulled her outside, closing the door behind me.

But it was too late. Others had heard her screams, and there was no keeping the thing secret, especially as some prowling nurse heard Dr. Balman and Dr. Hajek telephoning for the police and the coroner. The story was over the hospital in ten minutes and only the strictest measures prevented a panic. Terror-stricken nurses crowding into the halls and wing, the demands of the sick to whom the excitement seemed to have communicated itself, flaring, inadequate lamps and candles and their little flickering circles of light that made frightened faces whiter and the surrounding gloom blacker, horrified questions that no one could answer, stark fear in every pair of eyes — all this made it an hour not soon forgotten.

Fortunately Maida and I found that our own patients had not suffered from our enforced absence from duty. It was a difficult matter, however, to calm some of the more nervous ones and keep the knowledge of what had happened from reaching their ears. Olma Flynn's assistance was of the slightest as she refused to stir three feet from Maida or me, and her hands shook so that she spilled everything she touched.

We were very busy and I did not see the

coroner and the police when they arrived and went directly to Room 18. Along about half-past three I slipped into the diet kitchen and made some very strong coffee which I shared with Maida and Olma Flynn. We felt a little better after that though still weak and sick and controlling our fears by sheer strength of will.

Somehow the weary gray hours dragged along. Dawn came through still gusty rain and wind and the cold light crept reluctantly into the sick rooms. Breakfast was late that morning owing to the cook's not being able to find enough candles for adequate lights, but the day nurses finally came on duty, white and fear-stricken over what the night had held.

By that time, however, policemen were all over the place and I must say that their broad, blue backs gave me a welcome sense of security. Dr. Letheny had not turned up yet; at least, if he had I had not seen him.

The breakfast trays came up at last and Maida, Olma Flynn, and I washed our hands and faces and descended to the dining room in the basement. We said little. The candles on the long table flickered; the rain beat against the small windows; our uniforms were wrinkled and looked cold; our eyes were hollow and our faces drawn and gray, and already we were starting nervously at sudden sounds and were beginning to cast furtive glances over our shoulders as if to be sure there was nothing there.

But it was not until I had finished drinking some very black coffee and playing with my toast that the reason for our strained silence made itself clear to me.

Only someone connected with the hospital could have known that the radium was out of the safe and in use in Room 18. Only a doctor or a nurse would have known how to administer morphine with a hypodermic syringe.

It might be — anyone! It might be one of us!

The thought threatened that remnant of courage I still maintained. I rose, pushing back my chair. It scraped along the floor and at the sound heads jerked in my direction too quickly and someone cried out nervously.

I hurried from the room, up the stairs and to my room in the nurses' dormitory. I am not ashamed to say that I locked the door. But though I needed rest I could not sleep.

3

Dr. Lethany Does Not Return

From sheer fatigue, however, I must have dozed for I awoke at the sound of a repeated knocking at the door. It was a frightened little student nurse wanting to know if all training classes and lectures were to be suspended.

"Suspended?" I said, the horror of the past night sweeping over me. "Suspended? I — why, Dr. Letheny will tell you."

She blinked.

"But Dr. Letheny — we — they — nobody knows where Dr. Letheny has gone."

"What!" I was fully awake.

"No, ma'am. They can't find him anywhere." Frightened though she was, she yet appeared to take a naïve relish in being the first to tell me the news. "They can't find him at all. Miss Letheny has telephoned everywhere that he might be and the police are working on it and they have been asking us all kinds of questions."

I reached for a fresh uniform.

"I'll come down immediately," I said.

"About the training classes, did you speak to Dr. Balman?"

"No. Miss Dotty said to find out if you knew what was to be done." Which was like Miss Dotty, she being amiable but not very clear-thinking.

"Dr. Balman is Dr. Letheny's assistant. I have nothing to do with it."

The little student nurse rustled away and ten minutes later, refreshed by a bath and a clean uniform, I followed her.

I found the main portion of the hospital fairly shuddering with excitement. To my extreme annoyance it appeared that the moronic fraction of our nursing staff was beginning to take a melancholy satisfaction in the tumult and posing freely for the reporters who, with their flashlight affairs, were swarming over the whole place. I might say here and now that I soon stopped that and did not mince matters in so doing, though I could not prevent the headlines that had already found their way into the city newspapers.

In the main office Dr. Balman and Dr. Hajek, both looking worn and haggard, were literally surrounded by our board of directors who, it seemed, had descended in a body and were determined to hold somebody responsible for the terrible thing that had occurred. I learned later that there was some trouble in convincing them that Mr. Jackson's death was not due to a mistake on the part of the nurses. Some policemen were in the room, too, and the chief of police, himself, a burly fellow who looked habitually as if his darkest suspicions were about to be verified.

This expression intensified itself as I entered the room, which, by the way, was the first indication of a fact that later became all too painfully evident, namely that I, Sarah Keate, occupied a prominent place in the list of suspects, for had I not been in the south wing? Had I not been in a position to administer the morphine that caused the patient's death? Had I not been the one to find him?

One or two of the board had the grace to rise as I entered, but most of them were, too agitated to remember their manners.

"What is this about Dr. Letheny?" I began.

"Are you Miss Keate?" asked the chief of police.

"Yes," I replied, none too graciously.

"We were just about to send for you," he informed me. "Now suppose you tell us everything you know of this affair. Mind, I say *everything*."

I turned to Dr. Balman.

"Hasn't Dr. Letheny returned yet?"

He shook his head slowly.

"Come, come, Miss Keate," said the chief.

"Doesn't Miss Letheny know where he is?" I insisted anxiously.

"Apparently not." It was Dr. Hajek who answered.

"Will you answer my questions?" demanded the chief loudly.

"Another time," I stated impatiently. Didn't the man see what the pressing issue was! "When did Miss Letheny see him last?"

Dr. Hajek shook his head. "She has not seen him since last night about twelve-thirty."

The chief rose.

"Now, look here! We'll have no more funny business," he began to bluster.

"Oh, *do* be still!" I may have spoken somewhat irritably; at any rate the chief turned purple. "Don't you see," I explained reasonably, "don't you see that we must find Dr. Letheny? That so much hinges upon our finding him? Why, so far as we know, *he* decided to remove the radium, perhaps he —" I stuck, appalled by the literal truth of my words.

The chief was quick to pick me up.

"So you have already formed your opinion. And quite right, too. It is very clear that this Letheny fellow has got away with the radium." The chief actually began rubbing his hands together and smiling. "Now, Miss Keate, just tell us why you suspect Dr. Letheny of this crime."

"But I don't!" I cried in exasperation. "I have not had time to suspect anyone yet. I have been too busy. The reason I spoke as I did of Dr. Letheny is that he is the attendant physician; he knew more of Mr. Jackson's condition than any of us. He may have decided that the radium was — er — not doing any good and may have removed it for that reason. It seems to me that our hands are tied without him."

"Just a moment, chief," remarked one of the most intelligent members of the board. "Suppose we follow your suggestion and leave all investigation until this man — what is his name?"

"Lance O'Leary," supplied the chief sulkily.

"Until this Lance O'Leary gets here. You seem to have great confidence in him and —"

"Him and me always work together," interpolated the chief.

"He is out of town at present," went on the board member, addressing me.

"Suits me," said the chief. "I've wired him and he will be here on the afternoon train. We've got everything under guard and can leave the room just as we found it."

"Then there is no need for us to stay any longer," remarked a particularly well-fed board member, getting fussily to his feet and kicking a little to shake down his trousers over his fat calves. "I've got to get to the office. And now see here, Dr. Balman — and you others — of course we don't say that this is your fault —"

"Well, I should hope not!" I interrupted tartly.

"Your fault," he repeated, eyeing me severely. "But at the same time it shouldn't have happened. There is something wrong somewhere. Here we go and put sixty-five thousand dollars into a whole gram of radium and now look what happens !" The other members shook their fat cheeks in sympathy.

"You seem to forget," I remarked with some asperity, "that there was also a murder in the hospital last night, which might have been prevented had we had an emergency gas line installed. We were without lights a good share of the night."

This was not quite true, in that the murder had been committed, I had no doubt, before the lights had gone out, but the subject of gas for emergency use had been a matter of contention between the board and the staff for some time and I was glad to note that the entire board looked distinctly uneasy as it filed fatly from the office.

"A splendid group of gentlemen," commented the chief approvingly.

"Then we are to do nothing until this detective arrives?" I asked impatiently.

"So it seems," said Dr. Balman, sighing wearily.

"Yes, and nothing is enough," said the chief, whose name, by the way, proved to be Blunt. "Once Lance O'Leary gets his teeth in anything it is as good as finished. Say — I could tell you things —"

"If only we could find Dr. Letheny," I reflected. "It is so strange, his disappearing like this and at such a time."

"Maybe it ain't so strange as you think," remarked Chief Blunt. "There is many a man would like to disappear with about sixty-five thousand dollars in his pocket. Say, what does that radium look like? How would you carry it anyhow? Wouldn't it burn you?"

"It is carried in a small steel box that is especially made to protect it — and you," explained Dr. Balman. As I glanced at him I was struck by the unbelievably drawn and haggard appearance of his face, which was intensified by a bruise on one cheek bone that was turning a dark, purplish green. "It would be a ticklish thing to dispose of," he added thoughtfully.

"Well, we shall have some disclosures in another night," said the chief comfortably. "And mark my words, this Letheny has had something to do with it. A man don't disappear like this for nothing. In the meantime we'll guard Room 18 and keep everybody away from it. And let nobody leave or come into the hospital."

"No visitors?" I inquired, with the first shade of approval I had felt for the chief so far.

"No visitors," he agreed.

"And in the meantime," said Dr. Balman, "business as usual. Eh, Miss Keate?"

"By all means. But Dr. Balman — you don't think that Dr. Letheny killed Mr. Jackson and got away with the radium —"

"Certainly not," said Dr. Balman. "There is nothing upon which to base such a conclusion."

"Don't be too sure of that," muttered Chief Blunt from the depths of the telephone transmitter.

It took a few moments for Dr. Balman and Dr. Hajek to arrange between them to take over Dr. Letheny's work in case, we were careful to say, Dr. Letheny did not come to St. Ann's that day, while Chief Blunt put the telephone to such good use that at the end of a few minutes he assured us that Dr. Letheny would be found within twenty-four hours. This I thought to be a somewhat sweeping prophecy but said nothing.

Leaving the office, I walked thoughtfully down to the south wing. It was a compliment to St. Ann's routine that, with the exception of a certain nervousness on the part of the nurses, all was quite as it should be. Morning baths had been given, breakfasts were all over and rooms dusted, and discipline in general had been maintained. However, there is no use saying things were just as usual for they were not. It was dark and cold that morning, with one of those quick changes of temperature for which our part of the country is famous. The electric service had not yet been repaired and there were lamps at intervals along the corridor. Miss Dotty, wisely for once, had doubled the number of girls on duty, and blue-striped skirts and white aprons of training nurses, as well as the severe white of graduate nurses, glimmered everywhere.

So far we had been successful in keeping the news of the murder from the ears of the patients, but of course they were aware of some kind of disturbance during the night, and several of them were quite fussy and upset and demanded to be moved to another wing, which naturally we could not do. We kept the newspapers from them, too, but one of the minor troubles of the day was the continual telephone calls from anxious relatives, which began as soon as the morning extras were out.

Oh, yes, the newspapers got out extras with all kinds of pictures and the most absurd statements that made St. Ann's appear to be something between a boarding school and a den of iniquity. This unfortunate impression was helped by the pictures of nurses in conjunction with the murder and radium theft.

And in spite of our efforts to carry on work the same as usual, in spite of cleaned rooms and spick-and-span corridors and careful charts, there lingered, somehow, pervading the very old walls of St. Ann's, a certain gloom, a sense of foreboding, that centred in the south wing.

Room 18 was closed and guarded by a stalwart policeman, who sat uncompromisingly in front of the door, but that end of the corridor was shunned as if there were live smallpox there, and when one of the nurses had to go to Room 17, opposite, or to the next room, Sixteen, she quite frankly sought the company of another nurse.

Old Mr. Jackson's lawyer had been notified immediately of the tragedy, I learned, and he, in turn, had notified the dead man's only relatives, a cousin and a nephew, living somewhere in the East. Along in the middle of the morning a rather impersonal telegram came from them to Chief Blunt, bidding him spare no expense and keep them informed of developments.

What with one thing and another I had very little time of my own until about two o'clock in the afternoon when, after firmly getting rid of Miss Dotty, who evidenced a distressing disposition to cling and whisper in horrified italics, I sat down at the south-wing chart desk, drew a blank chart toward me, and presenting as forbidding a back against interruption as I could, I tried to think. Until that moment the whirl of events had so caught me that I had had to act and had had literally no time in which to consider the matter.

I began, logically enough, at twelve-thirty, the time I had last seen Dr. Letheny. In spite of my defence of Dr. Letheny before Chief Blunt, I felt in my heart that his absence at such a time was, to say the least, rather strange.

It had been a queer night, even before its shocking development; that strange dinner at Corole's, where everyone had seemed strung to such a singular pitch of excitement, our walk home through the suffocating heat. Maida's preoccupation, my own disquiet, the storm — And now a memory recurred to me with such force that I almost jumped — that man with whom I had collided there at the corner of the porch! Who was he? What had he been doing?

And then, of course, I recalled the flat, smooth object I had found at the edge of the orchard, there below the kitchen window.

It took only a moment or two to hurry to my room and dive my hand into the pocket of my soiled uniform. Then I sank down on the edge of the bed, staring at the thing in my hand.

I recognized it at once.

It was Jim Gainsay's cigarette case.

The engraved fraternity shield winked at me as I turned it over in my hands and snapped it open; inside were two or three cigarettes; dazedly I noted the brand — Belwood's. Jim Gainsay! It was he, then, whom I had met there at the steps of the porch. What had he been doing? What had been his business about St. Ann's after midnight? And my breath caught and my heart began to pound as I recalled his words of the previous night: "If I can manage to lay my hands on fifty thousand dollars . . . can make as much money as I want . . . I can do it . . . *and I will.*"

And he had heard our discussion of the radium. He had even heard — yes, I remembered distinctly — he had even heard in what room the radium was in use and that the south door was to be left unlocked. To be sure, I might have been expected to lock the door following Dr. Letheny's visit, but there were windows and —

Someone was knocking at the door and I had barely time to slip the cigarette case under the pillow. It was Miss Dotty, her eyes fairly popping with excitement.

"Where is the key to the closet in the south wing?"

"What closet? There are several —"

"I mean the closet in Room 18, of course. Do you have the key?"

"No. And I don't know where it is. Who wants it?"

"They want it downstairs."

"They?"

"That little, slim detective. He has just come. And oh, Miss Keate, he is so handsome," she rolled her rather vacant eyes upward.

"Who is handsome?" I spoke somewhat snappishly. Miss Dotty's rhapsodies aggravate me.

"That Mr. O'Leary. Just wait till you see him. Such a way of speaking! Such clothes! And his eyes are simply wonderful!" Miss Dotty appeared to recall herself from Mr. O'Leary's charms with difficulty. "But I must hurry. They said if we couldn't find the key they would have to take the door off the hinges."

"Take the hinges off, you mean. Indeed they

shan't! That lovely gumwood door! They'll be sure to scar it. Maybe some of the student nurses locked it. Ask them. Or — wait! I'll come down myself."

But Miss Dotty's starched skirts were already scuttling away.

Before leaving the room, and not without a guilty feeling in my heart, I placed the cigarette case in a safe hiding place which was nothing more nor less than the bottom of my laundry bag. Almost without conscious volition on my part I had resolved to keep the matter of the cigarette case a secret and in my own possession, at least until I knew more certainly where my duty lay concerning it. It carried with it too grave an implication to act upon readily.

Then, still preoccupied, I took my way downstairs, through the main portion of St. Ann's, past the general office, and turned into the corridor leading to the south wing. As I approached the chart desk, one of the student nurses seized upon me tearfully with a tale of Three's hysterics, and wouldn't I help for she had not the least idea what to do. There was nothing for it but to go to her assistance, much as I was interested in the proceedings in Room 18. And it was a good thing for me that I did! Otherwise I should have been in the room when they opened the closet door.

Three's hysterics proved to be of an unusually stubborn kind, really virulent in fact, and though I was aware of a sort of subdued confusion and tremor of excitement outside the door I could not clearly understand what it was about. I heard faintly the sound of hammering, of feet running along the corridor, of a man's voice calling out something indistinguishable, and a hastily hushed, woman's scream which Three promptly and wilfully echoed. Then several people hurried through the hall, and as they passed the door I heard the unmistakable little metallic rattle of the wheels of the stretcher-truck, and caught the words — "Call Dr. Balman," and something about an ambulance.

This was too much for me and I left my patient as soon as possible. No one was to be seen in the corridor, however, so I walked hurriedly down toward Room 18. Just as I reached it a policeman opened it, saw me, slid hastily through the narrow aperture and, closing the door, stood squarely before it.

"You can't go in there, miss," he said firmly.

"But — what has happened? What is all the commotion about?"

"You can't go in there," he repeated stupidly. To my surprise I saw that the man was actually frightened. His eyes were staring, his weather-beaten face a sort of yellow-green, and his breath coming in gasps. "You can't go in there. You can't —"

He seemed capable only of keeping me out of the room, so without wasting time or effort I turned about and retraced my steps. As I passed the linen-closet door I saw a group of nurses inside. One of them was lying back in a chair in a dead faint and the others were clustered around talking excitedly in low voices and nearly drowning the recumbent one with cold water.

"What on earth?" I exclaimed and at my voice they turned; one of them was frankly sobbing and the other two were white as ghosts.

"Oh, Miss K-K—" began one, her teeth chattering so she could not speak, while the others just stood there with their mouths opening and closing like so many fish. Naturally it was very trying and I believe I shook her till her teeth chattered in good earnest.

"Now tell me what has happened," I said, releasing her shoulders.

"Oh, Miss Keate, the most terrible thing has —"

"Is this Miss Keate?" interrupted a clear voice from the doorway.

I whirled.

A man stood in the doorway; at the moment I was conscious only of a pair of extraordinarily lucid gray eyes; later I noted that he was slender and not very tall, that his gray business suit was well tailored, his gray socks of heavy silk and with a small scarlet thread, his scarf neatly knotted and chosen with care, his face clean-shaven, with clear rather delicately cut features, and that he wore an air of well-groomed prosperity. I knew at once that this was Lance O'Leary.

"I am Miss Keate," I replied.

"I am Lance O'Leary," he said (superfluously, but he did not know that). "I should like to talk to you if you have time. Will you come to the office with me, please — I think we shall be undisturbed there."

Being a woman of some strength of mind, I had intended to take a firm line with this detective whom everyone seemed to think so remarkable, but I found myself walking as meekly as any lamb at his side, and once inside the general office with the door closed, I sat as resignedly in a chair opposite him as if there were not a thousand and one things that I should be doing.

"You are the superintendent of the south wing?" He spoke very quietly and with what I found later to be a wholly deceptive air of detachment.

"Yes."

"You were on duty last night between

twelve and six o'clock?"

"Yes."

"Miss Maida Day was your assistant?"

"Yes."

"Dr. Balman tells me that Miss Day telephoned to him about two o'clock — possibly ten minutes before the hour. I judge that was only a few moments after you found that your patient was dead?"

"Yes. It must have been about that time. It was something after one-thirty when the storm broke and I hurried along the corridor and closed the south door. Then I closed the window in Room 17 and went directly into Eighteen." My voice was not quite steady at the recollection of those moments and he waited briefly, his clear eyes studying a pencil in his hands, before he went on.

"The windows in Room 18 were also open?"

"Yes. All the windows in the wing were open. It had been very hot and close before the storm began."

He nodded.

"Those windows are not far from the ground. Do you think someone from outside could get into the hospital without attracting your attention?"

"Yes," I said slowly. "It might be done but does not seem very probable. With the doors to the sick-rooms open and the night so still

79

I believe I should have heard any unusual sound. But the door to Eighteen was closed. I can't be sure."

"You heard no unusual sound, then?"

"Why, no — except that a few moments before the storm began I heard a sort of bang — as if a window had dropped to the sill. It was not very clear."

He was looking directly into my face, his eyes as clear as water.

"You are sure it was a window? It might have been a door closing."

"It was not the door for it was still open. I am not sure — I investigated but found nothing. The south door was still open — and as far as I could tell the windows were as they had been."

"Did you look in Room 18?"

"Yes."

There was a slight pause. Then:

"The patient was — quiet at the time?"

"The room was dark and still so I did not enter it. I just stood there for a moment holding the door half open; I was afraid if I entered the room I would wake him. He was asleep — that is —" I stopped abruptly as it occurred to me that he had not been asleep; that the incident had occurred not more than fifteen minutes before I found him dead.

O'Leary seemed to read my thoughts.

"Yes," he said quietly. "He must have been dead — then. Can you be certain of the time?"

"Yes. It was shortly after one-thirty. I remember because I had just noted the time on a patient's chart, when I heard that dull sound and went to see what it was."

He returned to his pencil, a shabby little red thing it was, which he rolled absently between his well-kept fingers.

"Was this sound sharp and loud?"

"No —" I hesitated, trying to recall just how it had seemed. "No — it was rather dull — muffled — and yet heavy. It was not very distinct."

"There were no other unusual circumstances? Nothing out of the ordinary?"

"Why, yes. There was someone — a man — " I broke off abruptly. That man must have been Jim Gainsay. I had no wish to involve him in the matter, at least until I became convinced that his movements should be investigated.

But Lance O'Leary's gray eyes looked straight through to my back hair.

"Yes?" he inquired.

"Yes." I spoke with an accent of finality, and gazed nonchalantly out the window as if the subject were closed.

"Where was he?"

"Running around the hospital," I replied

81

curtly, wishing I had held my tongue.

"Around and around?" inquired O'Leary blandly.

"No," I snapped. "Running along the east side of the wing. I — he — we collided."

O'Leary sat up straighter.

"What!"

"I had gone out on the porch for a breath of fresh air," I explained rather sullenly. "Just as I stepped off the porch I ran into him."

I stopped as if the incident were concluded.

"Go on," suggested the O'Leary man after waiting a moment; he was being very polite and very pleasant and altogether disagreeable.

"That's all," I said waspishly. I fastened my gaze on his extremely well-made shoes — an attention that I have found invariably disconcerts men — vain creatures! But this one was impervious.

"And what did you say?" he persisted with the most insulting good-humour.

"I said 'Well —' " I stared steadfastly at the shoes.

"And what did he say?"

I resisted an evil impulse to tell him literally and with feeling.

"I hope you don't think I'd repeat such language," I replied, and I'm sure he smiled.

"Then what happened?"

"He — er — set me on my feet again and

kept on running."

"Very chivalrous," remarked O'Leary. "So he kept on running — around the hospital?"

"No," I answered peevishly. "He ran along the path toward the bridge."

"What did you do?"

"I walked in the direction he had come from as far as the wing extends but saw nothing unusual."

"Did you not call anyone? Were you not alarmed?"

"I thought of calling Higgins, the janitor, but when I found that things seemed to be all right I decided it was not necessary."

"Then you came back to the hospital?"

"Yes."

"And all that time you saw or heard nothing uncommon?"

"Well — I smelled something."

He made a perceptible motion of surprise. "You smelled something? Did you say *smelled?*"

I nodded, taking a small degree of satisfaction in his discomposure.

"As I passed that clump of elderberry bushes I smelled ether. It was quite distinct. You know ether has a penetrating odour."

"But surely that was unusual?"

"Yes. But the night was so hot and ether out there in the apple orchard so impossible that I decided I must be mistaken, that it was just the mingled scents of alfalfa and clover and other growing things."

"Well — which was it? Ether or imagination?"

"I don't know," I said firmly. "I'm just telling you what happened. I know it sounds queer — but last night was a queer night. That dinner at Corole's and everything," I finished thoughtlessly.

"Dinner at Corole's? That is Miss Letheny?"

"Yes."

"Dr. Letheny was there?"

"Yes."

"Anyone else?"

"Yes. Miss Day, Dr. Balman, Dr. Hajek, and a friend of Dr. Letheny's — a Mr. Gainsay. He is an engineer who stopped for a day's visit with them."

"And you and Miss Letheny?"

"Yes."

"You implied that it was — 'queer,' I think was the word you used. How was it queer?"

"Oh — I scarcely know. It was very hot and oppressive you know — that sort of electric atmosphere that precedes a thunder storm."

"Aside from the — er — electricity in the air, was everything quite as usual?"

I paused for a long moment before replying.

"No," I said candidly. "I think we were all a little nervous and uneasy on account of the heat and suffocating air. That is, I was. And Dr. Letheny — and Miss Day —"

"But not the others?"

"Well —" It was difficult to define that curious tensity I had felt in the air all the night. "No one seemed quite natural to me. It may have been only I who was a little nervous. I really can't tell you anything definite."

"Why did you say definitely that Dr. Letheny and Miss Day were unlike themselves?"

"Dr. Letheny is a rather quick-spoken man — when you know him you will understand what I mean. He goes on his nervous energy, is very high-strung and temperamental. He seemed especially explosive last night. And Miss Day was a little abstracted, tired, I think."

"I suppose you talked — played bridge — had a little music?"

"Yes. All of that."

"Any special topics of conversation?"

"No —"

He noted the uncertainty in my voice.

"Radium wasn't mentioned?"

"Well — yes. But only in a general way."

85

"Didn't speak of using it? Having it out of the safe,"

"Yes," I admitted reluctantly.

"Didn't say for what patient it was being used? In what room?"

"Yes. But only casually." I explained Dr. Letheny's request to leave the south door unlocked.

"Anything else?"

"Nothing in particular. We just talked of general matters."

"Such as —"

I glanced at him impatiently.

"Such as?" he repeated.

"Oh — how warm it was, and how everybody longs for something that money will buy, and how St. Ann's is equipped with radios and expensive ambulances and a whole gram of radium and how much such things cost and all that — and then we played a few hands of bridge and then Dr. Letheny played the piano and then Maida — Miss Day — and I came back through the orchard to St. Ann's and changed into our uniforms and went on duty."

"You talked of money and how everybody longs for something that money will buy," mused O'Leary, adding with uncanny intuition, "I suppose several of you admitted a special desire for money?"

"Every single one of us," I confessed. "That is, except Dr. Hajek. He just listened and seemed amused."

He smiled. "Don't be alarmed over such an admission. That doesn't mean anything, that you all wanted money. Everyone wants money. But suppose you tell me, word for word, as much as you can remember of the conversation. Don't be afraid of implicating anyone, Miss Keate. I make the request only because I like to get as clear an idea of the general surroundings as possible." He smiled again. He had an extraordinarily winning smile; it brightened his whole face, for all that it was so brief, and I found myself warming under its influence.

Not seeing how I could possibly harm anyone I repeated as much of our conversation as I could remember, and since I have usually a good memory I think I omitted very little of it.

When I had finished he sat for some time turning and twisting his pencil. I might say that I never but once saw him use that pencil sensibly as a pencil is meant to be used. I even grew to cherish a notion that the pencil aided his mental processes and that if it were taken away from him his ability to think might go along with it. Like Samson's hair, you know. Then I aroused myself from such childish speculation.

"If that is all —" I hinted. "This is a busy day for us, you know."

"Not quite all, Miss Keate." The smile had completely gone from his face; his expression lost its youthfulness and was very grave. "When did you last see Dr. Letheny?"

"Last night, shortly after twelve-thirty."

"He had come to see Mr. Jackson?"

"Yes. He was here only a few moments."

"You saw him leave?"

"Yes."

"And he did not return, to your knowledge?"

"No."

"He said nothing of leaving town?"

"Nothing."

"He said nothing that would lead you to believe that he was — er — worried about anything? Had had any trouble?"

"Nothing. I really think, Mr. O'Leary, that he will return before the day is over. Some accident has detained him. There will be some explanation."

"You — admire Dr. Letheny?" Lance O'Leary was scrutinizing a dripping shrub outside the window as he spoke.

"Yes," I replied dubiously. "That is, he is a splendid surgeon, very cool and very daring. I like to assist him."

"You have known him for a long time?"

"Several years. That is, I have known him as everyone else knows him. I do not believe that any of us feel particularly well acquainted with him. He is rather distant, very much interested in some research that he is carrying on."

"You don't know the kind of research — the special subject of study?"

"No."

There followed a long silence; the rain beat steadily against the window; outside in the corridor I heard the sound of the four-o'clock nourishment trays being carried along, the glasses of orange-juice and egg-nogg clinking together. It was chilly there in the office and I shivered a little.

"I do wish that Dr. Letheny would return," I said. "It is bad for the head doctor of St. Ann's to be away at such a time."

Lance O'Leary turned slowly to me.

"Dr. Letheny will not return," he said, eyeing me keenly.

"Not return? What do you mean?"

He shook his head.

"He will not return," he said very slowly and distinctly. "Dr. Letheny is dead."

4

A Yellow Slicker and Other Problems

The slow words beat their way into my brain like so many dull little hammers. I opened my mouth, tried to say something, but could not seem to make him hear, felt curiously sick and dizzy, had a flashing memory of the first time I served in the operating room and all at once the table before me began to waver, the room whirled, and a great black blanket overwhelmed me.

Then, without any interval at all, I found myself lying on the couch in the inner office. I still felt sick but my face was wet and cold and my uniform damp around my shoulders and someone was saying in a dull voice: "Dr. Letheny is dead — Dr. Letheny is dead."

"All right now, Miss Keate?" inquired a voice anxiously.

Wearily I opened my eyes, saw a gray arm and met the gaze of a pair of clear gray eyes. Instantly my head cleared. I pushed away the supporting arm and sat up, feeling automatically for my cap, though my hands shook.

"That was beastly to shock you so," Lance O'Leary was saying with honest contrition. "I hope you'll forgive me, Miss Keate, I'm really awfully sorry."

"Did you say — Dr. Letheny is dead?" I asked, bringing out the words with the peculiar difficulty that one experiences in dreams.

"He is dead," he answered gravely.

"Not — not — Tell me how he died."

"Are you sure you can stand it? You've got to know sometime."

"Go on," I said, bracing myself.

"He has been dead for more than twelve hours. He was in the closet in Room 18." He paused, regarding me doubtfully, but at my horrified gesture continued: "He had received a blow of some kind. It fractured his skull. He must have died immediately."

"Wait." Rising I walked to the window, stared with unseeing eyes at the rain-drenched landscape, found my palms were stinging under the pressure of my fingernails, unclinched my hands, clinched them again and turned to face O'Leary. It was true that I had felt no fondness for Dr. Letheny — but I had often worked at his side.

"I say, Miss Keate," Lance O'Leary was protesting boyishly, "I'm awfully sorry to have been so brutal about it. But you see, I had to know whether this was news to you or not. Someone locked that closet door, you know. And in my business we suspect everything — everybody — the very walls themselves."

I was too deeply shocked to be indignant at the lack of compliment in his implication; after a moment he continued.

"There is nothing more for you to help me with now," he said. "We just found Dr. Letheny's body this afternoon when we pried the closet door off its hinges. I examined everything at once, called the ambulance, and now the room can be cleaned and used again. The only reminder you will have of all this, I hope, is that I shall likely be about more or less for a few days — or longer. That depends upon the luck I have." He smiled again. Evidently he was trying to be as considerate as possible and I found myself liking him. "Of course, there will have to be a coroner's inquest, but that is merely a matter of form and need not annoy you. That is all now, thank you, Miss Keate. Can't you take some rest? Do you have night duty again tonight?"

"Yes," I answered the last question. "Mr. O'Leary, do you have any idea as to who — who has done this?"

His face sobered instantly.

"No," he said simply. "Will you help me find out?"

"Yes." I spoke very thoughtfully. "It is only right and just to do so."

"Thank you." He seemed sincere. "You may be interested to know that you have helped me already."

"Helped you! How? There was nothing I told you —"

"I'll see you again, Miss Keate. By the way, I am leaving one or two policemen about tonight. It may help to steady some of the nerves in St. Ann's." He opened the door and before I knew it I was in the main hall with my question still unanswered.

I still felt ill and weak from shock, and it was fortunate that the exigencies of the situation demanded action. That was the only saving feature of these fearful days; we were all so busy that we had little time for brooding.

The news could not be kept from the nursing staff, of course, though I hoped that we could keep it from the patients, many of whom had been directly under Dr. Letheny's care. And there was Corole — in common decency I must go to her.

I snatched somebody's slicker from the rack near the main door and turned into the corridor leading to the south wing, intending to slip out the south door and along the path to Corole's cottage, it being much closer that way.

In the corridor I met Dr. Balman.

"I have heard," I said briefly. "I am going to see Corole."

He nodded.

"At the request of the Board of Directors I shall take Dr. Letheny's place — temporarily at least. I have just called a meeting of the whole nursing staff, Miss Keate. You were with Mr. O'Leary so I did not disturb you. I told them of the situation, gave orders that this thing must not get to the ears of the patients, suspended training classes for a few days, and doubled the number of girls on duty in the various wings and wards until we get a working routine established. I find that the girls are nervous over being alone." He spoke very calmly, but his extreme pallor caught my eye.

"You had better get some rest, Dr. Balman. And have that bruise on your cheek attended to — it looks bad."

He passed his hand over the bruise.

"I bumped it while running through the apple orchard last night. I wasted no time after I talked to Miss Day over the telephone."

"Oh — then you came by the side road?"

"Yes. Thought I'd save time by not going around by the main entrance. I didn't expect this." He fingered the spot cautiously.

"Put iodine on it," I advised.

"I'll sleep here in the hospital for a while," he said. "I'll be there on the couch in the inner office. So if there is anything wanted I shall be right here."

I nodded approvingly and went on, but while hurrying through the corridor I became conscious of something about the casual sentences that affected me disagreeably. What was it? Ah! "I bumped it while running through the apple orchard." To be sure he had followed the words immediately with a very reasonable explanation, but wasn't that in itself suspicious! On the other hand, however, I had been quite sure that the man with whom I collided had been Jim Gainsay.

Well, there was no way to make sure. And I resolved that I must not allow myself to become suspicious of anything and everything. The affair was strain enough on one's nerves as it was, without adding the horror of suspecting one's nearest associates.

Immersed in my own not too pleasant thoughts I passed the door of Room 18 without seeing it, an occurrence that I was to find unusual. On the porch stood a policeman, his broad back to the door, but he made no effort to stop me when I descended the steps. Once in the path the trees dripped steadily on my head, the wind blew the light slicker so that it was difficult to hold it around me, and I bent my head and ran through the damp welter of leaves and small sticks, with the branches of the trees sweeping so low as to brush my hair and cap, and the shrubbery reaching out thorny twigs to clutch at my white skirt. It was shadowy there in the orchard and the hospital soon disappeared behind the intervening shrubbery and trees and gray mist. It was nearing five o'clock by that time and already growing dark so that the path was not an altogether agreeable place in which to linger.

I turned another little bend that sloped rapidly down to the bridge and almost ran into a tall figure that was leaning upon the railing. At my startled exclamation it turned to face me. It was Jim Gainsay, a sodden hat pulled low over his eyes and the collar of his capacious tweed coat turned up. He was smoking (it was a pipe I noted, thinking of the cigarette case) and casting pebbles across the water, which is not a rainy day pastime.

"Oh. It's you." I said.

"Miss Keate! Say, you are the very person I've been wanting to see. Can you tell me something of poor old Louis?"

"Louis? Oh, you mean Dr. Letheny." I suppose I paled a little at the name. At any rate

Gainsay glanced sharply at me.

"I didn't mean to — disturb you," he said apologetically. "You see, I only heard of it an hour or so ago, and only what that fellow O'Leary told me. Don't talk if you would rather not."

"Then I know no more than you, for the detective, Mr. O'Leary, told me of it, too. Of course, it was a shock."

Jim Gainsay nodded, his gaze again on the little stream that, swollen by the night's rain, swept in a bubbling current almost to our feet.

"Poor old Louis," he muttered.

"You have known him a long time?" I said absently, my eyes too on the water.

"Since university days," said Jim Gainsay slowly. "I always liked Louis though I can't say I understood him; no one ever did. In the last few years I have seen him only a few times. It was terrible to — go like that. Do they have any idea as to who — who killed him?"

"Not that I know of," I said and shivered at the thought of the black night so recently past and of the unknown and ghastly presence that Room 18 had held. And I had taken that futile little candle and searched the room for the thing that some sixth sense warned me was there! I shivered again and caught my breath and Jim Gainsay turned to me again.

"Don't let me keep you out here in the

storm. You are cold in that slicker thing."

"A little. I am going to see Corole. How does she take it?"

Jim Gainsay's frown deepened.

"I hardly know. I can't understand her any better than I could understand Louis. She looked — sort of bad — this morning. Tired, you know. And kept saying Louis would return. But she was terribly nervous. Prowled over the house like a cat." He shrugged in distaste. "Fairly gave me the creeps to watch her. Then when they came up to the house to tell her that — that they had found him she sort of froze all up. Hardly said a word."

"Wasn't she dreadfully shocked?"

"Well — I don't know. You never can tell how Corole is feeling or what she is thinking about. Of course, she and Louis sort of got on each other's nerves a little. That is — you know what I mean —" He glanced at me uncertainly.

"I know."

"I suppose St. Ann's is awfully upset?"

"We are trying to keep everything going as well as possible. It is a bad situation, naturally. The nurses are doing their best but there is a sort of undercurrent of hysteria." My mind on Corole, I did not immediately note where his inquiries were leading.

"Miss Day was with you in the south wing

last night, was she not?" He knocked his pipe carefully against the railing.

"Yes."

"How — er — Is she feeling any bad effects from the fright?"

"I have seen her only for a few moments at lunch," I replied; at another time I should have smiled at his elaborately impersonal air.

"I — don't suppose I could see her? For a little while?"

"She will be free between six and seven o'clock. But we are allowing no visitors for a few days . . ." My voice trailed doubtfully into space.

"But see here, Miss Keate, I — it is important that I see her." He spoke rather defiantly as if he dared me to ask why. "Will you carry a note to her, then?"

Well, I was willing to carry a note to Maida, so I shivered under the folds of the flapping slicker while he stood with his back to the rain and wind, scribbling hastily on a bit of yellowish paper he pulled from his pocket. He held the paper close to him to protect it from the rain but I noted that it was an unused Western Union telegraph blank.

"There, and thank you, Miss Keate." He handed me he folded scrap of paper and I slipped it into my pocket.

But at the end of the bridge I turned.

"Why, Mr. Gainsay," I exclaimed. "I had forgotten. You were to leave this morning!"

His face had lost the youthful look with which he had begged me to take the note to Maida, and had become lined again, and his narrowed eyes were unfathomable under that shadowy hat brim.

"I shall not go for a few days," he said after a barely perceptible pause. "I can scarcely leave at such a time. Louis was a friend. They have no relatives here. Corole needs someone."

His disjointed explanation did not please me. I restrained a rather obvious remark as to chaperonage; after all, Huldah was a militant and vigorous enough chaperon to suit the most meticulous Mrs. Grundy.

I daresay, however, that my disapproval was apparent in my expression, for Jim Gainsay added hastily:

"My boat doesn't sail till next week."

"Your boat?"

"I'm to sail on the *Tuscania*."

"Oh," I said flatly, and there being nothing further I took my way on around the hill.

The Letheny cottage looked cold and grim as I approached it. Puddles stood along the turf path; the flowers were beaten down by the wind and leaves had blown all over the porch. Huldah answered the bell, her eyes red and swollen and the cap that Corole had forced her to adopt hanging dejectedly over one ear.

"Miss Keate!" she cried. "And so wet!" She took my slicker, holding it so it could not drip on the rug. "Oh, Miss Keate! Such a t'ing! Such a t'ing!" It is only when Huldah is tremendously moved that she forgets her digraphs.

"Yes, it is dreadful, Huldah," I said. "How is Miss Corole?"

Huldah shrugged her heavy shoulders oddly.

"There she is, in the study." She motioned toward the door without answering my question and then followed me, her china-blue eyes curious and round like a rabbit's between their pink rims.

"Oh, it's you," said Corole with not very flattering indifference. "For Heaven's sake, Huldah, take that wet coat to the kitchen. And close the door behind you," she added viciously. "I suppose you came to offer sympathy," she went on, moving a pillow to a more comfortable position under her arm. She was half-lying, half-sitting on the big davenport. A fire had been built in the fireplace but had burned down to a few sullen ashes with a red gleam here and there. There was no light in the room beyond the gray, rainy dusk from the windows.

Corole's hair was disarranged a little from its usual flat gold waves, and her eyes had great dark circles under them, and her face in the ghostly gray light was sallow and drawn. But she was gowned in a coppery-green silk thing that clung smoothly to her rather luxuriant curves. A heavily embroidered Chinese scarf, whose usual place, I recalled, was on the long table near her, had been flung over her feet and somehow, I presume because she glanced obliquely at it and reached surreptitiously to rearrange it, I got the impression that she had hastily flung it over her feet as I came into the room.

"Yes," I replied gravely. "I am very sorry that this thing has happened."

"Oh, of course, it is terrible," she agreed quickly. "The whole thing is simply unspeakable."

There was little for us to say; I offered the usual remarks; Corole told me that Dr. Letheny's body would be sent to New Orleans for burial with others of the family and thanked me perfunctorily for my offers of assistance.

"Jim Gainsay is staying on for a few days," she said. "Nice of him but I really don't see what he can do." There was a faint ring of resentment in her voice that surprised me.

Corole was not a woman to resent masculine company.

"I suppose Huldah is making you comfortable?" I said for lack of something better.

"Oh, yes," replied Corole discontentedly. "She does as well as usual. She was awfully upset about all this. Jumps every time I speak to her."

"Would you like someone to come and stay with you for a few days?"

"No," said Corole sharply. "No. Why should I?"

"Oh — in case of anything — er — happening. I should think you would be a little nervous." My explanation sounded somewhat lame and I recalled that Corole actually had no idea of the things we had gone through last night. . . . A swift recollection of that shallow, locked closet in Room 18 came to me and I arose suddenly, moved to another chair, and tried to think of something else.

". . . not that Huldah would be any good if something did happen." Corole was saying. "She would simply pull the covers over her head and shriek. But there's Jim." She added the last name grudgingly as if to say "such as he is," and lapsed into silence.

"I must get back to the hospital," I said presently, not seeing that my presence was vital to Corole.

"I don't suppose they have any idea as to what happened to the radium," she observed casually as I arose.

"No. I don't know what to think."

"It would seem natural to believe that who-ever killed Mr. Jackson and — er — Louis — did so in order to get the radium."

"So it would seem," I agreed. "For my part, I have not had time to speculate on possibilities. It is — too shocking."

"Don't you think that they will try to trace the radium?"

"I don't think anything about it," I replied caustically. Her interest in the radium annoyed me. I felt repelled at her callous lack of grief. Suppose she and Dr. Letheny had not been on the best of terms, nevertheless they were cousins and housemates.

"Well," she kept on, "it all seems very strange. Didn't you see or hear a thing while all that was going on?" Her catlike eyes, whose pupils shone large and flat and black in the semi-twilight, flickered over me with interest.

"No," I said shortly. I did not relish being questioned by Corole Letheny. "If there is nothing I can do for you I am going."

"No need to be in a hurry," she said in-dolently, yawning a little as she moved with a luxuriant stretching of muscles to a more comfortable position among the cushions.

"Good-night," I said curtly. "And do have some light!" As I spoke I reached abruptly for the lamp cord, pulled it, and the green light fell on the davenport.

Corole sprang upright with a startled half word, clutched the Chinese scarf and pulled it more securely over her feet.

"Good-night," I said again and left.

Huldah was waiting in the hall. As I took my coat it seemed to me that there was something hesitant in her attitude, as if she wanted to speak to me, but I was in a hurry and furthermore in no mood to condole with her. So I threw the slicker over my shoulders and splashed along the sodden path.

I scarcely noticed the rain, however, nor the cold discomforts of the path. When I entered the south wing and slipped quietly along its hushed length, I was still rotating in my mind a certain question.

When the light had flashed on there in Dr. Letheny's study, I had caught a brief but distinct view of Corole's slippers. They were beautiful pumps, high-heeled bronze kid with dainty, cut-steel buckles. But they were mud-stained and sodden with moisture and had wet leafmold clinging to them.

Where had Corole Letheny gone that afternoon? What errand had been so urgent that she had gone out of the house through the rain and storm in such haste that she had not had time to remove those dainty slippers?

Facing my own white, tired face in the mirror, I pushed my loosened hair together, removed little torn pieces of leaves from it and righted my cap. My shoes were soaked, so I changed them. Premonitory pangs of neuralgia began to shoot over my left temple, and I wished that I had not stood so long in the rain talking to Jim Gainsay.

With the thought came memory of the note with which I had been intrusted and I planned to give it to Maida at dinner; the bell was just ringing for the meal, then.

In my abstraction I had worn the borrowed slicker to my room; as I started down to the dining room I threw it over my arm. Idly wondering whose coat I had appropriated I ran my hand into a pocket, drawing out a man's handkerchief. It was large and white and had no distinguishing marks on it. But there was a faint scent — I pressed the square of linen to my nose, sniffed — and sniffed again with quickened interest. Faint but unmistakable, the scent of ether emanated from its folds.

I stopped midway on the stairs, stared at the thing and deliberately went through the other pockets. There was nothing more to be found; no identifying label or initials on the whole garment.

One yellow slicker is very much like another, and search though I did I found no means of discovering its owner. I felt, however, that I should like to have the ether smell clinging to that handkerchief explained. Possibly if I returned it to the rack and watched to see who came for it I should learn, at least, the identity of its owner. Thinking that no one would call for it during the dinner hour, the quietest time of the whole day, I replaced the handkerchief and hung the slicker on the hook from which I had taken it, and went down to dinner. But when I returned some fifteen minutes later, after hurrying over my dinner, the slicker was gone and I had not the faintest idea as to who had removed it.

I gave the note from Jim Gainsay to Maida when I met her in the hall outside the dining room and had the dubious satisfaction of seeing her crimson vividly as she read it. The crimson, however, was succeeded by a pallor that went to her lips as she finished reading the few sentences, and during the meal she kept her eyes steadfastly on her plate and ate practically nothing. And shortly after dinner, happening to be standing near an east window, I saw a slim, shadowy figure, crowned in a white cap, winding its way into the apple orchard. Something after seven o'clock, when I was catching forty winks in my own room,

Maida came in. The soft frame of black hair around her face had little beads of mist caught in it and I did not doubt that Jim Gainsay had succeeded in seeing her.

She did not mention him, however, but fussed around the room for a while, playing with the manicure things I had left on the dressing-table top, flipping through the leaves of the last *Surgical News*, and generally behaving as a woman does whose thoughts are elsewhere. She even picked up my tool kit, commenting on the curved bandage scissors and shining forceps and playing idly with the tiny plunger of my own hypodermic set.

We said nothing of the affair of the previous night; it was too recent, its developments too terrifying; we were both, I suppose, unconsciously fortifying ourselves against the ordeal of the coming second watch, which the memory of the last was not calculated to make easier.

Maida had two crimson spots on her cheeks — from the walk in the rain, I judged — but her eyes had slender purple shadows under them, her hands, usually so steady, fluttered a little over the tools she was fingering, she either spoke too rapidly of some trivial matter or lapsed into silence, and when someone passing coughed suddenly Maida started visibly, the pupils of her eyes darkened swiftly, and she cast a quick, apprehensive glance over her shoulder toward the door.

But since it was only to be expected that we both show the strain of the last twenty-four hours, I thought nothing of her evident uneasiness.

She had not been in the room more than half an hour when I was called to the third-floor telephone. The connection was poor and it took a few moments to find that it was Miss Neil who was wanted, and when I returned to my own room Maida had gone and I did not see her again until we met in the south wing at twelve o'clock.

Contrary to our unacknowledged apprehensions, second watch that night went much the same as on other nights. The electric lights had finally been repaired, though the utmost illumination was little enough to suit my taste. Just in front of the south door a policeman, tipped perilously back in his chair, slumbered spasmodically and I must say that, though he was no beauty, he was a most agreeable sight.

Fortunately for our piece of mind, it was a busy night. We actually needed the extra help, Olma Flynn and a student nurse, and the two extra uniforms, here and there about the wing, made it seem a little less silent and ghostly.

Along about two o'clock Sonny's light went

on and I answered it.

"Why, hello, Miss Keate," he said, as I turned on the light above his bed. "You haven't been in to see me since last night."

Was it only last night?

"I've been busy, Sonny," I replied. "How is the cast doing?"

"It was pretty bad last night." He moved a little to ease his tired body. "It is better to-night, though. Quite a lot more comfortable. What happened last night, Miss Keate? I heard somebody scream."

"One of the girls had a little fright." I made my explanation casually but Sonny's gaze remained puzzled.

"To-day has been so queer, too. So many people in and out and strange footsteps past the door. And this afternoon, about two o'clock, they shut all the doors and I heard the wheels of a truck being taken along the corridor. Did — did one of the patients die, Miss Keate?"

When I can't tell the truth I made it a rule to tell as near the truth as possible.

"One of the patients died, Sonny. He was an old gentleman."

"Oh," said Sonny, eyeing me doubtfully. I reached over to straighten his sheets. Through long hours of suffering, of lying helpless in bed and being at times rather nearer the other world than this, Sonny has developed a highly sensitive intuition.

"Oh," he said again. He was not satisfied but had good manners. "Did you have a nice time at the party?" he asked cheerfully.

"At the party — Why, no, Sonny. It — er — wasn't a very nice party. It was too hot."

"I guess Miss Day didn't get time to come in and tell me about it. I looked for her. But she must have been too busy."

"But I thought —" I checked myself abruptly, continuing: "Maybe she will come in to see you to-night. What is it you wanted, Sonny?"

"Just a fresh drink, please. And would you change my pillows?"

I brought the fresh drink and made him as comfortable as possible.

So Maida had not been in to see Sonny last night after all! And she had volunteered the information, I remembered; I had not even asked for it. I deliberated over the matter for some time before I came to the reluctant conclusion that only an affair of importance would have brought Maida to the point of telling a deliberate lie. Which conclusion did not lighten my state of mind.

The night didn't go so well after that.

From midnight until four o'clock are the dreaded hours of St. Ann's régime. They are

111

gray, cold, dreary hours — hours when pulses lag most feebly, when the breath comes most wearily, when life seems a burden that is all too easily escaped and the other world seems so near that the nurse must cling to her patients with all her will to keep them from making that quiet, easy journey. It is one of the demands of our profession that the most is asked of our strength at a time when it is at its lowest ebb.

Last night there had been two dead men in our wing — and dead by another's hands. Whose hand had it been?

Somehow during those black hours in that hushed and shadowy wing the thing that struck me with the most horror, that brought my heart, quivering, to my throat and gooseflesh all up my arms, was the memory of that locked closet.

Dead men can't walk. Dead men can't carry keys. Dead men can't lock doors.

Who had locked that door? We *must* believe that it was some intruder, someone outside our little circle at St. Ann's. And surely the police had searched the place and that fearful intruder could not still be about hidden in some recess of the dark old halls and passageways.

And yet — who would be familiar with the plan of St. Ann's? Who would know that the radium was in use? Who, indeed, would know of its value?

Eleven's signal light clicked and I hastened to answer, putting down the chart at which I had been staring without even seeing its red temperature line.

I found Eleven in a chill, which was followed, as I expected, by a raging fever under which he grew steadily delirious. Dr. Balman's orders for the night had included an opiate if conditions warranted it, so I went to the drug room.

The drug room is at the north end of the wing, directly opposite the diet kitchen. We always keep there a small supply of drugs for which we have frequent need. We do not keep the door locked as the drugs are in small quantities. In the drug room, too, we keep the various tools we are apt to need, among them a hypodermic syringe and a supply of needles. During the week past the syringe belonging to the south wing had got something wrong with its small plunger and Maida had brought her own outfit down for us to use, which had reposed beside the broken one in a drawer.

Pulling open this drawer I lifted the only syringe it contained and found it to be the broken one. Maida must be using the other, I reflected, and after waiting a few moments for her to return it I started out to find her.

She was in the kitchen, preparing a malted milk.

"May I have the hypo?" I asked hurriedly.

"The hypodermic syringe?"

"Of course. I need it at once."

"Isn't it in the drug room?" She was measuring the cream-coloured powder carefully.

"No. I thought you had it."

"I haven't used it to-night." She did not look at me.

"I'll see if Miss Flynn has it." I turned quickly away. But Miss Flynn did not have it, and had not had it. She hinted that I must have overlooked it and even walked back to the drug room with me, pulling out the drawer with her own hand.

"Why, there it is!" she exclaimed triumphantly.

And to be sure, there it was!

I was considerably chagrined, especially as Miss Flynn laughed and said something not at all witty about my eyesight.

And in the very act of filling the thing I caught sight of something that almost made me drop it. It was only a scratch across the bit of nickel where the manufacturer's name is engraved but it was a scratch I myself had made in order to identify it. In a hospital it is easy to get such things confused, so I had simply taken a pair of surgical scissors and scratched across the letter "K" which appeared in the manufacturer's name, Kesselbach.

My own hypodermic syringe! How had it got there? Like a flash my mind reverted to the memory of Maida, sitting on the edge of the window sill, looking at my tool kit and taking this same tool in her pink-tipped fingers.

I administered the hypodermic automatically, sterilized the needle and replaced it, and returned to Eleven.

But in that darkened room, listening to the gradually less rapid breathing of the sick man, and the still gusty wind and rain through which a slow gray dawn was beginning to make itself felt, I found myself possessed of new problems.

5

A Lapis Cuff Link

From that morning on I took an active interest
in the case — I mean, in solving the problem.
Indeed, Mr. O'Leary has had the kindness to
say, since, that I helped — well, I need not
repeat his words. However, it is true that I
did everything in my power, which was little
enough, to solve the mystery that confronted
us. While I am not at all inquisitive, nevertheless I do have an inquiring mind, due
doubtless to the fact that I have lived in a
hospital for a number of years and hospitals
are hotbeds of gossip. Not malicious gossip,
you understand, for nurses are one class of
women in the world who can keep the faith
which the ethics of the profession as well as
individual integrity demand.

But anything that happens in our small
world is of interest; the patient in the charity
ward who almost swallowed a thermometer
and had to be up-ended and shaken, the pre-
cipitate arrival of a new baby in a roadster
out in front of the hospital, or the alcoholic
whose language shocked — or diverted as the

case might be — a whole wing.

Besides the fact that the murders had occurred in the south wing, for which I feel a responsibility — the wing, I mean, not the murders! — there were other and as serious considerations. Chief among these was the affair of the hypodermic syringe and Maida's inexplicable behaviour the night of the seventh, and the presence of Jim Gainsay as testified by that gold cigarette case.

A hospital ought to be sanctuary and it seemed to me an offense against all the laws of humanity that this hideous thing should have happened within our walls of mercy. I deliberately tried to put myself in the frame of mind to be suspicious about anything and everything — and I trust it is no reflection on my character to say that I succeeded without much effort.

I found plenty to be suspicious about, and without going out of the way to do so. The only trouble was that, though I pride myself on being a keen and clear-minded woman and have more than the usual amount of determination, I could not arrive at any conclusion.

I worried all day about Maida, however, and when Lance O'Leary turned up about four o'clock, with a polite request for an interview, I did not know whether to be glad or sorry.

We went into the general waiting room to talk. It was a chilly place, with slippery leather-covered furniture and on the wall a none too cheerful picture of the burning of Joan of Arc. The weather had settled into a steady, dripping rain by that time, the clouds were still heavy, and the very concrete steps of the main entrance, just below the windows, oozed moisture. It was an added distress that not once during those strange days did we see the sun. Everything we touched was damp and cold and sweaty.

O'Leary was as meticulously groomed as he had been the day before, but there was about him a sort of quiet but intense concentration that seemed to detach him from ordinary affairs of the world. I have seen the same thing in the face of an artist I used to know — and in the face of a dear and saintly old nun under whom I trained.

There was nothing, however, of the poseur about him. He was ordinarily rather silent, was occasionally oddly boyish and young, was simple and direct — it was his unconscious absorption that marked him. And those extraordinarily clear gray eyes.

He asked a few commonplace questions as to how I felt, and were things going well, and was the policeman of any use. Then, he reached absently into his pocket and drew out the stubby red pencil.

"Miss Day was your assistant in the wing the night of the seventh?"

"Yes. We have second watch together this two weeks."

"How long has she been here at St. Ann's?"

"Three years."

"She is a good nurse, I judge? Cool and restrained?"

"One of the best."

"She is a friend of yours?"

"I admire her very much," I said warmly. "She is a girl of high moral character, thoroughly honourable and reliable."

"M'h'm —" He began to roll the inevitable little pencil.

"I suppose a nurse becomes fairly well acquainted with the other nurses, as well as the doctors, who frequent the hospital?"

"Yes," I said doubtfully, not seeing just where his questions were tending.

"Miss Day looks to be a girl of strong likes and dislikes."

Well, that was perfectly true so I contented myself with a nod.

"She was a good friend of Miss Letheny's and — of the doctor's?"

"Not — particularly," I said slowly. "We were all on friendly terms. Corole had us over there often."

"Did Miss Day work much with Dr. Letheny?"

"About as I did. She is a good surgical nurse."

"You mean she is efficient in assisting with operations?"

"Yes."

"I suppose that requires — nerve? Courage? A cool hand?"

"Yes." I was beginning to feel uneasy.

He paused for a moment, his gray eyes on the heavy clouds beyond the window.

"Tell me again, Miss Keate, just what you did when you first found that Mr. Jackson was dead."

"I left Room 18 and went to get a candle. When I returned Miss Day was in the doorway of Eighteen. There was a flash of lightning, and I saw her and she spoke to me."

"What did she say?"

"Just something about the storm: She had been closing windows in the wing."

"Did she know that Jackson was dead?"

"Why, no! Not until I lit the candle and she saw him."

"She was surprised, of course?"

"Yes."

"Then, as I understand it, she went through the dark corridor to the general office to telephone to Dr. Letheny. Was she willing to go?

120

Or was she — reluctant?"

"I — she —"

He caught my hesitation.

"She did not wish to telephone to him?"

"The corridor was so dark you could hardly see your hand before you," I remarked crisply. "And it was storming."

"Of course, of course," said O'Leary pacifically.

"Miss Letheny told Miss Day that the doctor was out," he went on quietly. "Then she, Miss Day, had the presence of mind to call Dr. Balman. I suppose she knew his telephone number? Or was there some kind of light in the office?"

"She asked Information for the number."

"Then Dr. Balman came out here at once?"

"Yes. He was here in just a few moments. He lives at the first apartment house off Lake Street and it is only a short drive."

"In the meantime you waked Dr. Hajek?"

"Yes. He sleeps in that little room that opens into the general office. He usually answers phone calls at night and — keeps an eye on things. Unless he is asleep," I added waspishly, thinking of how soundly he had slept when we needed him most.

"Why did not Miss Day call Dr. Hajek, when she called Dr. Balman?"

"She did try to but could not wake him.

But Dr. Balman was Dr. Letheny's assistant and should be called in a matter of such importance."

"Then you called Dr. Hajek yourself. I suppose you told him what had happened."

"No. I was so excited that I just told him to go at once to Room 18. I even pushed him toward the door." I smiled a little. "I took him by the coat and —"

"Took him by the coat? Then he was fully dressed!" O'Leary's gaze pierced mine.

"Yes." I paused as a certain recollection thrust itself upon me. "He must have been outside! In the rain!"

"Why do you say that?"

"His coat was damp."

O'Leary studied the pencil for a long time.

"Then what happened?" he asked finally in an inflectionless voice.

"Why — then — then I got hold of some lights and went back to Eighteen. They were all there, Maida and Dr. Hajek and Dr. Balman. They were just staring at the patient and doing nothing. Dr. Balman told me that he had died of an overdose of morphine. Of course, I knew that not a grain of morphine had been ordered. So that meant that it was done purposely. It was while we were standing there that —" I stopped. No need to tell that!

But he glanced at me quickly.

"Go on, Miss Keate."

"It was nothing."

"Then you should not object to telling of it."

"Well," I began reluctantly, "it was only that, as we were standing there, all at once there was a tiny bit of red that came from the hypodermic wound. You know the little pin prick where the needle has been inserted. It was —" I coughed to hide the tremble in my voice. "It was — very unusual."

I could see that Lance O'Leary, for all his professional frigidity, was somewhat shaken, for his hands gripped the pencil tightly and he drew a deliberate breath.

"That old superstition means nothing," he said. "But it must have been — grisly. And there were only you and Miss Day and Dr. Hajek and Dr. Balman in the room?"

My throat being dry I made an assenting gesture.

"And — Dr. Letheny in the closet," added O'Leary softly.

At that I must have gone quite pale, for Lance O'Leary, eyeing me with that oddly lucid gaze, spoke abruptly, as if to distract my thoughts.

"I believe you are a woman of some discretion."

"I ought to be! At my age."

"The fact inclines one to talk with you," he said drily. "Look here, Miss Keate, this is not going to be an easy job. In the first place it is obvious that the guilty person is very likely someone who is familiar with St. Ann's." I made some protestant motion and he went on: "Surely that has occurred to you?"

"Yes," I replied in a small voice.

"Why?"

"Because it must have been someone who knew that the radium was being used and in what room."

"And one who was familiar enough with the hospital routine to know the best time to enter the wing unobserved," said O'Leary.

"That eliminates Jim Gainsay," I remarked without thinking.

He regarded me keenly.

"We will come to him later," he said. "As to the radium — yes, I think we can assume that the radium theft was at least one of the motives. Its disappearance indicates that, though it might be merely a blind. But the radium is very valuable, a small fortune to many men. As a matter of routine we have taken steps to insure the immediate reporting of anyone trying to dispose of a quantity of radium. I do not expect to hear from this, however, for the person who has the radium will naturally wait until this affair has blown over before attempting to sell the stuff. Yes, the radium theft may account for the death of Jackson but not for Dr. Letheny. At least not unless —"

"Unless he caught the thief?" I interrupted eagerly.

"If that were true, how account for his stealthy return to St. Ann's and the fact that he did not call for help?" He paused but I said nothing and he continued: "Then there is the obvious conjecture that the person who administered the morphine must have been either so skilled that he could do so without awaking Jackson, or someone to whom the patient was accustomed. Dr. Letheny had charge of the case —"

"Dr. Hajek helped him some," I blurted. "And Dr. Balman was in to see him once or twice. And there were the nurses —"

"Then it appears to be between Dr. Hajek and Dr. Balman and you and Miss Day," said O'Leary all too coolly. I gasped and he went on: "And the unknown element which is always to be considered. We can't tell which died first — Dr. Letheny or his patient. We do not even know for certain whether Dr. Letheny met his death inside the walls of the hospital or not, but I have reason to believe that it was in Room 18. Otherwise it would have been difficult and purposeless, so far as

I can see, to convey his body into the room and into that closet. Almost impossible for a woman," he added as if in afterthought, and his eyes on that aggravating pencil. "I am inclined to think that the sound you heard and believed to be a window dropping to the sill was actually the blow that meant death for Dr. Letheny."

"Oh — !"

"Yes." His eyes were meeting mine, searching my face so intently that I felt as if my very thoughts were visible to them. "Now, Miss Keate, please tell me something of this Corole Letheny. I understand that she and her cousin were not on the best of terms."

"That is true," I acknowledged hesitantly.

"Don't be afraid of incriminating anyone," said O'Leary impatiently. "Clues are funny things. When they seem to point one way they are very apt, on close investigation, to point another way entirely. So please don't hesitate to answer my questions."

This reassured me somewhat; not that I have ever cared for Corole Letheny, but one does pause to consider one's speech in such a serious matter.

"Corole and Dr. Letheny never did get along well together. But I don't think she can be involved in this." Thinking of the oddly mud-stained slippers, I paused again.

126

That incident could have had nothing to do with the murders, of course, but still it was singular.

"What is it, Miss Keate?"

Before I knew it I had told him of the muddied bronze kid pumps.

"Indicating that Miss Letheny had some errand that took her hurriedly into the storm and that within a few moments following the discovery of Dr. Letheny's death. Suppose you ask this maid, Huldah, about it. She will be more willing to talk to you. Oh, yes" — he smiled a little — "we must investigate every incident, every straw, no matter how small and insignificant it appears. And moreover," he drew something from his pocket, "I am interested in Miss Letheny because of this." He placed the small, square object on the table before us. I stared. It was Corole Letheny's revolver. She had bragged about the thing often enough so I had no difficulty recognizing it. Someone had made her a gift of it, and it was very unsuitably decorated with some sort of silver trumpery and had her initials engraved upon it.

"We found this on the floor of the closet in which Dr. Letheny was found," said O'Leary quietly.

For a long moment I sat there in silence, my eyes fascinated by the dully gleaming thing. What could it tell?

"But — neither of the men was shot!" I said at length.

"No," agreed O'Leary, still quietly. "No. There is only the fact to go on that Corole Letheny's revolver was found in the room where two men met their death in one night. That is all. It only indicates her probable presence at some time in the room. And a revolver usually means that whoever carried it had reason to believe he was in danger — or expected trouble of some kind."

"But — Dr. Letheny might have brought it himself. He might have suspected that someone was planning to steal the radium."

Lance O'Leary smiled slowly.

"You are loyal, Miss Keate. It may interest you to know that on going through Dr. Letheny's deed box, I found that he was the beneficiary of a reasonably large income and that on his death it goes to Corole. I find, too — you see we detectives make our living by questions and answers," he interpolated, as I suppose I looked as I felt, very much puzzled at the knowledge he appeared to have secured — "I find, too, that Dr. Letheny kept his household down to the most moderate of expenses and gave Miss Letheny only a barely sufficient allowance."

"It is true that she has complained a great

deal about money," I admitted thoughtfully. "She is rather beautiful, you know, and loves to dress well."

He nodded.

"You have seen her then?" I asked.

"Yesterday. I talked to her. Yes, I suppose she does love clothes and finery. It is on account of her — dark blood."

"Her what?" I sat bolt upright.

"Good Lord, Miss Keate! Didn't you know that?"

"Know that Corole Letheny is a — ?"

"I think it comes to her by way of Haiti," he interrupted. "And a very beautiful mother."

"But — her light hair and eyes! You must be mistaken!"

"Her eyes are yellow, Miss Keate. A good deal like a tiger's. In fact she is a rather tigerish lady, on the whole. I suspected it when I first saw her brown hands, and was convinced when I found a reference to her in Dr. Letheny's papers; once he mentions her rather bitterly as 'my mulatto cousin,' and another time refers to her birthplace and his aunt, Jolbar, who, it seems, traced her lineage directly, if unobtrusively, to a cannibalistic royal line. Don't be so shocked, Miss Keate. A little mixture of blood doesn't hurt her. It only increases my difficulty."

"Increases your difficulty?" I murmured, feeling rather dazed.

"By increasing the complexities of a personality that I must classify and index. You see," he went on, as I still did not wholly understand him, "Corole is a factor to be considered along with the rest of the possibilities. And this fact warns me that she likely has a streak of savagery back of those yellow eyes; that the beat of tom-toms would stir her, for instance. She is apt to be rather indolent, too, and to seek what she desires in unconventional ways. Such as by the use of revolvers."

"Why, yes," I murmured idiotically. "Murder *is* unconventional."

"So you see, the counts against Corole are interesting, to say the least. Then, there are the others at that ill-fated dinner party. We shall have to consider the possible culpability of every single one of them — even of you, Miss Keate." He added this with a half smile but I did not relish his joke — if joke it was. I was inclined to think it was not.

"Corole Letheny," he checked her off on his fingers. "Because her revolver was found in the closet of Room 18, because she knew of the radium being in use and of the hospital routine and of the door being left unlocked and because she benefits by Dr. Letheny's death."

"But I'm sure she did not know what had happened to the radium," I said, going hastily on to tell him of her questions concerning it.

"She shows considerable interest, however," commented O'Leary. "And at an inappropriate time, too. Yes, we must consider Corole."

"But she — oh, she could not have done that!" I cried, revolted.

"We can't be sure of anything, Miss Keate, until it is proved," remarked O'Leary drily. "Then, there is Dr. Hajek; he was like the others, familiar with the circumstances, he had access to the morphine, being a doctor, and his coat was damp when, after some delay, you finally succeeded in rousing him, which, of course, leads one to believe that he was absent from his room and had recently been out in the rain."

"But," I objected, "Dr. Hajek was the only one of us who did not admit to wanting money — if we are to consider the radium as the motive."

"That does not prove anything. Indeed, it was more natural to admit a desire that everybody experiences at one time or another. Then, there was Dr. Balman. He, too, was familiar with the circumstances. Of course there remains the important questions of how Dr. Letheny comes into the puzzle, and whether Dr. Balman could have had time to drive to his apartment in order to be there when the telephone rang to call him back to the hospital."

"Why, yes," I said thoughtfully. "He could have done so. You see, just as the storm broke and I was at the south door, closing it, I saw the lights of a car on the lower road. That *could* have been Dr. Balman. But the idea is absurd. Dr. Balman is too mild, too kind — too — Oh! It is impossible!"

"Nothing is impossible," commented Lance O'Leary gravely. "But those lights may have belonged to another car. One driven by Jim Gainsay."

I may have imagined it, but it seemed to me, in view of my guilty knowledge of that cigarette case, that he eyed me rather closely as he spoke. However, if so he gained nothing by it, for I was honestly surprised.

"Jim Gainsay!" I cried.

"Yes," he answered, going on to explain. "The sedan owned by Dr. Letheny was seen standing in front of the Western Union office at about two o'clock that night. This information was brought to my ears and upon investigation I found that Gainsay took the Doctor's car — Huldah, in fact, saw him leave — and drove into the city, starting shortly before the storm began. He sent a message,

132

of which I shall have a copy before the day is over. We also know that Gainsay frankly said he intended to get hold of fifty thousand dollars — wasn't it that?" I nodded dumbly and he went on. "And he intended to go to New York this morning but is still here, work or no work. Also, as with the others, he knew something of the circumstances, and while his being able to obtain and administer morphine is a point to consider, still I understand that engineers almost have to have a practical working knowledge of medicine. But even if we could safely exonerate him from causing Jackson's death there is still the death of Dr. Letheny, for which somebody is responsible. And this Gainsay is a strong young fellow who looks as if he would stick at little."

"But he looks honest, too," I protested.

"They all look honest. Everyone of you."

"It seems terrible to consider people one knows in such a sordid connection. Why not all the other people in and around the hospital?"

He looked at me as if he were amused.

"But, Miss Keate, is it possible that you do not know that we immediately accounted for every soul in St. Ann's? And that every nurse and every patient has a perfect alibi, save you and Miss Day, Dr. Balman and Dr. Hajek? In a hospital run with such efficient routine as this one, it is a simple matter. The only person besides those I have mentioned, for whom we can't be absolutely certain, is Higgins, and that because he sleeps in the basement next to the furnace room and no one saw or heard of him during that night, since no one else sleeps in the basement. Of course, we shall have to include him in our list of suspects, but so far there is nothing but opportunity with which to suspect him."

"Then Maida and I are the only nurses who cannot prove just where we were between twelve-thirty and two o'clock that night?" I asked uneasily.

"We know *where* you were," said Lance O'Leary very soberly. "You were both in the south wing." He paused to look at his watch, a thin, platinum affair that reposed in a pocket of his impeccable vest, and I felt a quite warranted chill creep up my back.

"So you see our paths of search are limited," he said easily, replacing the watch, and returning to that abominable red pencil.

"Yes," I agreed weakly. "Limited." Altogether too limited!

"Of course, there is always what I spoke of as the unknown element. There might have been an outside intruder, but so far nothing has come to light that would indicate that possibility. The use of the radium seems to have been absolutely unknown to all but the hospital staff and the guests at Miss Letheny's dinner party. Now then, Miss Keate, there are three things that particularly interest me to-day. One of them is the identity of the man with whom you collided at the corner of the porch. Did you receive any sort of impression that would serve to identify him?"

Nervously I tried to think of something besides the cigarette case.

"He — I think he wore a raincoat. I seem to remember the slippery feeling of rubber. And I think he must have been wearing a dinner-jacket, for I seem to recall feeling his starched shirt front."

"Then it might have been one of the four men at Corole Letheny's dinner?"

"It might have been, of course," I spoke rather irritably, as I foresaw the next questions.

"Was it Dr. Letheny?"

"I don't think so. I can't be sure."

He was surveying me so closely that I found my eyes going toward the floor in spite of myself.

"Was it Dr. Balman?"

"It might have been. Though it seemed he was a little taller than Dr. Balman." I was studying the roses on the old-fashioned Brussels.

"Was it Dr. Hajek?" he went on mercilessly.

"I — I tell you, I can't be sure who it was. It might have been anybody."

He leaned back in his chair and I could feel his smile.

"I'm beginning to understand your — er — temperament," he said easily. "I suppose it was this Jim Gainsay. Now you may as well tell me what you were doing with his cigarette case in your laundry bag."

I blinked.

"How did you know it was there?"

"A policeman found it while searching your room."

"Searching my room!"

"Yes. We have had all the personal belongings of those in whom we are — interested — searched. We were at first surprised to find you were addicted to smoking — and more surprised when we traced its ownership. Now, please, tell me just how you came upon it."

In as few words as possible I complied.

"Will you hold Jim Gainsay?" I asked finally, as he turned and twisted the stubby red pencil thoughtfully in his hands.

"We shall watch him," he amended. "So far he has stayed of his own free will, a thing that is in itself strange. Of course, if he should attempt to leave I should be forced to restrain him."

The dinner bell rang just then and he looked at his watch, again frowning as he noted the time.

"Another thing, Miss Keate. That smell of ether interests me. Especially since to our knowledge ether was not used at all. Are you sure?"

"Yes." I spoke decidedly. "I am sure now, because of the slicker I wore yesterday afternoon."

"The slicker?" he inquired. "Yesterday afternoon?" And listened intently while I explained the whole thing.

"And you had no means of identifying it?" he asked, presently.

"No. Everybody wears a yellow slicker. You know how popular they have been the last year or two."

He nodded.

"I wear one myself," he said. "Well, thanks a lot, Miss Keate. You are a present help in time of trouble." He smiled at me with that engagingly warm and youthful look.

I started toward the hall, paused and turned around.

"Didn't you say there were three things you were particularly interested in right now?" I said. "What is the third one?"

"Oh, yes." He studied me for a moment as if to see how far the discretion with which he had complimented me might be trusted. Then he drew something from his pocket — something so small that it was hidden in his hand until he held it toward me.

And when I looked, I cried out and shrank back, my heart leaping to my throat. There on his outstretched palm lay a small cuff link; it was a neat square of lapis lazuli, set in engraved white gold.

"I see that you recognize it?"

Speechlessly, I made a motion of assent.

"You need not tell me that it is Miss Day's. I already know that. One or two of the nurses recognized it as I left it casually on the table in the general office. Oh, I watched it carefully — I suppose they thought she had lost it. They did not know where it was found."

"Where it was found —" I repeated, huskily, my voice losing itself somewhere in my throat.

"It was found — in Dr. Letheny's pocket." He spoke very deliberately, his clear, gray eyes searching mine. Then he turned. "Goodnight, Miss Keate," he said courteously and was gone.

As for me, I stood there quite still, staring at the gathering darkness outside the window, and at the slow rivulets of moisture trickling down the glass. Finally I aroused myself, straightened my cap, and moved toward the door. I was late for dinner, of course, and remember that someone was complaining about the steak being burned. It might have been ashes so far as I was concerned. Once I stole a look at Maida, across from me and down the table a few places. She was very white and tired-looking and it seemed to me that she avoided my eyes. I felt rather sick as I noted that, though it was a chilly day, she was wearing a uniform with short sleeves that had no need of cuff links.

6

I Make a Discovery — and Regret It

I must admit that I went about my duties somewhat automatically that night and could not help keeping an eye on Maida, not from suspicion, you understand, but simply because the matters of recent development troubled me considerably. Indeed, I had plenty to think of that night.

Corole's dinner party, followed by its terrifying sequel, had taken place on Thursday night. Early Friday afternoon the body of Dr. Letheny had been found. Friday night we had taken second watch with the policeman tipped against the sinister door of Room 18, and Saturday was the day just past. It was while I was sitting at the chart desk during second watch of Saturday night — really early Sunday morning — that the amazing idea occurred to me. I had been staring at the charts, absorbed in the baffling problems those days had brought, when all at once I began thinking of the morphine.

Might it not prove something if we were

to discover where that morphine had come from? Morphine is not something that one carries about in a pocket or vanity bag; it is very difficult to secure and in St. Ann's a most rigid check is kept on the quantities of the drug used. Would the morphine record for that week in the south wing balance?

With the thought I was up on my feet and starting toward the drug room. As I passed the door of the diet kitchen I saw Maida standing at the open window. Why do women bother with silks and laces and jewels when there is nothing that so sets off beauty as the severe, white simplicity of the nurse's uniform? Maida's face was like a proud young flower above the white collar of her tailored uniform. The stiff white cap perched piquantly on top of her head and contrasted nicely with her soft black hair. Her eyes were a deeper blue, her clear, gardenia skin and soft crimson lips were still lovelier above that plain white dress. I sighed, glanced down the corridor to see that there were no signal lights, and slipped into the drug room, closing the door.

A dose of morphine is a simple matter to prepare; it is the administering that requires skill. The preparation is a mere mixture of sterile water with the white morphine tablet, in the amount prescribed. At St. Ann's there is a careful check of the amounts used, and the drug room record must check with the doctors' orders. It was a simple matter for me to compare the two records with the remaining supply of morphine. And it was with a heart that dropped to my shoes that I found they emphatically did not check. And that the amount of discrepancy was more than enough to drug a person far more heavily than was safe.

When had this disappeared and how? A young, strong man might survive such a dose, or one accustomed to taking the drug. But an old man, whose heart reaction would be slow — well, it seemed all too apparent that the morphine that had killed Jackson might have come from our own south wing drug room. It was not a pleasant possibility.

Maida was still in the kitchen when I passed it again and I stopped. She was washing her slim, pink fingers vigorously.

"Eleven does get hungry at the most erratic times. He wants beef tea now and an hour ago he had malted milk," she said, drying her hands.

"Mr. Gainsay did not leave Friday after all," I said, coming directly to one of the things that troubled me.

She glanced swiftly toward me, lifted her

142

straight black eyebrows a little, and spoke rather coolly.

"Evidently not. He said his boat did not sail till next week. Is this beef extract fresh?"

"I think so. I suppose he is quite a comfort to Corole."

"Corole needs friends at a time like this," said Maida.

"Of course, he was such a good friend of Dr. — Letheny." For the life of me I could not speak that name naturally and easily.

"Yes," agreed Maida briefly. She turned to the stove, lit the gas flame, and held a small saucepan of water over the blue points of fire. I could not see her face.

"Maida," I said abruptly, "when did you last see Dr. Letheny — alive?"

She whirled toward me at that, and — well, it was not nice to stand there and see her face turn a dreadful, slow white with bluish hollows around her mouth and nose. But she answered at length, quite clearly:

"I last saw him at Corole's dinner party. When we said good-night and left."

She looked into my eyes for a moment after she ceased to speak, almost as if she were daring me to deny her statement. And I knew that it could not be true. Else how could her lapis cuff link have got out of the snowy cuff in which I had seen her place it *after* we were

143

safely within the walls of St. Ann's, and into Dr. Letheny's pocket?

"Oh — Sarah," she cried suddenly, throwing out her hands toward me in a gesture that was like an appeal and with a half sob in her voice. But as suddenly she drew her hands sharply backward and turned again to the stove. To this day the salty, meaty smell of beef boiling always brings to me a vision of those shining, white-tiled walls and the enamelled gas stove and Maida's straight, white-clad shoulders and beautiful, troubled face.

"Tell me," I said at last. "Is there anything you know that might help solve this mystery?"

But Maida turned an unfathomable blue gaze toward me.

"Nothing. Nothing that would help."

And it was not until she had departed with the beef tea steaming hot on a tray that I noted her ambiguous wording.

I could not disguise to myself the fact that I was deeply alarmed. Particularly because I had caught her, and wished I had not, in a deliberate lie. Either that or that abominable cuff link had simply jumped itself out of her cuff and into the pocket of Dr. Letheny's immaculate dinner coat.

I shall not conceal the fact that I gave voice to several expletives that made up in fervour for what they lacked in content. And I had

144

learned quite a vocabulary from my parrot, a nice bird who died last year on his ninety-sixth birthday, unless the dealer lied, and was much mourned by those of the nurses whose rooms are at the far end of the dormitory. Owing to the night air making the dear bird talkative there was a sort of feeling against him among the rooms within hearing distance of my own.

However, in this case the utmost of his vocabulary did not relieve my feelings.

All went as well as might be expected, and we did not once need a policeman, so it was as well that he had been withdrawn. Of course, I'm not saying it was a pleasant watch, for it was not. The south end of the corridor seemed darker than any other portion of it and the sinister door of Eighteen was somehow black and menacing and altogether unpleasant. But on the whole the night passed quietly, which was a mercy, for that was the last night that we pinned on our caps with any assurance of how long they would stay there. Dawn came at last, cold and gray, and with it the slow melancholy sound of the five o'clock bell for early prayers. The north wing of St. Ann's ends in a small chapel that is dignified with age and has a pipe organ, high walnut pews, and old, stained-glass windows. It is open on week days for prayer and meditation and on

Sundays the young assistant rector from St. B—'s down in the city comes to St. Ann's to conduct prayers and confession and church.

The Sunday then dawning was destined to remain long in my memory as a sort of interlude between what had been and what was to follow.

In the first place, Morgue, the basement cat, who is thin and ill-tempered and kept for utilitarian purposes only, surprised us all by having three healthy kittens. For some years the assumption had been that this was a feat biologically impossible and the news, brought to the table by a student nurse who had actually seen the kittens, caused quite a stir and for a moment distracted our minds from the too-absorbing problems of the last few days.

There were some disbelievers at table, this despite the student nurse appearing to clinch the matter by quoting Higgins's opinion that Morgue had displayed considerable talent in this connection, and after breakfast we all trooped down to the furnace room to see with our own eyes.

Higgins was down there, fussing around a grape basket which he had lined with an old duster, which, by the way, made the baby cats smell quite distinctly of cedar oil and must have puzzled their proud and complacent mother. The kittens themselves were not much to boast of, resembling, indeed, very young and scrawny rats and squirming vigorously and squealing when the girls picked them up and passed them from one to the other. There was a heated discussion over their names; it was felt they should bear some relation to the mother's name, and Morgue is not an easy name with which to relate. They settled on Accident, Appendicitis, and Ambulance. The kittens were all black, to my mind not a particularly happy or propitious colour, and Melvina Smith, who is pale and superstitious and would not touch an opal with a ten-foot rod, exclaimed in italics that trouble was coming to St. Ann's. Upon which someone murmured that trouble had already come and Melvina said, yes, but it always came in Threes and these three black cats were a sure sign that bad luck would come in threes here. She pointed out, reasonably enough, that Morgue could as well have had four kittens, or two, but no, she had had three. And that furthermore, who ever heard of Morgue having kittens before, and it was certain she had had them this time just to warn us of the third — er — trouble.

Well, for my part, I felt that Morgue would not go to so much bother, she being by nature unobliging and apt to mistrust our most friendly advances. But already the girls were putting the kittens in the basket and casting rather frightened glances into Morgue's inscrutable yellow eyes, and drifting toward the stairway. I could have wrung Melvina's foolish little neck, but naturally I followed them.

On the way upstairs Olma Flynn remarked earnestly that it was nice that Morgue hadn't had ten kittens. Upon which several of the less idiotic laughed and Melvina cast a look of pale reproach upon Olma, who, as a matter of fact, had spoken with single-minded gratitude.

As I reached the top of the stairs Higgins called to me.

"Miss Keate."

I turned. He was standing at the foot of the stairs, looking up.

"Yes."

"Can you spare some time now, Miss Keate? There was — something I wanted to — ask you about."

I hesitated. It seems to me that when anyone around St. Ann's has a complaint it is brought to my ears and I was in no mood that morning to listen to complaints.

"I was just going to get some sleep, Higgins," I said. "Will another time do?"

How often, since then, I have wished that I had stopped then and there. But I thought of nothing more important than leaky gut-

148

terpipes or the canna bulbs not doing well.

"Well — yes," agreed Higgins slowly. Something in his tone made me regard him sharply, thinking that he seemed quite reluctant and perplexed. However, as I say, I was tired and sleepy and had already more than enough problems before me, so I took my way upstairs.

On the way I picked up the Sunday paper. The supplement had the hospital pictures again, groups of nurses, a sort of history of St. Ann's, stressing its long years of service but winding up with a lurid résumé of the past few days, which is the way of Sunday supplements but not unpleasant. I even found a picture of myself taken some years ago when pompadours and bosoms were in style. It was not a flattering picture and neither was the caption below it, which described me as one of St. Ann's oldest nurses! Oldest in point of service, it went on to say tactfully, but the picture dated me indisputably and I flung the paper in the waste basket and tried to compose myself to sleep. And, I might add, did not succeed.

I found the noon service in the little chapel remarkably well attended, with prayer books in evidence and the nurses turning out *en masse*. The young rector preached a rather nice sermon about "Be ye not afraid," which I considered a little too apropos for comfort and good taste.

Sunday is usually a rather festive day in St. Ann's but that Sunday was anything but pleasant. No visitors were permitted, which made the patients fretful and hard to please. Moreover, we could not prevent an almost constant stream of morbidly inclined sight-seers whose automobiles splashed along the muddy road in front of the hospital, and who stared through the fog and pointed with melancholy satisfaction.

I drifted uneasily about the dismal corridors for some time before I found Maida, ensconced unhappily in a cold window seat with a magazine which she was holding upside down.

She had not been to see Corole yet, she told me, and was dreading the visit that convention demanded. Wouldn't I go with her? And though I had no relish for Corole's company I found myself following the blue and scarlet of Maida's nurse's cape along that sodden, desolate path, holding my own cape tight around me and wishing I had brought an umbrella.

On the porch we met Dr. Hajek, just leaving.

"Bad weather," he murmured as we passed him. His dark eyes slanted knowingly toward us; his face was very fresh and ruddy and his

150

square teeth gleamed under that small black moustache.

Huldah opened the door, her cap very properly on her head this time but her face sullen.

We found Corole comfortably seated in what had been Dr. Letheny's study, a warm fire glowing in the grate and the tea cart drawn up to the davenport and laden with her best silver tea service and some fascinating little French pastries that could only have come from Pierre's, a very exclusive and high-priced sweet shop. I registered the impression that Corole was not wasting any time enjoying her newly augmented income, and gave my cape to Huldah. Corole and Maida were murmuring polite sentences and, recalling my promise to O'Leary, I followed Huldah to the hall.

"Miss Letheny feeling any better, Huldah?" I asked.

She gave me an expressive glance.

"H'm!" she grunted. "There's not much mourning going on in this house! She —" she jerked her head toward the study — "dresses all up like a hussy every day and entertains callers. You know as well as I do that ain't any way for a lady to do!"

"I noticed she was wearing that green silk thing with her bronze slippers the other day," I remarked tentatively.

151

"She won't wear them bronze pumps again, anyhow," said Huldah in dour satisfaction. "She had to wear them out in the rain and now they are ruined."

"Had to wear them out in the rain?"

"Yes, ma'am! The very afternoon we heard the bad news. Not an hour after them gentlemen was at the house to tell her about the doctor being dead. Nice gentlemen they was, too — them police officers." She stopped, apparently musing on certain blue-coated figures. I had to prod her gently.

"Where was she going in such a hurry that she didn't change her shoes?"

"Goodness knows! As soon as they had gone she grabbed a shawl and ran out the back door and across the alfalfa field. The last I saw she was scooting into the apple orchard and she didn't get back for a full hour. It was raining, too, and she might have taken an umbrella at least. But not she! Catch her doing anything like a Christian!" concluded Huldah resentfully.

"Would you like some tea, miss?" she went on, after a moment's brooding. "Some tea and one of my own cakes I made myself yesterday before she ordered them silly French things? Like as not poison, too, with all such coloured candies on top."

"Indeed, I should, Huldah," I said soothingly, though her cakes are, as a rule, sprinkled too liberally with caraway seeds. "And let me have a small anchovy sandwich," I added, thereby winning her to a reluctant smile as she departed kitchenward.

I was not much wiser than I had been, and I really could not see that I could have questioned Huldah any further. Anyway it was likely she had told me all she knew, for Huldah's natural disposition is to spread anything she hears.

I joined the other two in the study in time to catch a strained something in the atmosphere that made me pause involuntarily and look from one to the other. Maida was standing very stiff and straight, her eyes flaming like blue fire, her fingers clutched together until the knuckles and fingernails were white, and her whole attitude breathing defiance and anger and — yes, alarm. Corole was lying gracefully back in her chair, her creamy lace teagown falling softly away from her brown neck, the topaz on one hand catching light from the fire, and her strange eyes narrowed lazily in an expression so like Morgue's that I almost gasped.

But as to that, resemblance to a cat or other animal is nothing to hold against a person, I argued reasonably to myself; there is a cashier in the City National who looks like nothing so much as a mild and woolly sheep and is yet, as far as I know, an upright and respectable man.

Neither Maida nor Corole seemed inclined to break that brittle silence, so I settled wearily into a chair.

"Huldah seems to resent the French pastries," I said. "Where did you get them, Corole? At Pierre's?"

"She resents everything," said Corole indolently. "Yes. At Pierre's. You must try them. I'll make some fresh tea. Do sit down, Maida. You make me nervous, standing there so stiff."

I think Maida was about to say something, but just then Jim Gainsay lounged into the room, straightened up with interest when he saw Maida, and she subsided into a chair while he greeted us with every evidence of pleasure.

It was, however, a very uncomfortable hour, with the conversation painfully limited to commonplaces, Jim trying in vain to catch Maida's eyes, and Huldah slapping down the tea things with venom and making it distressingly clear that I, alone of the company, was in her good graces. Corole was almost indecently easy and flippant in her manner, and Maida very quiet.

As for me, I was reminded vividly of the last time we had been together in that room, especially after Dr. Balman arrived. His coming made the gathering begin to seem too much like a party, so I prepared to leave. But Dr. Balman had come on business, and after speaking in a low aside to Corole he went to Dr. Letheny's desk, glanced hastily through a card index, and noted something in his small notebook. I remember thinking as he did so that Dr. Balman was not having an easy time of it; it is difficult enough to step suddenly into the position of head of a hospital, without having the burden of investigations into two murders on one's hands. And Dr. Balman looked as if he were feeling the strain of his duties, for his mild eyes had circles under them, his scant eyebrows wore a perplexed frown, and his pale cheeks were hollow. He looked as if he had not been eating much lately, and indeed, I didn't wonder at it. The bruise on his cheek had not receive proper attention, for it was dark and ugly-looking and I longed to take it in hand.

"Is that what you wanted, Dr. Balman?" asked Corole.

"Yes — yes. This is all." He was writing busily.

"You must have some tea," offered Corole graciously.

"What? — Oh, tea?" Dr. Balman compared the notes he had written with the original and raised his eyes to glance about the room with rather obvious distaste. He was always a man of keen sensibility and I daresay he felt much as I had felt on entering this room that spoke so clearly of Dr. Letheny.

He was about to decline, I think, when Huldah opened the door, said "Mr. O'Leary," as if she were firing a shotgun, and Lance O'Leary entered, his gray eyes twinkling a little at the manner of his announcement.

It was odd to see how the appearance of this slight, perfectly groomed young man, with his clear, gray eyes and thoughtful, well-shaven face, affected us all. Dr. Balman sat down slowly as if after all he had decided to stay. Jim Gainsay fastened a narrow, enigmatic look upon the newcomer and lit another cigarette, Maida's eyes widened a little and her hands sought each other in her white lap — and Corole adjusted the lace of her gown, smiled seductively at O'Leary, remembered she was mourning and sobered wistfully.

"No, thanks," said O'Leary pleasantly. "No tea, Miss Letheny. I hope you'll forgive my intrusion but I came on business."

Corole blinked but repeated warmly: "Business?" and motioned toward a chair.

"Yes. Thanks, yes, I'll sit down." He drew a chair nearer the glowing fire. "It's wet out," he remarked with a half smile.

"Would you like something besides tea?" asked Corole, her graceful brown hand on the tiny silver bell that decorated the tea cart. I could not help noting how pink her palm was, how brown her fingers, and how purple the shadows on the fingernails.

"No. No." The high-backed chair O'Leary had happened to choose, unpholstered in needlepoint tapestry, and with slim carved arms of softly gleaming walnut added somehow to his natural dignity. "How are you, Doctor? Not feeling this strain too much, I hope."

Dr. Balman smiled wanly. "No, thanks, Mr. O'Leary. It is quite a task though. However, Dr. — Dr. Letheny left everything in perfect order." He glanced at Corole apologetically as he spoke, but she was interested only in O'Leary.

The conversation dragged along very uncomfortable for a few moments, during which the only person in the room who was thoroughly at ease was Lance O'Leary. As soon as I decently could I rose to leave, for O'Leary had said he came on business and I naturally supposed that it was business with Corole.

Maida rose, too, and of course, the men.

"Just a second, Miss Keate," remarked O'Leary in a quiet and commonplace voice. "I only wanted to tell you all that the coroner's inquest will be to-morrow morning and that you are all to be called as witnesses. I'm sorry to have to tell you at such a time."

It just happened that I had my eyes on Corole as he spoke and thus saw her soft brown fingers grip the macaroon she held until it fell on the tea cart, a small, powdered mound of sugar. I looked quickly at O'Leary, but his gaze was apparently on the log in the fireplace.

It was an uncomfortable moment, there in that room of which the very books along the wall and the grand piano in the alcove spoke so vividly of Dr. Letheny. We were "all" to be called as witnesses then. And a few nights ago we had sat here in this room and listened to the Prelude in C Sharp Minor played by those strong white hands that would never touch a piano again.

I shook myself free from such morbid reflections, said a brusque good-bye to Corole, and left. Maida went with me, and somewhere along the path Jim Gainsay turned up.

As the path narrowed under the trees and I preceded the other two, I am sure I heard Jim Gainsay say rather huskily to Maida:

"I had to see you alone. You must do as I say. It is import—"

"Sh! I know!"

"Try to see it my way." (This in a still more urgent voice.) "It is dangerous to —"

"Hush!" she interrupted sharply again.

And just then I think that Maida stumbled over a branch that had blown across the path. At any rate I heard a quick motion and a sort of gasp and then Maida said rather breathlessly: "That branch — I nearly fell." And I turned in time to see Jim Gainsay pick up the stick, bow to it gravely and say: "Thank you, old fellow," before he tossed it off into the orchard. At which Maida turned quite pink and Jim Gainsay gave her a long look and laughed rather shakily.

Then we were at the south entrance and Gainsay swung on his heel with a brief "Goodnight."

And it was not fifteen minutes later that I glanced through the society section of the paper that someone had left on the chart desk, and my eyes fell on a small news item:

Mrs. J. C. Allen left Tuesday of this week for New York City. She sailed on the *Tuscania*, Saturday night, June ninth.

On the *Tuscania*, Saturday, June ninth. That was yesterday. And I was positive that Gainsay had said the *Tuscania*.

7

The Disappearing Key and Part of an Inquest

"Yes, I saw that this morning," said a quiet voice beside me. It was Lance O'Leary; I did not know he was near until he spoke. "Our friend Mr. Gainsay seems to be a little confused as to his dates."

I daresay my eyes reflected a question for he added, leisurely:

"He told me that he intended to sail on the *Tuscania* next week. I see that he told you the same thing. He is not a very discreet young man, else he'd have known that I should look up the *Tuscania*'s sailing date without delay."

I sighed; all those unpleasant little doubts of Jim Gainsay were returning in full force.

"If he has the radium, it is not in his room in the Letheny cottage," said O'Leary meditatively.

"How do you know?" I inquired stupidly.

"We have searched the rooms and personal belongings of each of those present at that dinner party last Thursday night."

"What!"

"In fact, I daresay that there is not a room in the whole of St. Ann's, as well as in the Letheny cottage, that has not been thoroughly ransacked."

I ran my tongue over dry lips. This was getting down to work with a vengeance.

"Why?" I stammered.

There was a glimmer of impatience in his eyes.

"For the radium, of course. Surely you did not think we were going to let it get away from us without a struggle."

There was a moment or two of silence during which I studied the polished glass surface of the desk before me without seeing it.

"Did you ask Huldah about Miss Letheny's errand through the rain last Friday afternoon?" inquired O'Leary after a contemplative pause.

"Yes." I told him in a few words the little that Huldah had told me. "And there is something else I have discovered," I went on miserably. "I've got to tell you, though I must say I do not want to do so. It is — that morphine. The morphine that killed Mr. Jackson, you know. I — I know where it came from!"

"You — what!" O'Leary was for once startled out of his usual composure.

"I know where it came from," I repeated

reluctantly. "At least, I think that I do. You see, — there is morphine missing from our south wing drug supply."

I had to tell him the whole thing, of course, under his searching questions and no less searching gaze, and even explain our system of keeping account of the drugs. He had to see the drug room and the charts and the records for himself. It was while I was showing him the drawer in which the morphine was kept, that I made my regrettable slip about the hypodermic syringe.

I had started to show him how the needles were fitted into the small mechanism, and I reached for a hypodermic syringe. It turned out to be my own.

"This one is mine," I said thoughtlessly, fitting the slim, hollow needle into the tiny instrument. "The other one that we were using disapp—" I stopped so suddenly that my breath came out in an explosive little pop and O'Leary's face hardened slightly. It was an expression that I was growing to recognize.

"You may as well finish. So the other one disappeared, did it? When and how? Whose was it? There is still one in the drawer. What about the one that disappeared?"

"I don't know," I said flatly. "Then, you see, we take the sterile water and measure the liquid into —"

O'Leary looked at his watch.

"I haven't much time," he said pleasantly. "But I have enough time to wait right here until you tell me about the hypodermic syringe that disappeared. Or if necessary I can dog your footsteps the rest of the night, reiterating my question at frequent and embarrassing intervals. Of course, I can have the whole hospital searched extensively and every hypodermic needle accounted for, especially if missing. I can follow you to your meal — isn't that the bell? — and keep on asking you." He added meditatively: "I suppose it might cause considerable interest among the other nurses."

I regarded him furiously. The thing was that he would be quite capable of doing just that. I began to understand the force of the words of the chief of police when he had said — "Once Lance O'Leary gets his teeth into anything, it is as good as done."

"I suppose you'll have to know sometime, anyway," I said sulkily.

The flicker in his gray eyes was like a ripple across a very calm, deep lake.

"You are right, Miss Keate. So why not tell me now?"

Well, to make a long story short, I told him of the missing hypodermic, which after all, was little enough: barely the fact that Maida's syringe had been removed and my own sub-

163

stituted, but this without my knowledge. And that Maida had had the opportunity to take my own, and if she had wished to use it, all that she needed to do was ask me for it.

"Which she conspicuously did not do," commented O'Leary. "Oh, by the way, Miss Keate, have you ever attended an inquest?"

"No."

"Well, don't get bothered. Our coroner is a decent old fellow but he does love to be pompous. Just answer what he asks, tell your story as briefly as possible and don't — er — volunteer anything. You see there are some things that you and I know that will not come up at the inquest."

"You mean — they would warn the guilty one?"

He nodded briefly as he turned away.

Maida was already in the south wing when I rounded the right angle of the corridor leading from the main office at exactly twelve o'clock that night.

"I locked the south door," she said, hanging the key on its customary nail above the desk.

"That was right," I approved, glancing over the charts. It appeared that Eleven's digestive apparatus was still doing business at the old stand, so to speak, but otherwise all was well and I settled briskly into the business of second watch.

Midnight temperatures had scarcely been taken, however, when Olma Flynn developed a sick headache, worse when I was within hearing distance, and had to be excused from duty. We didn't actually need the extra help, as Maida and I had been accustomed to care for the whole wing ourselves, but nevertheless it was a little annoying, especially as, about two o'clock, the little student nurse burned her wrist over the gas flame in the diet kitchen, and the burn had to be salved extensively and the nurse sent to bed with an aspirin tablet.

Thus Maida and I found ourselves alone in the south wing for the first time since those terrifying events of Thursday night. This precarious situation was a matter that was, I think, predominant in our thoughts but neither of us mentioned it; we even manufactured an artificial sort of — not gaiety, that would be asking too much — but of brisk attention to work and a determined avoidance of conversation that might lead back to things we were anxious to forget.

All went well, in spite of our hidden fears, until about three o'clock. I was pouring out a small dose of bromide for Three, who had made up her mind not to sleep that night and naturally was not doing so, when Maida opened the door of the drug room.

Her face was so ghastly white that at first

glimpse of it my hand began to tremble and the medicine poured all over the spoon. Blindly I set the bottle down.

"What is it?"

"There's something in Room 18!" she gasped through ashy lips.

"Room 18!"

"Just now — I saw something go into that room from the corridor!"

"Someone — is sleep-walking." I grasped at the first rationality that presented itself.

After the light in the diet kitchen the long corridor seemed peculiarly dark and shadowy and the green light over the chart desk was miles away. It never occurred to me to call for help, and we sped along toward that dark end of the wing that we had good cause to fear.

But we stopped stock still as we came close enough to see the door of Room 18, and a cold shiver crept up from my back.

The door of Room 18 was standing wide open!

It had not been opened, so far as I knew, since the police had left that room. It had been shunned by all the nurses. Who had opened it? Who would dare open it?

Who was inside that dark place?

A long, shuddering sigh came from Maida beside me and I felt her cold hand grip my wrist. The contact nerved me and I did what, I afterward realized, was a very foolish thing.

I took a few steps forward, advanced to the very door of that grisly room, reached a shaking arm through the open doorway, groped for the electric-light button, found and pressed it.

The cold white dome on the ceiling flooded the room with light.

There was nothing out of the way to be seen. There were the plain dresser, the bedside table, two chairs, the folded burlap screen and the high, narrow bed — nothing else. Something caught in my throat as I glanced at the bed and toward the closet doors.

"The — closet —" breathed Maida at my side. "Oh! You are not going to open that!" as I took a more decisive step forward.

It was no easy thing to do, for I knew well that those shallow closets were yet large enough to hold — what one of them had held.

They were both unlocked this time. And there was nothing in them!

I turned to Maida, whose white face had been beside me during the ordeal. Without saying a word we retreated to the corridor.

"Are you sure you saw something?" I asked, my voice hoarse.

"I am positive," whispered Maida. "You see, I was just answering Fourteen's light,

167

which brought me fairly near to Eighteen. I came out the door and was starting down toward the chart desk when something — I don't know what — some rustle or sound, perhaps, made me turn around, facing this way, so I could see the south door. And I was just in time to see a sort of movement at the door of Eighteen." Her hands went to her throat as she spoke and I did not feel very comfortable myself.

"It couldn't have been one of the patients?" I murmured.

"No! There isn't a one of them who is able to walk."

"Then who —"

"Or — *what* —" said Maida.

A remnant of common sense saved me, I think, from stark terror. I took a firmer hold on my imagination.

"Nonsense," I spoke decidedly but still, for some reason, in a whisper. "There are no such things as — as — I mean to say, the shadow you saw was either an optical illusion or a living, breathing person."

"Certainly," agreed Maida, adding inconsistently: "I don't see how a living person could have got past us, through this long corridor without one of us seeing him — *it*."

My eyes fell on the south door near at hand; the tiny panes of glass winked blackly at me as I crossed to it, grasped the brass latch and pulled. The door swung slowly open, letting in a current of cold, mist-laden air.

"There, you see?" I said to Maida. "Only a real, material thing needs a door to go through."

Maida was looking at me strangely.

"I don't see that that helps matters any," she said. "I locked that door myself, to-night. It just proves that someone was actually here. That the murderer is still about the hospital."

"Not necessarily," I said, though my heart was pounding in my throat. "You are sure you locked it?"

"Positive."

"And you hung the key there on the nail above the chart desk?"

"Yes."

We both swung hastily around. At the other end of the shadowy corridor gleamed the green-shaded light over the desk. With one accord we started toward it.

The key was not on the nail above the desk!

But even as our frightened gaze took in that amazing fact my eyes fell on the glass top of the desk. There on its shining surface lay the key. We stared at it for some time before our eyes met. Then I picked up the key my fingers seeming to shrink from the cold, clammy metal, returned to the south door, locked it securely and put the key in my pocket.

And as I did so, a thought struck me. The person who had got into the wing by means of the south door must also have got out again. He couldn't have gone through the corridor and south door for Maida was, by that time, in the hall.

The light was still glowing in Room 18, and I crossed the room, not without a queer feeling in the region of my knees, as if they would give way with me, without notice. Sure enough, the window was unlocked; it was even open a fraction of an inch at the bottom, though the screen, which has a spring snap, was closed.

I pushed the window the rest of the way down, locked it, not without an unpleasant impression that something was out in that gleaming darkness back of the window pane watching my every move, turned off the light, and closed the door again. Maida was standing in the corridor and we walked slowly toward the more cheerful region of the chart desk and diet kitchen.

"I suppose," she mused at length, "that someone could have taken the key from the nail and returned it when we were in Room 18."

"But who? It would have to be someone

in St. Ann's. And that is unthinkable."

"There are likely ways in and out of St. Ann's," she said finally, and with that a signal clicked somewhere. I recalled Three who would be in a tantrum by this time, and we separated.

We were very busy for the rest of the night, and dawn was never so welcome a sight. But during those slow hours I came to the conclusion that there were only two things we knew without doubt. The key to the south door had been removed from the nail and left on top of the chart desk, and the sinister door of Room 18 had been opened and left open.

Who had done this and why was a matter of conjecture, and I resolved to say nothing of it save to Lance O'Leary. I should leave it to O'Leary.

Leave it to O'Leary! I had so far recovered from my fright that I smiled faintly at the phrase, but I could have embraced the day nurses when they came on duty, and the rattle of the dishes in the small, rubber-tired dumb-waiter, as it came up with the breakfast trays, sounded like music to my ears.

On the way to the basement for breakfast, I had time for a word or two with Maida.

"We'll say nothing about it, save to O'Leary," I murmured in a low voice and she nodded, just as Miss Dotty joined us with one of her insufferably bright good-mornings.

Miss Dotty keeps a book at her bedside, entitled *Every Day a Sunny Day*, and memorizes verses from it. Her verse that morning was:

If you're lonely, sad and blue,
Keep smiling.
Luck will bring you someone true
Who understands and loves just you.
Keep smiling,

which seemed not only inane but downright offensive, as coming from one old maid to another.

The inquest was set for nine-thirty. We had an early operation and at eight o'clock prompt I was tying Dr. Balman into his white apron and hood and counting sponges in the operating room. The patient's appendix proving to be elusive, turning up, in fact, on entirely the wrong side, the operation was more interesting than we had expected. Dr. Balman looked haggard from fatigue and worry, his thin hair and beard were dishevelled and his eyes were hollow, but his hands were steady, if rather slow, and every last detail was thoroughly attended to.

The inquest was held in the nurses' library

in the basement. It is not a cheerful room, particularly on wet, rainy mornings. It was chilly in the place; the white-washed walls looked cold and bare, even the medical books along the walls had none too happy titles. The linoleum rug caught dismal highlights, the chairs borrowed from the dining room were slippery and uncomfortable, and moisture dripped steadily down the small windows. Someone had turned on the lights but they did not improve matters.

At a little table sat a stout, elderly gentleman, whom I had no trouble identifying as the pompous coroner. He wore a pair of noseglasses attached to a button on his broad vest with an important black ribbon. The board of directors were ranged near at hand, some of them constituting the jury, which would have surprised me had I not known the weight in politics and otherwise that some of those names carried.

Corole Letheny was there in a soft brown frock daringly tailored and very short so that her silk-clad — er — ankles and so forth were much in evidence; she wore a small green hat pulled low over her eyes and carried a large and gorgeously beaded bag which made a spot of vivid colour in that neutral gray room. Huldah, very stiff in her Sunday black silk, sat beside her.

A little way off among a group of nurses sat Maida, her beauty and the distinctive air of breeding in the very lift of her chin making her stand out from the others as if they were only the frame for a picture. Jim Gainsay stood at the back of the room with a group of reporters. He wore an air of ease that was a shade too deliberate; his impenetrable eyes looked at nothing in particular but, I had no doubt, missed not the smallest movement in the room. He was attractive, clean, young, vigorous, but I could have wished him less restrained — less poised — less wary.

There were the staff doctors, of course, talking to Dr. Balman and Dr. Hajek. I was interested to note that a bit of Dr. Hajek's ruddy colour had deserted him; he said little and his black eyes darted here and there about the room, occasionally lingering upon Corole. Save for those restless eyes he was as unmoved and stolid as was usual with him.

There were several policemen, too, Higgins, the cook and a few curious student nurses sitting with Miss Dotty, who being something of a simpleton took that occasion to shed a few tears, presumably for Dr. Letheny. And there was O'Leary, of course, gray and quiet, sitting near the coroner's table.

It being the one and only inquest I had ever attended (for which I am truly thankful), I was not able to compare it with others and did not know whether the undercurrent of excitement, the low whispers, the white faces, the nervous little movements and darting glances here and there, are typical of all inquests or peculiar to that one.

All at once the coroner put down the papers he had been studying, took off his nose glasses, and began to talk. I did not notice what he said, for at the same moment O'Leary rose quietly and moved toward the back of the room. As he passed me he dropped a small bit of folded paper in my lap. Under the cover of my wide cuff I read the brief message it contained. I read it again; it didn't seem to make sense, but of course, I was willing to obey the terse request. Just as I slipped the paper into my pocket I heard my name being called and I rose and walked to a chair indicated by the coroner.

After convincing the coroner and the jury that I was actually Sarah Keate, superintendent of the south wing and on duty the night of Thursday, June seventh, I was allowed to proceed.

It was not so difficult as I had feared it would be; I was allowed to tell my story in a brief and straight-forward manner. The only time I became confused was when I got to the incident of the arrow-like projectile that had

175

whizzed over my shoulder while I stood for a moment there on the little south porch. It was then, for the first time since the night it occurred, that I recalled the trifling incident, and I was already launched upon it and could not head off the coroner's questions. I caught a reproachful look from O'Leary but had to continue; however, the coroner's questions could prove nothing for there was little I could tell of the matter.

The coroner questioned me rather particularly, too, as to the man with whom I collided, but I had expected this and gave guarded replies. He also tried to make me identify the owner of the cigarette case which lay there on the table before him, but I refused to commit myself beyond telling how and when I found the thing.

As I say, it was not difficult — that is, until I reached the actual events leading to the crime. It was then that my voice faltered.

"It was while I was sitting there at the chart desk, at exactly one-thirty — I had just entered the time on a chart — that I heard a sort of — bang. It sounded like a door closing." I went on speaking with more and more difficulty. "So I got up and walked along the corridor but the south door was still open. Then I went back to the chart desk and was there when the storm broke and I had to run to close the door and the windows. When I went into Room 18 to close the window I found —" I stuck and had to clear my throat. — "I found that the patient, Mr. Jackson, was dead. The lights had gone out but a flash of lightning lit the room and I felt for his pulse and knew that he was dead. I ran to the diet kitchen, found a candle, and ran back to Eighteen. Miss Day had been closing the windows in the wing and had just got to Room 18 when I returned with the candle. It was after we knew we could do nothing for him that we found the radium had been stolen."

My testimony continued for some time after that, but I simply answered the coroner's questions as briefly as possible and volunteered nothing, and presently resumed my seat, feeling that, with the one exception, I had conducted myself creditably.

Then Dr. Balman and Dr. Hajek were called in turn, to testify as to the causes of death, first of Mr. Jackson's, and later of Dr. Letheny's. They used technical terms, and told the methods of determining the length of time each had been dead before discovery. It was a difficult half hour for both of them, knowing Dr. Letheny as they had, and they both looked quite exhausted when the coroner had finished with them. Dr. Balman was frankly mopping his high forehead and even

Dr. Hajek's stolidity was shaken, for his eyes darted nervously about him and he retreated to the back of the room, where he lit a cigarette with unsteady hands.

Then Miss Maida Day was called and as she took the witness chair my hands gripped each other and I watched her with strained attention.

She testified very coolly, though. No, she had not seen Dr. Letheny when he called to visit his patient at twelve-thirty. She had been busy in one of the sick rooms. Yes, she had stepped out on the porch for a breath of air. Yes, she had attended the dinner party given by Miss Letheny. The coroner seemed to be supplied with all the topics of conversation of that dinner and Maida agreed imperviously to every one of them, even to the fact that she had said she wanted money.

"I believe your words were 'I'd give my very soul for money'?" inquired the coroner nastily.

"I think I did say something like that," said Maida quietly, though a tiny flush mounted to her cheeks. "Of course, I didn't mean exactly that. One often exaggerates one's statements."

The coroner did not comment on that but looked expressively at the jury.

Then she corroborated, under his questions,

178

every detail I had told of our finding of the body of Mr. Jackson and of our subsequent actions. He made his questions very searching and important indeed, and I felt something between a fool and a liar during the process; I am not accustomed to having my word doubted.

"Miss Letheny answered the telephone, when I called for the doctor," Maida explained, "and said that she couldn't rouse him, and when I said we must have him immediately she went away from the telephone and when she came back told me that he was not in the house and she didn't know where he had gone."

"Then you telephoned to Dr. Balman?"

"Yes."

"Did he answer immediately?"

"No. I think he must have been asleep. When he did answer I told him simply of Mr. Jackson's unexpected death and that we could not locate Dr. Letheny."

"About how long was it until Dr. Balman arrived?"

"I'm not sure. I was — agitated naturally. But I should say about fifteen minutes."

"How was he dressed when he arrived?"

"In — a dinner jacket, I think — and slicker. It was raining, you know."

"Miss Day, have you lately lost a cuff link?"

asked the coroner, without warning.

I was watching Maida closely and saw the little flush that had been in her face drain steadily away; her eyes darkened but did not falter in their steadfast gaze.

"Yes," she replied quietly.

"Is this it?" He placed a small object in her hand that I could not see but had no doubt was the square of lapis.

"It — seems to be," she said, after a pause during which we others scarcely breathed. "It resembles the one I lost."

"Do you think you can say that it is your cuff link?" asked the coroner smoothly.

"Why — yes. At least, it is identical with mine."

"Can you explain its presence in Dr. Letheny's coat pocket when he was found —dead?"

"No," said Maida steadily, her steel-blue eyes meeting the coroner's directly.

"When did you discover its loss?"

If possible, Maida went still whiter, and her nostrils took on a pinched look.

"Shortly after I had returned from the porch," she said steadily enough, but her eyes went to the back of the room for a brief instant.

"How did this get into Dr. Letheny's possession?" persisted the coroner.

"I do not know. I suppose I — dropped it. Lost it from my cuff, and Dr. Letheny must have — found it."

"In the dark?" inquired the coroner suavely.

Maida flushed again but her chin went higher.

"I do not know."

He continued to question her at some length but with no success, and finally he dismissed her, with a grudging "Thank you."

Corole Letheny was the next witness and I settled myself more comfortably in my chair to listen. She was extremely self-possessed, and sat down as gracefully as if she had been paying a call. She looked rather nice, or would have, but for the clear beauty of the face that had just preceded her. Maida's immaculate uniform, her clear white skin, her amazing blue eyes under their straight black eyebrows, that little, aristocratic air which somehow always surrounded her, made Corole seem a little tarnished, a little tawdry, a little theatrical, in spite of her perfect grooming and her expensive clothing.

By that time the repetition of the details of that oft-referred-to dinner party were growing stale and I did not pay the strictest attention to the first questions of the coroner. I was aroused, though, by hearing him say suavely:

"You will pardon me, Miss Letheny, but were you and Dr. Letheny on the best of terms?"

181

She stared at him, her yellowish eyes widening and reflecting green lights from her hat brim.

"What do you mean?"

"Following the departure of your guests that night, did you not have a heated disagreement?"

Her eyes slowly left the coroner and went to Huldah in an exceedingly unpleasant gaze.

"I suppose my maid told you that. Yes, we did quarrel. Louis — was not an easy man to get along with."

"What was the subject of your quarrel that night?"

"About as usual. Nothing in particular."

"Can you recall any of the exact — er — subjects?"

"Why — no," said Corole slowly. "That is, he told me I was running the house too extravagantly. He always said that."

The coroner surveyed her for a moment or two.

"Is this your revolver?" he said suddenly, reaching for the shiny revolver and holding it before her.

She started, quite visibly. One brown hand, with a great topaz shining on it, reached out as if to clutch the thing, and then drew slowly back.

8

A Gold Sequin

"Does this revolver belong to you?" the coroner repeated.

"Why, yes," Corole said huskily. "That — is mine."

"Can you explain its presence in the closet in which your cousin's body was found?"

She ran her tongue nervously over her lips.

"No," she said. "No."

"When did you see it last?"

"I — don't know. It was usually kept in the drawer of the table in Louis' study. I — don't remember just when I saw it last."

"You didn't bring it to the hospital, then?"

"Certainly not," flashed Corole. Her eyes narrowed so suddenly that I almost expected her to flatten her ears and spit like a cat.

"When did you last see your cousin, Dr. Letheny?"

"When I went upstairs at a little after twelve." Mentally I figured that their quarrel must have been short and to the point.

"Where did you leave him?"

"He was sitting in his study."

"When you answered the telephone when Miss Day called, did you search the house?"

"Yes."

"Had his bed been disturbed?"

"Apparently not."

"You can swear, then, that he was not in the house at — two o'clock?"

"If that was when Miss Day telephoned, yes. I did not look at my watch."

There were a few more, rather unimportant, questions, then Corole was dismissed.

After that the inquest rather dragged for awhile, although Huldah telling very succinctly of Jim Gainsay taking out the Doctor's sedan a short time before the storm broke was one of the points of interest. Several policemen had to tell just what they found; during the description of finding Dr. Letheny's body, I saw Corole wince for the first time and raise her laced handkerchief to her face.

Then Dr. Balman was summoned to tell of his movements following the dinner party. He had gone directly to his room, it appeared, and was asleep when the telephone rang.

"Asleep?" said the coroner astutely. "Not in your dinner jacket, Doctor."

"I was very tired that night, having worked hard all day. I sat down in an armchair to rest and went to sleep. The first thing I knew the telephone was ringing."

"And what did you do then?"

"Miss Day sounded frightened — and it had been my impression that Mr. Jackson was doing very well indeed. I took my coat, for it was raining, got into my car and drove as fast as I could to St. Ann's."

Dr. Hajek, too, corroborated as far as possible every feature of the testimonies Maida and I had given. No, he had not heard any knocks on the door of his room, until I knocked. The lights were out and he did not understand at once what was wanted. However, when he did understand that there was some trouble in Room 18, he hurried to that room. He had only time to make the briefest of examinations, when Dr. Balman arrived. Dr. Balman came by the south door into the wing, instead of going around to the main entrance. The south door had been closed and the key in the lock and Miss Day had let Dr. Balman into the corridor. Yes, they had immediately agreed as to the cause of death.

Mr. James Gainsay was the next witness. As he advanced a queer little stir crept over the room.

He admitted freely that he had been walking in the orchard previous to the storm. The night was hot and sultry, he said, and he had thought it might be cooler outdoors. As freely he admitted that the cigarette case belonged to him.

"I'm certainly glad it was found," he said, grinning a little. "I value that cigarette case and did not know where I had lost it."

The coroner frowned; this levity was out of place. He moved the slim, gold case to the side of the table farther away from Gainsay.

"Was it you who collided with Miss Keate, there at the porch steps?" he asked.

Jim Gainsay's sun-tanned eyebrows drew closer together, but his mouth retained a half-amused smile.

"I think it likely," he said easily. "At least I — collided with some one."

His candid air did not remove, to my mind, any of the significance of his presence near the hospital.

"Why were you running?"

"I was in a hurry," said Gainsay simply.

"Where were you going?"

"To Dr. Letheny's garage."

"Did you go directly to the garage?"

There was the barest possible hesitation. Then:

"Yes."

"What did you do, then?"

"Took Dr. Letheny's car and drove into town."

"How long were you gone?"

"About an hour, I should say. The roads were new to me and the rain made it bad driving."

"You wanted to send a telegram?"

If Jim Gainsay was surprised, he gave no sign of it.

"Yes," he said quietly. I don't know what it was in the tightening of his mouth and the quality of his voice that made me quite sure that the question had, in some manner, put him on his guard.

"What was the telegram?"

"A matter of business," replied Gainsay smoothly.

At this point Lance O'Leary reached over the coroner's table and pushed something across it to the coroner. The coroner took it in his hands, a slip of yellow paper, and adjusted his spectacles. After reading what was written there, he glanced disapprovingly over his glasses at Gainsay, deliberately read the message again and finally spoke.

"Was this the message you sent?"

"I'm sure I don't know," said Jim Gainsay, good-naturedly, though there was a wary look in his half-closed eyes.

A little gust of laughter was frowned upon by the coroner, who poised his spectacles again to read in a measured way: " 'Delayed owing to unexpected development stop cannot make the *Tuscania* stop may not get away soon signed J. Gainsay.' That yours, huh?"

I was astounded to see that Gainsay had gone rather white and his jaw was set.

"Yes," he said very quietly.

"What do you mean, 'unexpected development'?"

"I — am not at liberty to state."

Something in Gainsay's manner seemed to irritate the coroner.

"Not at liberty to state! Well, see here, young man, you'd better be at liberty to state and that mighty fast! You've admitted to skulking around St. Ann's, at a time of night when respectable people are in bed and leaving cigarette cases —"

"Now, now," remonstrated Jim Gainsay gently. "I object to the word 'skulking.' "

"You object! You object!" The coroner removed his eyeglasses for freer gesticulation and somehow they detached themselves from the ribbon and flew out of his hand. He paused in slight discomposure and Lance O'Leary stooped, returned the eyeglasses, and as he did so, leaned over and said something in a low voice.

"H'm-m. R'r'h'm!" remarked the coroner weightily, fixing a profound gaze upon Jim Gainsay, as if his blackest doubts of this young man had been justified.

188

"That is all, Mr. Gainsay. For the present."
He surveyed Gainsay unpleasantly and added,
as if he liked the sound of the words: "For
the present."

The rest of the inquest was not interesting
and was mostly a matter of repeating things
that I already knew. The coroner seemed
rather addled but very determined to catch
somebody in an untruth. I knew where his
trouble lay; it was not that he lacked clues,
it was rather that he had too many of them
and they all seemed to point in different di-
rections. I was glad that Lance O'Leary appeared to have kept his own counsel about
certain matters of which I had told him,
though I should have liked to see the faces
of the board members if it had been brought
to their attention that the morphine had
very likely been stolen from our own south
wing.

The bell was ringing for lunch when the
coroner concluded his somewhat pointless inquiries, and after a few moments in which the
room was in utter silence the decisions were
given. I was not surprised to hear that Dr.
Louis Letheny had come to his death at the
hands of a person or persons unknown. And
a little later, in a hush so tense that we could
hear the dripping of rain from a gutter pipe
outside the windows, the same decision was

given as to the death of our patient, old Mr. Jackson.

We stirred our cramped muscles, rose slowly and straggled out of the room by twos and threes. To tell the truth I felt as if nothing but a formality had been accomplished. But as I left the room I turned for a look backward and saw Lance O'Leary's smooth brown head bending close over the coroner's bald spot in earnest consultation. That one glimpse convinced me that O'Leary actually, if not openly, controlled the inquest and did so to suit his own inexplicable motives. I longed to tell him of the mysterious visitor the south wing had had the previous night but had no opportunity until later in the day.

What with one thing and another troubling me I did not rest well that afternoon. By the time I had napped spasmodically, had a bath, and got into a fresh uniform and cap it was four o'clock and I wandered through the curiously hushed corridors, down the stairs and into the general office. Miss Jones was writing in the record book of incoming cases and I paused to find out who had been entered. It was something to know that even the disagreeable publicity we had been given had no affected St. Ann's prestige.

"I'm putting him in Eighteen, in your wing," she said as I bent over her shoulder.

"In Eighteen!"

"Why, yes. The room is available for use, isn't it? He wants a downstairs room and that is the only one left."

"Whose patient?"

"Dr. Balman's, I think — yes." She referred to the typed card.

At the moment Dr. Balman entered the room from the inner office.

"Just copy this history, please, Miss Jones, and let me know if —" he glanced at the record she was preparing. "Are you putting him in Eighteen?" he asked sharply.

"Yes. Isn't that right, Doctor?"

His long fingers sought his beard perplexedly.

"This affair is so recent —" he said doubtfully. "But, if there is no other room?"

"He especially asked for a downstairs room."

"Very well, then," he agreed after a moment during which his thoughtful, rather kind eyes studied the record. He spoke wearily. "Put him in Eighteen. We will have to use the room sooner or later, in any case. Oh — Miss Keate. Better warn the nurses to say nothing of Eighteen's — er — history. The patient will be here at least two or three weeks, perhaps longer."

"Yes, Doctor," I said as meekly as if I

shouldn't have known that I must do that, anyway. And I must say I did not relish the idea of a patient in Eighteen, knowing, as I did, that if it proved to be a surgical case with no private nurse, much of the care would fall on my shoulders, which meant many errands into Room 18.

"Very good," he said and turned toward the door.

"Oh, Dr. Balman," Miss Jones called him back hastily. "Did you not want me to copy that history?"

Dr. Balman wheeled, glanced at the typed paper still in his hand.

"I forgot," he said abstractedly. "Thank you, Miss Jones." He handed her the paper. "The patient will be in about six o'clock, I think," he added, as he disappeared.

He had not any more than got out of the room, when Dr. Hajek entered.

"Was there a telephone call for me — thank you," as Miss Jones handed him the pad with a number scribbled on it.

He took down the telephone.

"Main 2332, please," he said into the mouthpiece, adding aside to Miss Jones, "Any new cases this afternoon?"

"Yes, Doctor. A Mr. Gastin is coming in. I have put him in Eighteen."

"In Eighteen! What? Oh, yes — Main 2332

—" he turned again from the telephone. "Did you say you put him in Eighteen? Eighteen in the south wing?" he asked sharply.

"Why, yes," said Miss Jones. "That was the only downstairs room left."

"But —" began Dr. Hajek, only to be interrupted by the operator's voice again. "Yes. Main 2332 — Oh, there you are. Yes, this is Dr. Hajek. What's that? . . . Did you take his temperature? Oh — yes I see. Try a hot water bag and a little warm milk. . . . Yes. . . . Yes." He hung up with a click. "About that new patient, Miss Jones, I really don't think it wise to put him in Eighteen. If he is inclined to be nervous —"

I was tired of discussing the matter.

"He will not know a thing about what has happened there," I interrupted very rudely and not at all in accordance with professional etiquette. "We've got to use the room sometime. Why not now?"

"Yes," agreed Dr. Hajek, surveying me absently. "Yes, I suppose so. Yes. Did you say he comes this afternoon?"

"About six o'clock," said Miss Jones, and with a nod he swung toward the inner office.

Thinking that I must see that Room 18 was in order, I hurried toward the south wing. The room had not been cleaned beyond a brief straightening up, so I sent two nurses to clean it and went along myself to superintend the affair.

It was not pleasant to open that door, but I had opened it under still less agreeable circumstances. The room was very gloomy and cold with dismal shadows on the white walls, and the window panes so beaded with moisture that the gray light from outside filtered but faintly into the place. I relented so far as to turn on the electric light, which threw the whole room into sharp relief, and the two girls set to work.

The air was stale, so I crossed to the low window near the porch, unlocked the catch and flung it wide, letting in the damp mist. I stood there, thinking of the intruder of the previous night. Who had been in this room? What had been his purpose? What would O'Leary say when I told him of it? Had the visitor escaped by this window? I looked at the wide sill. There was a screen there, to be sure, but it worked on a spring catch and could easily be opened from either side, this to facilitate the shaking of rugs and dusters and the adjusting of awnings. Idly I pushed back the screen, running my finger along the sill. I was about to close it again when a faint reflection of light from something in the corner of the sill caught my eye. I leaned toward that corner to look more closely, reached out

194

and slowly turned the tiny flat thing over with my fingernail.

It was a gold sequin!

I should never have seen it save for that minute reflection of light, for the upper surface was all tarnished and stained, though the under side was still bright. A wisp of frayed green thread still clung to the small hole for a needle at the top of the flimsy bit of metal.

I needed no one to tell me from where the thing had come; the night of June seventh Corole Letheny had worn a dress of gold sequins cunningly arranged over net with flashes of green here and there.

And it did not seem probable to me that she had worn the gown since that night.

By the time I had digested this amazing fact the girls, to whom fear seemed to lend astonishing speed, had got the room cleaned.

"A patient is coming," I explained to them. "That is all now." They were glad to be dismissed and hurried away.

I did not remain alone in that room. Strolling down the corridor, the tiny sequin still in my hand, it occurred to me that it would be a fine thing to be able to tell Lance O'Leary, when I gave him the sequin, whether or not Corole had worn her gold gown since the night of her dinner party. Huldah would know, and somehow in the face of this last development, I had no scruples as to inquiring of Huldah concerning the affairs of her mistress.

It was a matter of only a few moments until I was on my way.

The path through the orchard squdged wetly under my feet; the trees dripped steadily on my starched, white cap, and the mist lay so heavy and close that I could not see more than ten or fifteen feet ahead of me. The shrubs massed around the trees were hazy, shadowy outlines, and the raw air fairly hurt my throat.

I walked on slowly through the wet alfalfa field, passed the clump of pines that made a black blot amidst the fog, and through the gate. The porch of the Letheny cottage still looked dreary and Huldah had not swept it that day.

Corole came to the door.

"Oh," she said unenthusiastically. "Oh, hello, Sarah. Come in. I was boring myself over a book." She threw my cape on a chair and I followed her into the study.

"You decided not to go to New Orleans, then, with the — that is, for the funeral?"

"There was no need to." Her face darkened. "He has relatives there who — never cared for me."

"Mr. Jackson's body was sent East," I said.

We lapsed into silence. Presently Corole stirred.

"I'd give you tea but Huldah is in bed with a headache. She went to sleep right after lunch but I suppose is awake by now. I told her not to worry about dinner; I'll drive in to the Brevair. I've been wanting to get out, anyhow, and they say there's a wonderful new chef there."

"Well, for goodness sake, Corole, don't make yourself conspicuous. There's that matter of the revolver at the inquest, you know."

Corole glanced curiously at me and laughed.

"But my dear, I don't know a thing about that revolver getting over to St. Ann's. And I do happen to know that there are other, far more intriguing things that might bear a little investigation." She smoothed the flat wave in her hair gently. "A little investigation, at least," she murmured as if amused, but her expression was not pleasant. Indeed a look in her flat, yellow eyes reminded me that this woman had lived in strange places, had seen strange things, was likely familiar with dark secrets and black rites and primitive passions — product of the twentieth century though she seemed, with her laces and jewels and sophisticated eyebrows. Jungle nights, tom-toms and the word "voodoo" came into my mind — and though I have never been at all sure just what voodoo means, I found my skin crawling.

"I think I'll go up to see Huldah," I said, rising abruptly, and feigning a professional interest.

"Do," said Corole, smiling not at all tenderly into the fire. "You know the way to her room? I'm too lazy to go along." At my nod she continued indolently: "Huldah highly approves of you, Sarah. She has never quite trusted me, you know." She laughed again.

I found Huldah very drowsy and her headache worse.

"It is on account of the cloudy weather," I said, and we talked for some moments very pleasurably of our experiences with neuralgia; my own were much more interesting than Huldah's but I listened forbearingly to her tale.

"I felt better for awhile after Miss Letheny gave me some medicine she has," went on Huldah. "I went right off to sleep. She gives it into your arm so it doesn't take long to —"

"Into your arm!" I cried, struck by the phrase. "What do you mean?"

"Why with one of them — what do you call them? Sort of like a needle."

"You don't mean a hypodermic needle?"

"Yes!" Huldah smiled happily. "That is it. I just couldn't think of what she called it. It is fine. You see, that way the medicine goes directly into your —"

"Huldah! Do you mean to say that Miss Letheny gave you a hypodermic?"

She nodded, pulling up the sleeve of her outing-flannel wrapper and showing me the tiny scar. I scrutinized it closely. It had been most deftly done. There were no skin abrasions, the vein had been carefully avoided, the needle quite evidently had been thrust into the flesh by a practised and unfaltering hand. And that hand belonged to Corole Letheny!

"Wasn't that all right, Miss Keate? It didn't hurt at all —"

I recalled myself to the present.

"Huldah," I said severely, "never let anyone but a doctor or a trained nurse give you a hypodermic. Never!" And as her face turned rather green I added, "That was likely just some headache medicine that Dr. Letheny, or some one, had given Miss Letheny. So it is all right this time." And, indeed, I could tell that Corole had actually given her only a mild opiate to relieve, most unwisely, her headache.

"Now," I went on, as I caught sight of my wrist watch pointing to five o'clock. "Can you tell me something that I want to know, and forget that I asked you?"

Huldah is shrewd; she raised herself on one

gray flannel elbow and looked at me keenly.

"I can keep a secret, Miss Keate. There's many a thing I could tell if I wanted to."

"What I want to know is this: Has Miss Letheny worn her gold dress lately?"

"You mean that green and gold, snaky thing with the scales on it?"

"Yes."

"Let me see. She wore it last the night Dr. Letheny was killed."

"Are you sure, Huldah?"

"Yes'm. I remember well. Poor Dr. Letheny!"

"Feeling better, Huldah?" said a voice from the doorway.

It was Corole, of course.

9

Under the Barberry Bush

I left rather abruptly. But on the darkening path toward St. Ann's I decided that Corole could not have heard our conversation. Feeling that I must get these last two pieces of news, as well as the occurrence of the previous night to O'Leary as soon as possible, I walked rapidly along through the fog. I crossed the little bridge and was hurrying through the apple orchard when I came face to face with O'Leary.

"You are the very person I want to see, Miss Keate," he said at once.

Taking my arm he drew me a few steps from the path; he motioned and following his gesture I found I had a view of the south door and small colonial porch.

"Tell me, Miss Keate, exactly where you were standing the night of June seventh when the — er — arrow-like affair was thrown over your shoulder?"

"I had truly forgotten that — I should have told you."

"That's all right," he brushed my apology

aside. "Can you recall about where you were standing and the line it took over your shoulder?"

"I think so," I replied slowly and thoughtfully. "It seems to me it should have fallen somewhere about that clump of barberry. Over there." I pointed with my finger toward the shrubbery that edges the apple orchard. "I suppose you are trying to find what it was."

"If no one else has found — or retrieved it yet," agreed O'Leary.

With O'Leary going ahead and holding back the more importunate branches and shrubs, we made our slow way to the spot I had indicated. I remember that we took some pains not to be seen from the hospital and, bending over as I did, to keep my white cap invisible from those windows, I had an absurd feeling that I was playing a grim game of hide-and-seek. In the excitement of the search I did not notice my soaked shoes and my wet hair, and remember only how I groped along the sodden leaf mold, and around the slippery brown roots of the shrubs and trees. If we had known what to look for, it would have been an easier task, O'Leary informed me, after some twenty minutes' vain delving in the wet underbrush. He was inclined to be a little pettish about it, implying that I might have noticed the thing more carefully. That remark was made the time he slipped on some wet leaves and flung his hands into a barberry bush to keep his balance. He looked amazingly human and ordinary, picking out the thorns. It was just a few moments after that that I heard him utter a sudden ejaculation of pain. He was on the opposite side of a large clump of barberry bush and I crawled cautiously around to discover what had happened.

I found him squatting on his heels, with his thumb in his mouth and the other hand clasping a small object that, from his glance, seemed to have pleased him inordinately.

"I've found it, Miss Keate," he said, achieving triumphant utterance in spite of the thumb. "Look! Could it have been this?"

It was a mercy I was so near the ground for my knees simply caved in under me. In his hand was a small hypodermic syringe. The nickel on it was rusted a little from the weather.

This syringe whizzing over my shoulder was exactly what I had seen. It was heavy enough to acquire considerable velocity and, as I peered through the shrubbery and trees to the porch, I knew that it would have fallen about here. The trouble was that it looked very much like the south wing's missing syringe. Of course, all hypodermics are much alike, but I knew a certain way that it could be identified, for Maida had taken a cue from me and marked all her tools with a small scratched "D."

"Let me see it," I said.

Without a word he handed the thing to me. On the top of the little flat button was a rudely scratched "D," rusty but still distinct.

"I see you recognize it," said O'Leary, taking his thumb out of his mouth, and regarding it as thoughtfully as if he had not another object in the world. "It is Miss Day's, is it not?"

I nodded.

"Everyone in the wing had access to it. The fact that it may have originally belonged to Maida doesn't mean that she threw it out here."

"No — no, of course not," he said contemplatively. "Well — we found it, Miss Keate. Though I could wish that I had not run into it so forcibly."

He regarded the scratch on his thumb. "You don't suppose that rust harbored any tetanus germs?"

"It has bled enough by this time to clean itself," I said without much sympathy, feeling indeed that if he *would* find things it served him right to get stuck!

"You nurses!" he said, looked at me and laughed. "I wish you could see yourself, Miss Keate."

Conscious not only of my undignified posture but also of an increasing dampness penetrating my skirts, I rose. He followed me through the shrubbery toward the path.

"This is as secluded a place in which to talk as we can find, Miss Keate," he said. "Have you come upon any new developments that I'd like to hear about?"

"How did you know I had?" I asked, not any too pleasantly.

He smiled. "By the look in your eyes and your general aspect of — er — having swallowed the canary, so to speak."

"Well, as a matter of fact there is a thing or two." As briefly as I could, I told him of the gold sequin and of the fact that Corole had last worn that gown the night of June seventh. I also told him that she was an adept at the use of a hypodermic needle. And then, somewhat reluctantly, and glancing rather nervously into the foggy shadows that were increasing under the dripping trees about us, I told him of the visitor to Room 18 of the previous night. He asked several questions, seeming to be extremely interested.

"It goes without saying that the person, whoever it was, who entered Room 18 last night had some purpose. That there was — or is — something yet in Eighteen that he wanted." He frowned. "I don't see what I

205

could have missed."

"There was the sequin," I suggested.

"Yes, there was the sequin. You said it was under the screen? Yes, I missed that. But somehow I don't see Corole Letheny coming back for it."

"She has likely not missed it — there are hundreds of the things on that dress."

"Huldah was positive she hadn't worn the dress since Thursday night? She might have left it there last night, you know."

I shook my head.

"No. Huldah was sure. And it must have been then, for the side of the sequin that lay uppermost is all tarnished from the rain."

"That is true. Then the question is, Who was in Room 18 last night? And what did he want?" His gray eyes were like two clear lakes.

"Miss Keate," he said suddenly. "This radium: I've been hunting through encyclopedias about the stuff, but there is something I want to know. Could it be carried about in a pocket? Without burning, you know."

"Yes, if it were in the box made for it. Radium is used in a variety of tools, for many purposes. But in this case it was in a sort of boxlike container, quite small."

"And could be carried in a pocket or in one's hand?" he insisted. "Or even hidden in one place or another?"

"Goodness, yes!" I replied. "I've seen tools containing it carried about in doctors' bags often enough."

He did not speak for a moment or two, studying me in the meantime with thoughtful eyes that did not in the least see me.

"I should think that it would be hard to dispose of — though as to that —" He broke off abruptly. "Look here, Miss Keate, how is it that such a valuable thing is used with so little precaution against theft?"

"In some hospitals radium is guarded," I explained. "There is one very large hospital, to which patients come from all over the world, where guards are placed in the sickroom whenever radium is used. But it was not deemed necessary here at St. Ann's. Nothing of the kind has ever happened before and our class of patients is, as a rule, of the most respectable. St. Ann's, you know, has really the best standing —" I stopped in the middle of my rather snooty remark as I saw the half smile on his face.

"Still it did happen," he said softly.

"Yes," I retorted. "And it is your business to recover it."

His face sobered instantly.

"Not an easy task, Miss Keate," he said at once and most amiably. "And I'm grateful for the help you give me. In return I shall tell you, since you ask it, that there are a few possible premises that interest me. You might give me your opinion of them. For one thing — we have found that there were three possible means of death, in or about Room 18. There was a revolver, ether, and a hypodermic syringe and enough morphine missing from the drug room to more than accomplish — what we believe it did accomplish. Three weapons where only one was necessary! Dr. Letheny met his death by a fourth means. Three weapons! Does that not indicate that there was more than one person interested in your patient's death?"

"Three!" I gasped. "Three!" In consternation I went over the list of names of that dinner party of ill memory. "But there were only six of us at that dinner to whose personnel you limit your suspects."

"Seven," corrected O'Leary. "There is Dr. Letheny, you know."

"But Mr. O'Leary, it sounds like a club." I was very much in earnest but the man had the impudence to laugh.

"It *does* sound like an association of some kind," he said coolly. "The cuff link and the affair of the disappearing hypodermic needle point to Maida. The presence and continued presence of Jim Gainsay, plus that somewhat ambiguous wire, point to him. Possibility includes you and the two doctors. And as to Miss Letheny, we have several counts against her. So you see it does look rather like a conspiracy."

"Nonsense," I said irritably. "I assure you that all six of us did not band together for the purpose of doing away with Dr. Letheny and his patient."

"Of course not," agreed O'Leary soothingly. "Though you must admit, Miss Keate, that there are a good many clues — no, we'll call them merely facts that intrigue the curious mind — that seem to include all of you."

"Coincidence," I said with considerable decision.

O'Leary's eyebrows went up a little.

"Have it as you will," he agreed amicably. "You have forgotten the fact that Fred Hajek's coat was wet that night when I finally aroused him. Why didn't you inquire about that at the inquest?"

"I had already done so," said O'Leary. "He explained that the window in his room was open and that the coat was lying across a chair beside the window when the rain began. He did not waken immediately and it rained on his coat."

"H'm," said I skeptically. "How about Dr. Balman? Are you going to take his word for it that he was in his own apartment during the time all this took place? What about that bruise on his face that he said he got running through the orchard? Mightn't he have got it earlier in the night?" Though my heart reproved me as I spoke, for Dr. Balman, torn from his beloved studies, forced into a thousand responsibilities, worn and haggard and tired and troubled, was a pathetic figure.

"Dr. Balman is too busy a man these days to bother much with questions," said O'Leary simply. "However, since you have inquired, I have proved his statement. According to the elevator man at the apartment house in which Dr. Balman lives, Dr. Balman arrived from the Letheny's at twelve-fifteen and did not leave until the same elevator man, who also attends the switchboard during the night, gave him a call from St. Ann's. The elevator man obligingly listened in to the conversation, had the elevator at the door of Dr. Balman's apartment immediately, and took the doctor down to the first floor at exactly three minutes after two."

"Now then," he continued after a short silence, "about this hypodermic needle: I should like to have a little talk with Miss Day. And also I want to visit Room 18 again."

"There is a patient in Room 18."

"Already!"

"Yes. I don't think Dr. Balman, or Dr. Hajek either, wanted to permit the room to be used, but there was no other place for the patient."

O'Leary's clear eyes considered me absently for a moment.

"It isn't likely, then, that there will be a repetition of last night's affair," he said finally. "But suppose you let me go over the room again, when I can do so without disturbing the patient."

A figure moving through the mist caught our eyes. It was Maida, her white cap gleaming above her blue and scarlet cape.

"Good-afternoon, Miss Day," said O'Leary, stepping into the path.

I think Maida was a little startled, for her eyes darkened and she glanced hurriedly along the path toward the bridge.

But: "Good-afternoon, Mr. O'Leary," she answered composedly enough. "Oh, there you are, Sarah," she went on as her eyes fell on me. "I was wondering where you had gone." Her eyes travelled to my hair, and she exclaimed: "How wet your hair is! You'll get neuralgia, won't you?"

I put a hand to my hair. It was wet and very draggled where the branches from the trees and shrubs under which I had crept had pulled it. I straightened my wilted cap and tucked up the more adventurously straying locks.

"I've been looking for something."

"I think you must have been," agreed Maida, a flicker of mirth in her blue gaze. "You must have looked for it under the barberry bushes."

As a matter of fact I had done just that. But before I could say anything O'Leary took up the conversation.

"Did you lose your hypodermic needle, Miss Day?" he asked without prelude.

Maida's face sobered instantly and she glanced swiftly at him.

"Why, yes, I did lose it," she said immediately.

"Is this the one you lost?" he asked, holding the syringe toward her in his outstretched palm and keeping his extraordinarily clear eyes on her face so keenly as almost to read her thoughts.

So I am sure he saw her lips tighten, as I did, and her chin go up defiantly.

"It seems to be," she said. "I had scratched my initial on mine." She reached for the syringe and turned it so she could see the small plunger with its marked top.

"Yes," she said quietly. "That is my own syringe."

"I found it just now in a clump of bushes.

Do you know how it got there?"

"No," said Maida flatly.

"Why, then," said O'Leary very softly, "did you replace it with Miss Keate's needle?"

Maida turned toward me at that, her eyes again unfathomable. But before she could reply Jim Gainsay, whose approach we had not noted, swept impetuously between us.

"Hello, Miss Keate — O'Leary. Here you are, Miss Day." And without any ado about it, he simply took Maida's arm and hustled her away from us and along the narrow path toward the bridge before we had time to blink.

It was rather astonishing, and O'Leary and I stood there in silence for a moment until the fog hid the gleam of scarlet from Maida's cape.

"Well," remarked O'Leary then, turning to me; I saw that his eyes were twinkling with a sort of unwilling admiration that was half amusement. "Well — somewhat piratical is Mr. Gainsay. I suppose he brazenly listened to what we said. It is evident that he did not want Miss Day to answer my last question — also, that he is more or less in her confidence and that he was meeting her by appointment. Or" — he paused for a moment — "or it might be that he has reasons of his own for not wishing it to be known just why Miss Day substituted your needle for her own.

At least," he concluded briskly, "he knows more than an innocent man should know."

And with that I had to be content, for he would not say another word and we walked silently along the dusky path until we came to the colonial porch of the south wing.

"I'll go on around to the main entrance," said O'Leary, then. "I want to use the telephone in the general office. I'll be around to your wing later; there is something about Room 18 that I must know." He took off his cap as he walked away from me — a nice gesture that was somewhat marred in effect by his very dirty hands.

10

A Midnight Visitor

I slipped unobserved into the diet kitchen, where I left my cape and to some degree repaired damages. I found, on emerging from the kitchen, that the new patient in Eighteen had arrived. It is a rule with me personally to superintend the installation of a new patient, so I went at once to Room 18. I still found it unpleasant to enter that room, especially since the figure on the narrow bed reminded me forcibly of that other figure that had lain there.

Mr. Gastin was an elderly man, somewhat peevish at being thrust into bed, and quite to my liking. He must have been a person of some importance, for flowers galore had already arrived, among them a potted lobelia, a sinister-looking flower that I have never liked.

He replied rather bitterly that he was as comfortable as might be expected and asked for the evening papers.

"I'm sorry," I said, "but we don't have them."

"Don't have them!" he exclaimed, eyeing me shrewdly. "Oh. Oh, yes, I see why. Where did all this trouble occur, anyway? And see here, what's the matter with this radio? The thing don't work. Is it turned on at this hour? I want the stock reports. I want to tune in myself."

"The radio is in the general office," I explained hastily, fearing he would return to the question I did not wish to answer. "The speakers in the different rooms connect with it. It is usually turned on at this hour, but I don't know whether they have got the stock reports or not."

"Well, bring me a speaker that works, anyhow," he said, hitching himself on one elbow among the pillows and then flopping back again. "Anything for amusement. I suppose it will be bedtime stories. Well, bring 'em on. And you might slip me a cigar."

I felt rather sad as I took the loud speaker, pulled the plug from its connection above the bed, and started away. It doesn't take five minutes to place a new patient in his correct category and I knew all too well where this one belonged. Someone had labelled them "crippled captains of finance," and the title stuck.

Being in a hurry I took the faulty speaker into Sonny's room. He was engrossed with

216

a new block puzzle and paying no attention to the radio so I exchanged the speakers, taking the one in Sonny's room to Mr. Gastin for the time being. Once connected, soft and dulcet tones rang through Number 18: ". . . and then Bunny Brown Eyes — scampered along . . ."

"Oh, hell," remarked Mr. Gastin.

"The dinner concert comes on at seven," I suggested.

"Think I can stand this till then?" he asked, but left the plug in. "Can you bring me a — er — blanket or two, nurse? Somehow this room seems sort of — I don't know — cold, I guess. You might turn on that light up there — yes, and the one over the dresser, too."

The light over the bed was already glowing, but I did as he asked. Which only goes to prove that Room 18 was already getting in its work. I left the door open and remember that I spoke very earnestly when I told him to turn on the signal light if he wanted anything.

He did not have to listen to the bunny story after all, however, for I met Miss Jones coming along with a truck and she told me that she was taking Mr. Gastin to Dr. Letheny's — that is, Dr. Balman's office for an examination.

"He hasn't had his supper tray yet, has he?" she asked anxiously.

Meeting O'Leary in the hall I told him that Room 18 was vacant for a few minutes; I went on downstairs to eat, however, and did not accompany him. But when I sat down to glance at the charts of the south wing an hour later, O'Leary stopped beside me.

"No luck?" I said.

"Not a thing," he replied.

There was a distinctly puzzled look in his face.

"Keep your eyes open to-night, Miss Keate. If anything occurs like last night, 'phone to me immediately. Here's my number. I'll sleep right by the telephone. Thanks. Good-night."

But before taking five steps he whirled back to me.

"By the way, Miss Keate," he said in a low voice so that the little cluster of white-clad nurses around the dumbwaiter could not hear him. "By the way, it seems peculiar that after the inquest when the matter of your seeing this hypodermic needle was brought to light so publicly, no one tried to retrieve it. One wonders why. And another thing — I should like to know where this Jim Gainsay spent the time between your meeting him at the corner of the porch, and his starting to town in Dr. Letheny's car. There are, according to your story, about fifteen minutes unaccounted for — Good-night, again."

I did not return to the south wing until midnight. I found only Maida there for second watch, Miss Dotty having arranged the schedule of nursing hours on its old basis, thus depriving us of our temporary increased help. I thought it somewhat presumptuous of Miss Dotty, who, after all, is only superintendent of nurses and has no jurisdiction over our wing. Olma Flynn had been placed on first watch, as formerly, and on relieving her she assured me that everything was going well and though the new patient in Eighteen was a trifle restless, I had expected that, so I thought nothing of it.

Olma had locked the south door and its key hung peacefully on its customary nail. Under Maida's understanding gaze I took the key from the nail and slipped it under an order pad on the chart desk; if anyone wanted it that night he should have to ask for it!

I hadn't been on the floor ten minutes when Eighteen's light went on; upon answering it I found my patient sitting bolt upright in bed, with the small light over the bed glowing brightly.

"I don't like this bed, nurse!" he said. His rumpled gray hair gave him a rather ferocious aspect and his pajama coat was all wrinkled and twisted from flouncing around on the bed.

His words gave me rather a turn for, as far

as that went, I didn't like the bed myself. But I advanced coolly enough and began straightening the tossed sheets and blanket.

"What is the matter with it?" I asked, in my professionally comfortable voice. I was not prepared for his reply.

"It feels like a coffin," he said, staring gloomily at his feet.

"Like a coffin!"

He glanced at me sharply.

"Like a coffin," he repeated stubbornly. "I don't like it."

"Nonsense," I said, recovering myself and reaching for a pillow. "You aren't used to it, that's all."

"What do they make them so high for?" he said peevishly, peering over the edge of the bed. "If I'd fall out I'd have a long way to go."

"You're not going to fall out," I reassured him. "And if they didn't make them high we nurses would break our backs. That is the greatest life-saver for nurses that anybody ever found. You see, if they were built at the height of ordinary beds we would have to bend away over —"

"Well, they don't have to be so narrow," he interrupted sulkily. "Every time I turn over I have to grab to save myself from going out."

"Oh, it isn't that bad, is it?" I plumped the

pillows briskly, replaced them and pulled the draw sheet straight. "Now, that will be better. Try to relax and lie quiet."

He subsided on the pillow, still muttering childishly. It seemed close in the room, so I raised the window higher and brought him a fresh drink of water. Of course, if the window had already been up I should have lowered it; I make it a point to fuss around the room a little just to make the patient think I'm doing things for his comfort, and nine times out of ten he will drop off to sleep at once.

This was the tenth time, however, for within half an hour Eighteen's light flickered on again. Maida answered it that time and when she came out she looked very peculiar.

"What is the matter?" I asked, meeting her in the corridor.

"It is Eighteen. He is very restless."

"Yes, I know that he is."

"He —" she hesitated. "He does not seem to like the room."

Our eyes met but I tried to keep the little tremor of fright out of my voice as I replied: "He isn't accustomed to a hospital room yet, that is all."

"I hope so, I'm sure," said Maida somewhat morosely and went on about her errand.

I myself am so accustomed to the hospital

that is home to me that it is only once in a while that I see it as it impresses a stranger. For a singular moment or two that night I saw it with alien eyes, so to speak: the corridor was long and strange and dark with the vases of flowers along the walls making grotesque shadows against the lighted region of the chart desk at the extreme end of the wings; the hush that always surrounds a hospital, particularly at night, seemed unfamiliar and grim; the doors swung noiselessly; the little thud of our rubber-heeled shoes along the rubberized floor-runner seemed stealthy. Our hushed, low voices had a furtive note. The hospital odours of antiseptics and soap and medicines and sickness, with under it all a lurking, faint but ever-present breath of ether, came to my nostrils with the clearness of novelty. The dim red gleams of scattered signal lights, above the black voids that were doors, seemed strange, too, and weird. I caught myself staring up and down the corridor, puzzled and wondering and faintly frightened as if I were in a new and terrifying place. Then all at once, things resolved themselves into the old, familiar wing. But the feeling of uneasiness persisted.

The patient in Eighteen finally turned off his light and must have gone to sleep, for we heard nothing of him for an hour or two. We were fairly busy, with little opportunity for conversation. Along about two o'clock I found that Sonny had managed to acquire a sore throat, a hot, flushed face and icy feet. I was hurrying for camphorated oil and a hot-water bottle when Eighteen's light shone redly above the door. I hastened to answer it.

"Nurse," said our patient firmly, his eyes quite swollen from lack of sleep, and his bedclothes more tousled than ever. "Nurse, I do not like this room. I want another."

I sighed inwardly even as I went again about the business of straightening him and the bed.

"There isn't another on the floor, Mr. Gastin," I said quietly. "And anyway we can't move you in the middle of the night."

"But I insist upon being moved," he said, with an odd mixture of childish pettishness and adult command. What would be the result if the world at large knew these important business men as we know them! Big babies, they are, most of them!

"This room is exactly like any other room," I said.

"I don't like it!" he reiterated. "There's — there's noises." His eyes roved about the room uneasily. "There's noises! Sounds like whispering."

I'll not deny that these extraordinary words stirred my hair at its roots.

"Non—sense!" I brought out jerkily. "Nonsense! You are nervous."

He was regarding me with shrewd little eyes. I stared back at him, trying to appear steady and at ease, but it was no use. He raised his hand to point a square forefinger at me, shaking it emphatically in my face.

"I'll bet you ten dollars — I'll bet you a hundred dollars, right there in my pants pocket, that this is *the room!*"

Fascinated, I kept my eyes on the square finger. He did not need to say what room, for I knew well what he meant. I moistened my lips.

"How about it?" he went on more briskly. "How about it? Do I win?"

And at my continued silence he chuckled, lying back again on the pillow.

"I can see that I win." he said. He pulled the sheet up over his shoulders, and stuffed the pillow more comfortably under his head. "Now that I know what the trouble is, I can go to sleep all right," said this amazing man. He laughed softly. "I'm no nervous woman," he went on with a touch of swagger. "Turn out the light, will you?"

He closed his eyes with the utmost unconcern.

"The whispers won't bother me now that I know what they are," he said casually as I moved toward the door.

Still feeling shaken, I walked slowly along the corridor. What could the man mean?

Resolving at length to take a lesson from my patient's sang-froid, I tried to shrug the matter away as a fancy on his part, and proceeded to take care of Sonny's needs, applying the hot-water bottle to his throat and the camphorated oil to his feet in the coolest fashion until Sonny remonstrated with a hoarse giggle.

By three o'clock things had quieted down all over the wing. The patients were either asleep or resting and the windows dark with the blackest hour of the night. Maida was sitting at the chart desk, her white-capped head bent over Eleven's chart, and I had gone into Sonny's room to make sure he was all right. The whole place was as quiet and hushed as a city of the dead.

I took my thermometer and shook it vigorously. And in the very act of placing it between Sonny's lips, I lost hold on it, dropped it and whirled facing the door. For without any warning at all a scream was rising from somewhere in the wing.

It rose and swelled to the very old roofs, choked horribly at its height and ceased.

It was a scream of stark terror!

A woman's scream!

Somehow I got into the corridor. Maida was there, too, running toward Room 18, and I followed her.

It was Maida who reached for the light. It revealed our patient half out of bed, staring with blinking eyes at something on the other side of the bed.

We followed his gaze. Huddled there on the floor was a woman. We saw a dark cloak, a brown hand outflung and metallic waves of hair. We both leaned closer.

"It's Corole!" cried Maida sharply.

We turned her on her back. For a horrible moment I though that Eighteen had added another victim to its list. But all at once Corole opened her eyes, sat up dazedly, saw Mr. Gastin still sitting on the edge of the bed, and at the sight her mouth opened, her eyes glared, and she pressed her hand tight across her mouth as if to prevent an outcry.

The relief of seeing that she was alive was so great that Maida sank limply to a chair and I turned in natural reaction to anger.

"What on earth are you doing here, Corole?" I asked warmly. "What happened to you? Are you hurt?"

She ignored my questions.

"Who is that?" she whispered hoarsely, pointing to the bed. There was such urgency in her tone and gesture that I replied.

"That is a new patient."

"A new patient? *Here?*"

"Certainly. Why not?"

She looked at me; her eyes were green and shone.

"When did he come?"

"Late this afternoon. Why? What is the matter? Tell me what happened!"

She groped for the cloak, pulled it absently around her and rose to her feet in one long, sinuous motion.

"He frightened me," she said. "I thought — I saw him lying there on the bed — I didn't know you had a patient here. I thought it was — I thought —" With a visible effort she controlled herself, passed a hand across her pallid face. She looked terrible — grim, hag-ridden; her lips were blue, her face ashen and her eyes like a frantic cat's.

And at the moment we heard hurrying footsteps in the corridor and Dr. Hajek, clutching a bathrobe around his pajamas, followed by Dr. Balman, burst into the room. Dr. Hajek had a revolver in one hand, and at sight of us he paused abruptly, his eyes met Corole's for a long moment, and I experienced the strangest feeling that they were corresponding, without words or motions, there in front of my eyes. It was the briefest of impressions, gone before the thought had more than come to me, and I saw Dr. Hajek slowly dropping the revolver into his bathrobe pocket.

"What is it?" inquired Dr. Balman. In a few words I explained the situation, as far as I could. Dr. Balman surveyed us all for a space during which I could hear my own heart thudding, then he walked to the bed, drew the patient gently back and pulled the covers over him. Mr. Gastin submitted without a word, his gaze still on Corole.

"I was frightened," said Corole, her voice harsh. "I thought — Never mind what I thought. I —" She tried to smile and the grimace she made was dreadful. "I must have fainted. I'm sorry. Sorry to disturb you."

This apology was not like Corole. I started to speak, stopped myself, started again. No one seemed to hear me.

Dr. Hajek cleared his throat.

"Was there — anything wrong?" he asked in what struck me as rather belated inquiry.

"I —" began Corole again. Her face was looking a little less hideous, and by the time she had finished she seemed more like herself. "I did not know that there was a patient in the room. I saw his figure in bed, there. It frightened me. I screamed. And fell. I suppose I roused the whole hospital. Really, Miss Keate, I do not think you should have put a patient in this room."

It was like the hussy to try to blame me, and indignation almost choked me. While I was stuttering for a suitable reply Maida spoke. At the first word I glanced at her in amazement and saw Dr. Balman and Dr. Hajek follow my gaze.

"And what were *you* doing in this room?" asked Maida. Her eyes were like twin swords, her straight black brows stern. "You had no honest business in this room, Corole Letheny! Why did you come here?"

Corole's head jerked toward Maida with a flash of green light from those crafty eyes.

For a moment the two women surveyed each other, neither faltering in her steadily inimical regard. I moved uneasily and in the hush I heard one or two signal lights clicking. At the sound I pulled myself together; we should have another panic on our hands if we did not take care.

"Yes, Corole," I said decisively. "Why did you come here? And how did you get into the room?"

"I think your presence demands an explanation," added Dr. Balman quietly.

She looked at me, she swept Dr. Balman's mild brown eyes, she flickered a green glance at Dr. Hajek, she drew her silk wrap more closely about her, she moved her brown hands uneasily up and down its collar, and she finally replied.

"I couldn't sleep," she said. "I got to think-

229

ing of Louis and somehow — got the idea that if I came over here I might be able to — to —" Her excuse died away from very lack of body, she took a long breath, and raised her eyelids insolently. "I felt I must see Room 18. So I came. I got in at the window. If you have nothing more to say — Good-night." Her strange eyes swept us and actually they harboured a gleam of amusement. Then she drew the cloak tightly about her, walked to the window, put one hand on the sill, and with a long, graceful movement swung herself over the sill and through the window. It was done with the nonchalance and ease of an animal and she did not even glance back at us. For an instant her gold hair shone beyond the window, then the screen came down upon a black void and she was definitely gone.

No one left in the room spoke. Dr. Hajek made a motion as if he thought to accompany her but thought better of it. Dr. Balman reached for Mr. Gastin's pulse. Maida crossed the room swiftly and went into the corridor. As her starched skirts rustled past the bed Mr. Gastin took his eyes from the window.

"I think," he said feebly. "I think I should like to have an upstairs room."

"We'll see in the morning," I said absently.

"In the morning!" observed Mr. Gastin with

feeling. "Do you think I'm going to stay in this haunted room for the rest of the night!"

And believe it or not, we had to give up and bundle him on a truck and take him to a temporary bed in the charity ward! This was the first time in all my years of nursing that I was so influenced by a patient and this was not accomplished without resistance on my part and extremely sulphuric language on his. In fact, he proved to be versatile in the latter respect, attaining heights that made my hair stand on end. Dr. Balman was quite scarlet at the end of one climactic triumph and sent Dr. Hajek hurriedly for the truck.

So, all in all, it was not until I was back in the wing, and our patients had been assured by the story of a mouse that Maida in a burst of unexpected mendacity brought forth, and things were quiet and peaceful again, that I began to wonder what had been the purpose of Corole's visit.

And it was clear to me, all at once, that she was looking for something.

What could that something be — the radium? Could Corole believe that the radium was still in Room 18? And if so, what reason had she for her belief?

And at the same time I recalled my promise to O'Leary to telephone to him if the night brought any disturbance. It was with some trepidation that I convinced myself that he could do nothing till morning anyway, and it was as well that I had forgotten my promise.

I did not for a moment believe Corole's faltering attempt at an explanation. But at the same time it occurred to me that had she been of a mind to lie she could likely have invented a much more plausible and convincing tale than the one she told.

11

By the Light of a Match

It was near morning by that time, and Maida
and I had to work rapidly to get our patients
washed and tooth-brushed and ready for the
breakfast trays. To my satisfaction no one
from the other wings appeared to have heard
Corole's scream, or to know that there had
been any disturbance in the south wing.

The morning passed quietly. I took a long-
needed rest and did not see O'Leary until I
came downstairs about the middle of the afternoon. Somewhat to my disappointment, for
I had anticipated telling him myself, he knew
all about Corole's visit. Dr. Balman had told
him of it. O'Leary said briefly that he had
talked to Corole; I gathered that she stuck to
her story of the previous night, even to the
extent of embroidering rather elaborately on
her cousinly affection for Dr. Letheny and her
anxiety to know the cause of his death.
O'Leary seemed somewhat perturbed, a result
that would have delighted Corole had she
known it.

"We have got bolts on the window," said

O'Leary. "Dr. Balman suggested it; at least there'll be no more such visitors as last night."

He did not linger. An hour or so later I slipped out the south door for a breath of fresh air. I glanced in at Room 18 as I passed. Sure enough there were shiny new bolts on the window. Mr. Gastin had evidently preferred the charity ward to Room 18, for he had not returned, though the pot of lobelias still stood on the table looking more jaundiced than ever.

If cold and damp, still the air was refreshing and I walked at a brisk pace along the path toward the bridge. I did not see that Higgins was following me until I paused to lean on the railing and stare at the muddy, swollen little stream below my feet. There the shrubbery grows so close to the bridge that it hangs over it and the water, and I was amusing myself by pulling dead leaves from a willow, bending near and tossing them into the little, swirling eddies of water when Higgins spoke suddenly at my elbow.

It startled me and I whirled to face him.

"Miss Keate," he began again. "I — Could you — There is something I want to tell you." He spoke in a hesitating, reluctant manner as if he here not sure he wanted to tell me, after all.

"What is it?" I inquired crisply.

He swallowed audibly and cleared his throat.

234

"I — I've been wondering — It is this way, Miss Keate. I want to know what you think I had better do."

I squared around for a better look at him. He was rather pale and played nervously with his furnace-stained cap.

"What about, Higgins?" I said kindly.

He made a motion to speak, checked it and peered furtively up and down the path. Owing to its twisting he could not see very far either way, so he leaned over toward me and spoke in a half-whisper.

"It is about the night of June seventh," he said mysteriously.

The words focussed my attention sharply.

"June seventh!" I exclaimed.

"Sh — sh —" he made a quick gesture for silence, and peered again all about in the semi-twilight made by the still dour, cloudy sky and mist and dripping, close-growing shrubbery. "Yes. The night of June seventh. I don't know what to do. I don't know what my duty is. I don't want to get nobody into trouble. But I can't go on no longer without telling somebody. I thought you, Miss Keate, would know what to do."

"What is it?' I asked quickly.

He did not reply at once. Instead he looked uneasily all about us, examining the surroundings with an intensity that impressed upon me the need for caution as to the matter he was about to relate. Unconsciously I drew nearer him.

"Go on," I said.

He surveyed me doubtfully.

"I wish I knew whether I was doing right or not," he mused with a worried air. "You see — I don't want to get into trouble myself, either."

Poor Higgins!

"I'll see that you do not," I promised rashly, little knowing how impossible it would prove to be to keep my word.

He cleared his throat, glanced toward the path again.

"You see, I saw it," he whispered.

"Saw what?"

"Saw who killed the patient in Room 18!"

For a breathless second I wondered if the man had taken leave of his senses. His gray face, his evident fright, the way his eyes shifted about, first peering in one direction and then another, convinced me of his sincerity. He must be speaking the truth. It was evident, too, and I did not wonder at it, that he was in a mortal terror of his knowledge.

"How was it? What did you see?" I whispered too.

"Well, it was this way," he began so slowly as to nearly drive me frantic with impatience.

"It was this way: I had a bad toothache that night. It wouldn't let me sleep and the hot night seemed to make it worse. I finally got up and came upstairs to get Dr. Hajek to give me something for it. I knocked and knocked at his door but I couldn't wake him, so —"

"What time was that?" I asked.

"I don't know exactly. I think about one o'clock. Anyway I went back to the basement and still couldn't get any peace from the tooth. It ached and ached and I got up and tried to rouse Dr. Hajek again. I couldn't wake him — you see, he wasn't there at all. So I let myself out of the main door and walked around the corner of the hospital. Sometimes Dr. Letheny would sit up late and I thought that if there was a light in his study, I could get something for my tooth from him. It was the darkest night I have ever seen."

He paused to shake his head dolefully.

"Anyway, pretty soon I saw a sort of green light up there on the hill, and knew that Dr. Letheny was reading late. Well, I started toward the path and it was so dark I could hardly find my way. When I got to the end of the south wing, I could see that the south door was open, and could see the light over the chart desk. The wing looked almost as dark as it did outside." He stopped, drew out a blue bandanna handkerchief and wiped his forehead, though it was chilly out there on the bridge.

"Then — I heard something, a sort of sound like a footstep — I don't know exactly what it was. But it seemed to come from there near the door of the wing. It flashed through my mind that someone was prowling about St. Ann's and, all at once, I remembered about the radium being used, though I didn't actually think that anyone was stealing it. Anyway, I felt my way through the dark, past the porch of the wing. I went very cautiously and stopped when I heard, just on the other side of that big elderberry bush, two parties talking." He stopped and used the bandanna again, and inwardly, I cursed that ambiguous word of his class: "party."

"Go on," I said impatiently. "Who were they?"

"I heard a little of what they said," he continued, impervious to my eagerness. "I'll tell you about that later. I must have made some sort of sound, for all at once they stopped talking and went away. I followed them but lost them in the darkness, and thinking from their talk that they would be coming back to the hospital, I felt my way back again, too. I was just in time to see a little light through the window of Eighteen. It was the light of a match and by it I saw the face of the party that" — he was whispering — "that killed Jackson. I saw the radium being hid. Yes, miss, and I know where the radium is right now."

I think I seized him by the arm and shook it, for I remember he drew back.

"Tell me, quick, Higgins. Hurry. Who was it?"

"Not so fast, now, Miss Keate. I've got to tell my story in my own way. Miss Keate, there was three in Room 18 that night. Yes, ma'am, three."

"Three? Who were they, Higgins? Didn't the same man kill both Jackson and the doctor?"

He shook his head slowly and with the most exasperating stupidity.

"No, Miss Keate. No, that couldn't hardly be."

"Could hardly be! What on earth do you mean? Who was about that night? Whom did you see? Who was in Room 18? Speak up, man!"

I suppose I succeeded in confusing him.

"Wait, miss, till I finish my story. I was standing in the shadow, staring with all my eyes at that dark window waiting for the party I had seen to come out — when I just knew that someone was near me. I didn't hear a footstep nor a breath but all at once somebody was just there. And I was holding my breath to listen when there was a sort of a scramble at the window and I sneaked up closer to the wall. I stumbled over a coat or something right at the window and just as I caught myself I heard a crash from inside Room 18. That scared me, Miss Keate." The man paused again to scrutinize the dripping, green curtains about us, and I caught my breath.

"That scared me, so I stayed right there where I was, listening. I heard a kind of a scraping sound, then it was all quiet for a minute or two, and I thought I'd better get out of the way. I sneaked over to the corner and stood just around it. It was so black that I couldn't see my hand in front of my face, but I've got good hearing, ma'am, and I heard *only one party* slip out that window and close the screen and go away, walking light like a cat through the orchard. And it was just then the wind came up with a bang and things began to whiz around and I thought I'd better get back to my room. I knowed there was some skulduggery going on, ma'am, and I didn't want to be in on it." He blew his nose vigorously. I realized that my mouth was hanging open and closed it with a snap.

"Who was about, Higgins? Tell me at once." I spoke very sternly, trying at the same time to keep my teeth from chattering. The recital had recalled all too forcibly to me the events of that black night.

"Well, there was Dr. Letheny — of course. Then there was that Gainsay fellow, the one that is staying up there at Letheny's. Then there was Corole Letheny and there was Dr. Hajek —"

"Did you recognize all these people, Higgins?" I cried incredulously.

He regarded me with scorn.

"Say, didn't I tell you I got good ears?"

"But you could hardly recognize Mr. Gainsay, for instance, with your ears."

"I didn't," said Higgins. "I saw his face in the light of a match."

"Go on," I urged. "Who else? Who was it you saw in Eighteen? Where is the radium?"

Unfortunately I placed an impatient hand on his arm; he glanced down and saw my wrist watch.

"I've got to hurry," he cried. "It's nearly six and the fire's not —"

"Wait!" I seized his coat sleeve. "Tell me. Who did it?"

He jerked away. "It's late! I must hurry. I'll see you to-night." Eluding my grasp he scurried away and out of sight, around the little bend!

Slowly my hands dropped to my sides. For some time I simply stared in the direction he had taken and let my thoughts whirl.

What had he seen? What had he heard? Who . . . ?

It was curious how slowly I became aware that the green curtain within an arm's reach was wavering. The slender leaves of willow were trembling, shivering, dancing. The elderberry swayed gently.

There was no wind.

I blinked — frowned — realized its oddity — and in sudden, quick suspicion I took a step forward, thrust the bushes aside with my arms, brushed back the willows, took a few steps along the water's edge and saw Jim Gainsay vanishing into a little thicket of evergreens.

He did not look back. He seemed to have no idea that he had been seen. He wore no cap. I saw him clearly and unmistakably.

So Jim Gainsay had been behind that willow curtain! Jim Gainsay had heard Higgins's faltering, reluctant revelations. And after brazenly listening to the whole thing, Jim Gainsay had furtively and stealthily slipped away, without intending that I should even be aware of his presence.

Concerned almost as much with this evidence of Jim Gainsay's duplicity as with Higgins's tale, I stood stock-still there in that thicket, with wet branches and leaves pressing against me on all sides. Aware finally of a spe-

242

cially rude one scratching my neck I roused myself, pushed out into the path, and took my way back to St. Ann's.

The thing to do, I realized, was to let O'Leary know at once of Higgins's story; if anyone could worm the whole tale from the janitor it would be Lance O'Leary. But I shall have to confess that baffled curiosity overcame me, and I resolved to get hold of Higgins immediately and try to make him tell me, at least, whom he saw there in Room 18.

The supper bell was ringing when I entered the south wing. I am not one to slight meals as a rule, but that was one time when I ignored the summons. However, Higgins was not about and upon inquiry someone said she thought he had gone into town. Reluctantly, then, I went to supper.

At the door of the dining room I met several training girls. Melvina Smith was among them and they were talking excitedly in low voices which they hushed as soon as they saw me, and one and all looked guilty.

"Well, what is it?" I said briskly.

Melvina Smith fastened hollow eyes upon me and said in a sepulchral voice:

"Accident has died."

"Accident!" Having for the moment forgotten the christening party I was at a loss to understand her cryptic utterance, and wondered if she was quite right.

"Accident," confirmed Melvina. "The third tragedy is on its way."

"I must say I don't in the least know what you are talking about," I remarked acidly. Melvina is very trying and carries an element of conviction in her tones that makes one feel as if she is well informed.

"Accident. The kitten, you know. The black kitten," volunteered one of the girls hurriedly. "It died and Melvina says —" her eyes got larger and she lowered her voice — "Melvina says — it is a *sign!*"

"Oh, the kitten! What nonsense!"

"He was not sick," said Melvina in a measured and undisturbed way. "He was not sick at all. He was, in fact, the healthiest of the whole batch. But — he died."

And would you believe it I felt gooseflesh coming out on my arms? Melvina was never intended for as matter-of-fact a profession as that of a nurse; her talents are wasted.

"Nonsense," I said again, and repeated it. "Nonsense."

"It is a sign," remarked Melvina in that quietly positive way. She reached quite casually into her capacious pocket and drew out before our very eyes the kitten. It was, to be sure, dead and quite stiff and stark. All of us shrank back at the sight of the poor little black body with its stiff claws outstretched and its mouth open and grinning, but Melvina regarded it familiarly. "It was a perfectly healthy kitten," she went on, in the manner of the scientist who weighs facts impartially. "It died. All at once. Just died. No reasons for it. But it died. *It is a sign.*"

A little gasp went over the group and I found my tongue.

"Melvina Smith," I said, "take that kitten out into the orchard and bury it. Then change your uniform and scrub your hands with antiseptic soap. How long have you been carrying that thing around? Not that it matters," I went on hastily as Melvina opened her too-gifted mouth to reply. "Don't ever let me catch you doing such a thing again. Moreover, if I hear of you saying such foolish and — yes, wicked things again I shall have Miss Dotty give you fifty demerits and that means no Sundays off for the rest of the summer."

"Miss Dotty already knows about it," said one of the other girls. "Melvina had it on the table showing it to us at theory class and Miss Dotty didn't see it and put her hand on it."

"She was sick," added another girl solemnly. "She was real sick, all at once. We wanted to practice 'What to Do for Nausea' on her but she didn't give us time."

"She is in her room now," concluded the

first girl with a passionate devotion to detail. "She is in her room with a hot-water bottle and an ice bag and a bottle of camphor."

"Well," I said abruptly, feeling very much as if I were going to imitate Miss Dotty, "take that — er — kitten outdoors at once, Melvina."

"Yes, Miss Keate," said Melvina dutifully. "Do you have second watch in the south wing to-night, Miss Keate?"

"Certainly."

"My-y-y!" Melvina sucked in her breath. "Something will be sure to happen. May I help you, Miss Keate?"

"Good gracious, Melvina!" I cried, revolted. "Do you mean to say you would want to be there if anything *did* happen?"

"Oh — no," she said reluctantly, eyeing the kitten fondly. "But something *will* happen. Soon. It is a sign."

"Melvina!" I must have spoken firmly for Melvina wasted no time in going about her burying and the rest of the girls hastened on down to supper.

It was just after supper that I was called to the telephone.

It was O'Leary, and his voice seemed very far away.

"Is there anyone else in the office?" he asked.

"No."

"Is this line private? Is there a way for anyone to listen in?"

"No."

"Then listen, Miss Keate. I can't get out to the hospital right now and there is something I want to know. Has anything — any article of furniture — any — er — bed linen — blankets — pillows — anything of the sort, been taken out of the room we are interested in?"

"Only the soiled linens," I replied.

There was a long silence, so long that I repeated my answer.

"Yes, I heard you," he said hastily. "Are you positive about that? Think hard, Miss Keate."

"Not another thing — oh, yes, last night I exchanged the loud speaker in that room for another."

"You did!" His voice was eager. "When? Before or after I was in the room?"

"Before!"

"Sure?"

"Yes. The patient complained that it wasn't working very well."

"What did you do — where is it now?"

"In Sonny's — that is, in the room where I put it, I suppose."

"Lord, I'm a dumbbell," said O'Leary heartily. "Miss Keate, listen carefully, please.

Take that loud speaker, *just as it is,* to some safe place and don't let anyone have it until I come. Understand?"

"Yes," I said slowly. "But I — do you think — could it possibly be —"

"That's all, Miss Keate," he interrupted. "Thank you very much." And before I could tell him of Higgins he had hung up the receiver and I was left shouting "Mr. O'Leary," into the mouthpiece.

Feeling somewhat put out I telephoned immediately to the number he had given me. A man-servant answered and told me rather superciliously that Mr. O'Leary was out. On my saying the message was urgent he brightened up, however, and took my number and name with alacrity, promising to have Mr. O'Leary telephone me as soon as he came home. It seemed evident to me that O'Leary believed the radium to be in the loud speaker, and though at first I was disinclined to agree with him, for it seemed to me that that was altogether too prominent a hiding place, by the time I had reached the south wing, I had had time to recall the "purloined letter," lying there in plain sight, and was beginning to feel considerably excited and eager to get my hands on the loud speaker. Those loud speakers that we have at St. Ann's are, as Dr. Letheny had complained, specially made at the advice of a board member who deals in radios; they are built a good deal like a small round hat box on a standard. You've seen them. The parallel sides, or what would be the top and bottom of the hat box, are made of some sort of fancifully decorated parchment paper. They are quite attractive and have a clear, soft tone, very nice for a hospital. The more I thought of it the more clearly I realized that here would be a place to hide the radium. There would be plenty of room, the speaker was inconspicuously prominent, if I may indulge in the paradox, and while appearing to be so permanently constructed, nevertheless one of the sides could doubtless be removed and replaced with little evidence of tampering.

It could not have been more than a minute or two later that I entered Sonny's room and got the loud speaker. I suddenly remembered that it was out of order and had not been fixed, but fortunately Sonny had not asked to have the radio turned on since I had transferred it from Room 18. Or at least if he had, I hadn't heard of it. As I left the room the corridors were deserted. I met Maida just outside my own room and she saw what I carried but said nothing. I went on into my room and closed the door.

I had fully intended to remove one of the sides of the loud speaker at once, but in the very act of doing so I checked myself. So far as I knew I might thus destroy some important clue. Lance O'Leary had said nothing about examining it; he had said only to place it in safekeeping. It was with some disappointment that, after staring at the thing for some time and shaking it tentatively at my ear, I placed it face downward on the lower shelf of the chifferette and locked the door.

Now to find Higgins!

Higgins was not easy to find, however. I hunted all through the basement, the ambulance rooms, the kitchens, even went out in the twilight to the garage, but Higgins was not to be found. It was dark by that time so I took my way back to the hospital. Not willing to give up I made another rapid search through the basement, but the only living beings I saw were Morgue and the cook who was just going to bed with a stack of forbidden newspapers under his arm.

The cook, however, had seen Higgins.

"Not twenty minutes ago," he said positively.

"Where?"

"Let me see now — seems to me he was walking down toward the apple orchard. That tall fellow, the one that is visiting up at Letheny's, was with him."

"Mr. Gainsay was with him!"

"Sure." The cook was immediately interested. "Sure. Walking down toward the apple orchard, they was. Do you want to see Higgins, Miss Keate?"

"Oh, it was of no importance," I said, and somewhat disconsolately departed.

12

Room 18 Again

Still feeling that I must get hold of Higgins, it was hard to compose myself to rest and I didn't sleep a wink. About eleven o'clock I got up and made my way again to the basement. It was dark and spooky and very empty down there and after knocking at Higgins's door a few times and feeling, while I waited for the reply that did not come, as if all the ghosts in Christendom were prowling in the furnace room and thereabouts, I retreated precipitously to my own room. I was sure that Higgins was in his room, for where else would he be at that hour? But the surroundings were not those to encourage persistence on my part. The unused corridors are very desolate at that hour and those of the sick-room wings little less so.

I was still wide awake when the twelve o'clock gong sounded.

By that time I was convinced that Higgins was deliberately keeping out of my way and that in itself made me the more anxious to get in touch with O'Leary. I stopped at the general office as I passed it on my way to the south wing, and telephoned again.

The same servant answered my ring, sleepily at first, but he awoke in a hurry when I told him that it was Miss Keate at St. Ann's and that I must speak to Mr. O'Leary at once.

"You might try the police station," he said guardedly. "I think he was investigating some telegraph messages that just came in."

So I looked up the number in the telephone book and tried it. But though I tried and tried, the line was busy and kept busy and I had to give up in order to be on time at the south wing.

Olma Flynn was waiting for me and Maida already busy about twelve-o'clock temperatures.

"Eleven is doing pretty well to-night," said Olma as we bent over the charts. "Three has a degree or so of fever but has been fairly quiet. Oh, by the way, have you the key to the south door?"

"No."

She frowned.

"I couldn't find it. I had to leave the south door unlocked."

"Couldn't find it!"

"No. It wasn't anywhere about the desk."

"Did you look in the lock?"

"Of course, Miss Keate. And I asked the other girls. No one has seen it since morning."

In view of the existing circumstances, I suppose it was natural that I should feel immediately alarmed. After Olma had gone wearily away to bed I gave the chart desk and its vicinity a thorough search.

"What on earth are you doing?" asked Maida, coming along just as I had taken all the charts out of the rack and was feeling about with my fingers in the recesses left empty.

"Looking for the key to the south door," I replied. "Have you seen it?"

"No. I have not seen it since last night."

She waited for a moment, watching me rearrange the charts.

"I wish this trouble were all cleared up," she said, her voice sombre.

"So do I." I replaced the last chart and turned to face her. The greenish light from above the desk made her face worn and colourless and cast a sickly green glow over our white dresses.

"If we don't find it to-morrow I shall have to have a new key made. I suppose we can leave the south door unlocked to-night," I decided irresolutely. "I don't like to; I have had enough of people prowling through our wing."

Maida's shadowed eyes met mine and she shivered slightly; she attempted to smile but her lips pulled tautly.

"It is getting to disturb me more and more," she admitted. "Think of this, Sarah: it has been only four days since that dinner party of Corole's. Is it possible! So much has happened. It seems like months."

"This is Tuesday," I calculated, "That was last Thursday night — no, Maida, five days."

"Well, five days then," she assented lifelessly. "What a five days! If it would only turn warm and summery and sunshiny again, I do believe things would be better off. I'm sure I should be at least!"

"I dislike this constant drizzle," I agreed, without much spirit. "There is something honest and wholehearted about real rain, but weather like this is wretched."

"Everything I touch is clammy like — like a dead man." She whispered the last words and I think they came as a surprise to her, for she looked frightened and a little shocked.

A small red light shone down the corridor above a door and I started to answer it.

"Don't forget to — er —"

"Keep my eyes on the south door?" finished Maida with a bleak smile.

"Exactly." I tried to smile, too. I remember thinking, as I walked briskly toward the signal, that our words were not unlike those of soldiers going into battle — in spirit, at least. I saw something of that in 1918; I was in a hospital that was once, mistakenly I hope, shelled. In a choice between the shelled hospital on that lurid front and the dreary, clammy nights of second watch at St. Ann's, where every stir made your breath catch, and every whispering noise made your skin crawl, I'd much prefer the shelled hospital. There the terror was expected; its source was known. Here, every doorway was a silent menace; every room and every turn and every alcove might harbour death. The hospital seemed too roomy, too large, too dark. Our very skirts seemed to whisper and hiss with fear along those blank corridors and empty walls and half-lights and shadows.

I had left the door of the general office open and while going about my work listened for the telephone. Dr. Hajek is supposed to answer it at night, having his room off the office for that purpose, but I hoped that if I heard the ring when O'Leary first called, I would be able to get to the telephone by the time Fred Hajek, who is a heavy sleeper, was aroused.

And when I finally heard the subdued buzz I happened to be at the chart desk and simply dropped pen and all and ran through the corridor that connects us with the main portion of the hospital.

I took the receiver off the hook and was

panting so heavily that I had to wait for a second to catch my breath before answering. The door to Dr. Hajek's room remained closed and Dr. Balman, in the inner office, had not been aroused either, so I must have made the distance in nothing flat — whatever that is — I picked up the term from a patient who was interested in sports and believe it to mean a very rapid pace.

It was O'Leary, of course.

"This is Miss Keate," I said in a low voice, hoping that the sound of it would not carry past those closed doors. "I am very anxious to see you."

He must have caught the urgency in my voice.

"Shall I come right out?"

"Yes. At once."

"Very well. In fifteen minutes."

The receiver clicked, I hung up my own softly, straightened my cap and walked back to the south wing. Maida was not to be seen. I sat down at the desk and found that in my haste to get to the telephone I had upset the red ink I was in the act of using. It was meandering gayly across the desk, reddening everything it touched, and I seized some trash out of the waste basket for a blotter. It was while I was mopping up the ink that all at once, without even a warning flicker, the light above the desk went out, leaving me in total darkness. It was so unexpected that I gasped and cried out.

Then I turned as if to look down the corridor, but nothing but a close black curtain met my eyes. There was not a gleam of light. Every signal light was gone; there was not even a glimmer of light from under the doors of kitchen or drug room or linen closet. I was suspended in a breathless black void.

And down that black emptiness, only five nights ago, two men had been violently done to death!

My breath began to come in painful, rasping gasps. I must do something. I must find Maida. I must get a lamp. Must make my way to the basement switch-box and replace a burned-out fuse — or find what had caused the trouble.

Or was it an accident? Had a fuse actually gone? Could it be that the lights had purposely been disconnected?

The terrifying question had not more than entered my head when from somewhere down the corridor a cold current of air struck me.

I shivered. Some door or window had been opened. Some door — the south door! Was it the south door?

I was standing, gripping the chair back, loath to leave that firm, stationary thing and venture forth into the surrounding blackness that was alive, now, with foreboding and the menace of unspeakable things. Was something moving? Did I hear a stealthy footstep? Was it the thudding of my own heart?

I strove to move, to force my horror-drugged muscles to advance that length of grisly blackness toward — toward Room 18.

I tried to call out: "Maida — Maida —" I kept saying and finally realized that my stiff lips were only shaping the words.

What was happening down there? Was Room 18 claiming another — Was — I took a step into the darkness, tore my reluctant hands from the chair, and groped for the wall to guide me past the yawning emptiness of those intervening doors.

With outstretched, shaking hands, I was feeling for some stable thing to guide me, when, in that dead silence, there was a shattering crash of sound.

It was a revolver shot! The crash reverberated through the halls, echoing and reëchoing in those empty spaces and about those blank doors.

Then gradually the frightful echoes died away. The blackness pressed in upon me, more suffocating than before, and again dead silence reigned.

For a moment I must have been numb with

shock. Then there were footsteps running, a cry, the clicking of signal lights that did not light, and I was running, stumbling, gasping, bumping into doors, trying to reach the end of the corridor. And Room 18.

Along the way I collided with something, something moving that twisted away from me and cried out. It was Maida and at my voice she answered.

"What is it! What has happened! Was it Room 18?"

"Room 18! What can we —"

"We must have a light. In the kitchen — there's a candle —" I heard the swift, soft thud of her feet as they moved away and I kept on, feeling along the cold, dank wall, groping my way past open doors. It seemed an eternity before I reached the end of the corridor and felt the small panes of glass in the south door under my fingers. I turned sharply to the left. Beyond that black void stretched Room 18. I paused at its threshold but something drove me on, into the room.

Here was the wall. Here was the electric light button. Here the bedside table. I bent, feeling along the rough weave of the counterpane on the bed, took a few steps further, trod on something hideously soft and yielding, and sprang backward in stark terror.

Afraid to move, afraid to breathe, my heart

clamouring in my throat choking me, my hands pressed against my teeth, I could not even scream.

What lay there? What was in that room?

Then I realized dimly that Maida was coming, that a small circle of light was at the door, that a hand was holding a lamp unsteadily and the wavering flame was casting grotesque shadows on Maida's chin and mouth. Above them her eyes were wide and black and mirrored my terror.

I saw her hand advance, pointing at my feet. It shook. Her mouth opened in a voiceless cry and I forced myself to look downward.

It was Higgins, sprawled there at the foot of the bed. He had been shot!

Neither of us spoke. Neither of us moved. At last Maida withdrew her hand.

"Set the lamp down," I heard someone saying — it must have been I. "Set the lamp down before you drop it."

We did not hear O'Leary enter the south door. All at once he was there with us, staring at the thing there on the floor, holding his electric torch to illumine it.

"When did it happen? How? Come into the hall. Tell me. Was I too late?"

Somehow we were out in the corridor; the lamp was left on the table in Room 18. The light from its small flame trembled and cast eery, creeping shadows.

"Quick," said O'Leary. "Take that lamp to the basement, Miss Day. The light switch has been pulled out. You know where the switch-box is —"

I saw Maida flinch but she took the lamp, averting her eyes from the floor.

"Hurry! No, Miss Keate, stay here, please, at the door. If anyone tries to get in, stop him! Scream! I'll not be far away."

In a flash he was gone, out the south door. I was still standing as if petrified, there in front of the south door, when the green light over the chart desk at the opposite end of the corridor flashed up and the little red signal lights gleamed suddenly all up and down the hall. I breathed a sigh of relief; Maida was all right, then. And in another moment or two her white uniform came into view at the chart desk.

"All right, thank you, Miss Keate," came a voice at my elbow. It was O'Leary, his hat gone, his hair ruffled, his eyes shining like phosphorescent flashes on a deep-lying sea. "Come with me, please," he said.

"Was the fuse burned out?" asked O'Leary as we met Maida, who was hurrying to answer the signals.

She shook her head. Her eyes were hollow and dark and her face as white as her cap.

"The main switch had been pulled out."

"What I expected," muttered O'Leary, as we sped along the corridor.

Lights were gleaming from the north wing, and the night-duty nurses from that wing were clustered in a frightened group in the main hall. As they saw us they ran forward.

"What was it, Miss Keate — we heard a shot — what has happened?" And down the stairs tumbled several nurses in uniforms and kimonos and Miss Dotty with her hair in paper curlers and her eyes distracted.

O'Leary paid no attention to them. I followed him into the general office. He rapped sharply, first at Dr. Hajek's door, then at the door of the inner office. Then he put his hand on the latch of the door to the inner office and pushed. It was not locked and opened readily; the light from the office streamed through the door.

"O'Leary! What has happened? What is it?" Dr. Balman, his eyes blinking anxiously in the light, was tossing back the covers and springing from his bed.

"There has been another murder in Room 18," said O'Leary.

"Another what! Who?"

"The janitor — Higgins." And at that second the door to Dr. Hajek's room opened and Dr. Hajek, his bathrobe hugged about him, ran toward us.

263

"What was that? What did you say? Higgins? Dead?"

In a few, terse words O'Leary explained and by that time we were all hurrying back to the south wing, Dr. Balman's white pajamas leading the way. I did not enter Room 18 again with them.

There was plenty of work waiting for me in the wing. As if to make bad matters worse the nurses from all over the hospital were crowding into the south-wing corridor, their pallid faces and wild questions adding to the confusion. The excitement was becoming tumultuous when Dr. Balman came into the corridor, a strange figure in his pajamas and bare feet, his thin hair rumpled and his eyes worried.

"There has been an accident," he said. His voice carried though it was very low. "Please return immediately to duty. Do not be alarmed." And it was curious to see the nurses scattering hastily like frightened children caught in mischief.

For a while I had not time or eyes for anything but work. It was difficult enough to calm and soothe the patients of our wing and I paid no attention to the closed door of Eighteen, the flying trips through the corridor made by the two doctors, or O'Leary's gray suit and thoughtful countenance and shining eyes here and there about the wing.

When the police began to arrive, entering the wing by the south door so as not to be seen by those from other wings, it was a great deal like the repetition of a bad dream. It continued so until along about four o'clock when an ambulance, gleaming oddly white and distinct in the cold gray dawn, was drawn up at the south door. I did not see them leave.

I was trying to control my still shaking hands in order to get the neglected charts written up before turning things over to the day nurses, when O'Leary paused beside me and sat down in the vacant chair.

"What is that on your hands?" he asked suddenly as I wrote.

I glanced at my hands and jumped.

"Oh!" I remembered. "It is only red ink. I was cleaning up some that I had spilled when — when the lights went out."

"When the lights were turned out," he corrected. "How soon will you finish that thing?"

"I am through now." I verified the chart hastily and thrust it in its place in the rack. "Have you — found anything?"

"Yes." He spoke coolly. "I have — found a good deal. First, though, why did you telephone for me?"

"Why, it was Higgins! It was Higgins and now it is too late!"

His gray eyes studied me.

"What do you mean?"

My heart began to thump as speculation aroused within me.

"Higgins," I said, dropping my voice to a whisper. "Higgins saw the face of the man that killed Mr. Jackson."

There was a moment of silence so profound that the very walls seemed to whisper and echo my words; someone in the kitchen nearby dropped a spoon and at the metallic little rattle O'Leary stirred.

"Higgins — saw the face of the man who killed Jackson," he repeated slowly. "How do you know, Miss Keate?"

As rapidly as possible I repeated to him the whole of my amazing conversation with Higgins. Then, more reluctantly, I told him of Jim Gainsay's presence back of the willows where he could overhear every word we had spoken. I told him also of what the cook had said.

His inscrutable eyes studying me shrewdly, O'Leary said nothing until I had finished.

"Then Jim Gainsay heard Higgins not only admit his dangerous knowledge but promise to tell you tonight the name of that man. *Tonight.*"

"Yes." Then as I caught the emphasis, I went on hurriedly: "But Jim Gainsay had nothing to do with his death. I saw nothing of Jim Gainsay to-night. I — am sure . . ." My voice trailed breathlessly away under O'Leary's sharp regard.

"And as far as we know now Jim Gainsay was the last person to see Higgins alive?" He continued quite is if I had not rushed to Jim Gainsay's defence.

"As far as we know *now*," I pointed out. "We may find that someone talked to him after he was seen with Jim Gainsay."

"Gainsay overheard your conversation. The man whose face Higgins saw had everything to lose at such evidence. No one but Gainsay and you, Miss Keate, knew of its existence. I'm sorry; Gainsay seems to be a decent enough young fellow." He paused, fumbled in his pocket, drew out the shabby stub of a pencil and began turning it over and over in his slender, well-kept fingers.

The light above my head was paling in the slow, gray light of early morning which was struggling in through the windows and making the whole place more desolate and more grim and forbidding than it had been in the dark of night.

"It is a difficult situation," he said presently.

I pushed my cap farther back on my head and rubbed my hand across my eyes — eyes that were tired and weary with what they had seen that night.

"I dread the effect of this night's doing; it will almost demoralize our staff, to say nothing of its effect upon outsiders. We are looking to you to straighten out this hideous tangle. And it must be soon."

His face was very sober.

"I hope to do so," he said gravely. "I think I am not saying too much when I tell you that I have good reason to hope for success."

There was a restrained little throb of exhilaration in his voice.

"Do you mean —" I began sharply. He interrupted me.

"I mean only that I am beginning to arrive at some conclusions." And without giving me a chance to ask what those conclusions were he continued at once: "Are you sure Higgins said it was a *man's* face that he saw?"

I went back in my memory, over that brief and baffling conversation, now never to be finished. Poor Higgins!

"No," I said thoughtfully. "He did not definitely say it was a man. I — I'm afraid I just assumed it to be a man."

"Assuming is dangerous," said O'Leary quietly. "But he did say that he saw three people?"

"He said he knew that there were three people in Room 18 that night."

"And that there were four people — Corole Letheny and Dr. Hajek and Jim Gainsay and — Dr. Letheny in and about St. Ann's that dark midnight?"

I nodded confirmatively.

"He said, too, that he saw Jim Gainsay's face by the light of a match. And that he saw the face of the man — or person — who killed Jackson by the light of the match."

"But that doesn't prove —" I began hotly.

"No — no, of course not," he said absently. "You say he was of the opinion that the man —"

"He kept saying the 'party'," I interpolated.

"Who killed Jackson and the — the party —" with a rather grim tightening of his lips, O'Leary adopted Higgins's terms — "Who killed Dr. Letheny was not the same person."

"He said 'no, that couldn't hardly be.' " Strange how vividly I recalled his hesitating confession.

"It is apparent, of course, that the man in Room 18 must have had some sort of light, if only for a second, in order to conceal the radium. Higgins knew where it was all the time. He swore to me that he had slept through the whole night. Well —" O'Leary's shoulders lifted a little.

"We will never know now what Higgins saw," I commented, my thoughts sombre.

O'Leary raised his eyes from the pencil for a moment.

"Don't be too sure of that, Miss Keate. Did you get the speaker for me?"

"Yes."

"Put it in a *safe* place?"

I nodded. "I longed to look inside it but did not."

He smiled.

"Suppose we look now."

The rustle of my starched skirts echoed against the empty gray-white walls. The general office was deserted, likewise the stairs and corridors. Once in my room I unlocked the door of the chifferette, withdrew the speaker, and holding it carefully, hastened back to the south wing. O'Leary was still sitting beside the chart desk, his gray gaze on Maida, who was bent over an entry she was making on Three's chart. If she wondered what I was doing with the loud speaker she did not say so but returned immediately to Three.

I set the speaker down on the shining glass top of the chart desk. My hands were shaking a little and I held my breath while O'Leary removed one of the sides of the speaker. We both peered into it. Then O'Leary put his hand inside and groped around.

We stared at the compact arrangement of

wires and tiny coils and screws, then met each other's gaze.

"Nothing!" I said.

"Nothing!" confirmed O'Leary. He studied the thing thoughtfully for a moment.

"Did anyone see you take this to your room?"

"No one. That is, no one but — but Maida. I met her at the door just as I was carrying it to my room."

"Miss Day — h'mm." And after another pause: "Are you sure that this is the same speaker that was in Room 18?"

"Why, yes. No. That is —" I hastened to explain as he cast a decidedly irritated glance at me — "that is, I mean that this is the speaker that was in Sonny's room and I just assumed it to be the one that I had left there."

"Assuming again," remarked O'Leary with dry disapproval. "It might have been one from another room, then?"

"Yes. It might have been. But I think —"

"Did you know that the speaker at present in Room 18 has been torn open, probably during the night?"

"What!"

"Evidently the — er — visitor in Room 18 to-night thought what we thought and did not know that the original speaker in Room 18 had been removed. Or else —" He left his sentence uncompleted, turned abruptly and strode down the hall to Sonny's room.

I followed him to the door. Sonny was awake.

"Good-morning," said O'Leary kindly. "It is rather early in the morning for young fellows like you to be awake. Look here, Sonny, the other night Miss Keate brought in a loud-speaker for the radio attachment, just like this one in my hand. She left it here and took away the one that you already had on your table. Then last night, she came in and took away the speaker she had left with you. I want to know whether the loud speaker she took away last night was the very same speaker she brought in here."

Sonny looked bewildered and O'Leary repeated his question patiently and clearly.

"Why, no," said Sonny finally. "That speaker she brought in wouldn't work."

"What happened to it, then?"

"Why" — Sonny frowned — "Miss Day was in to see me and I told her the speaker wasn't working so she took it away and brought me another. The one she brought in worked fine. But Miss Keate came and got it last night." He looked reproachfully at me.

"Thank you, Sonny," said O'Leary briefly.

I have never seen O'Leary showing any feeling or excitement, but there were eighteen rooms in that wing and I don't think it took him eighteen minutes to examine all the loud speakers in the whole wing. He did not omit one save, of course, that already rifled speaker in Room 18.

When he had finished, still without any results that I could see, he went to Maida.

"Miss Day," he began, "you took a loud speaker exactly like this one" — he still carried under his arm the instrument that I had so futilely treasured — "from Sonny's room last night. What did you do with it?"

Maida put back a wisp of black hair that had strayed from under her immaculate cap; her blue eyes regarded us steadily from the weary, dark circles about them.

"I put it on the table in Room 18," she replied at once. "It was out of order somehow, and I thought likely Room 18 would be unoccupied. So I simply exchanged the speakers."

"Thank you, Miss Day. You did not — er — examine it closely to see what was wrong with it?"

"No," she said. "I know nothing of such things; I couldn't possibly have repaired it."

She went on about her errand.

"A strange case," mused O'Leary, his clear, gray eyes following the slim, white-clad figure moving away from us. "The speaker in Room

18 was the right one, after all. The question is, was the radium in it and if so who took it? Who has it now? When we know that answer we will know who shot poor old Higgins." He went to the window over the chart desk, flung it up to the sash, and took a deep breath of the fog-laden air. His intent young face, his curiously lucid gray eyes, showed no hint of a night without sleep.

"A strange case," he repeated absently. He turned from the dripping gray orchard beyond the window, fingered idly the bronzed surface of the loud speaker there on the desk.

"Another thing, Miss Keate — did you notice that when Dr. Hajek came from his room to-night, presumably from his bed, he wore trousers under that bathrobe that he held so tightly to him? And that those trousers had fresh, wet mud stains about the cuffs?"

I murmured something, I don't know what, and O'Leary met my shocked gaze quietly.

"And furthermore," he said softly, "I found fresh mud stains on the window sill of his room. Really, Miss Keate, this hospital of yours should have been built with its first floor higher from the ground. Entrances and exits are too easy."

13

The Radium Appears

How true it is that time, in retrospect, is measured by the events occurring therein. By which I mean, of course, that while the whole sequence of mysterious and shocking events that so deeply troubled us there at St. Ann's really occurred during a period of only a few days, when I look back at the affair it seems to have extended over weeks. It was true, too, that every day seemed to bring its problems and those before yesterday's problems were solved. In fact these problems so crowded each other that the only way in which I can recall their exact sequence is by referring to the days on which they took place. For instance, I see that in my account book where I have an orderly habit of noting certain things such as birthdays of relatives, dates when my insurance falls due, and such matters, I have noted several items under Wednesday, June 13th:

Higgins killed in Eighteen during second watch, last night. No clue so far as I know. Wish J.G. would go on about his bridge building. Whole hospital much upset; several nurses threatening to leave. Police underfoot everywhere and suppose it means the whole thing over again. Sent laundry this A.M. Am getting nervous about second watch. Twelve pearl buttons. Wish this affair were safely over.

The "twelve pearl buttons" entry, of course, referred to the fact that I had forgotten to take them out of one of my uniforms before it went to the laundry and must remember to telephone the laundry about them. It was owing to these buttons, however, that one of the most singular and troublesome facts of the whole week came to my attention.

If the second watch of the previous night had seemed like a repetition of a bad dream, then that day, Wednesday, was its continuation. The directors, irate and fussy and hysterically horrified, descended upon St. Ann's. There were the police, O'Leary, and newspaper men just as it had been before. The only difference was that this last development seemed more terrible than that other — if that were possible. There was a rather grisly fear stalking through the hushed hospital corridors: Who would be the next victim?

The inquest was held at once, that very morning. It was a brief and formal affair, held in the main office with only a few present. Nothing was proved beyond the immediate fact of Higgins's death and nothing was mentioned that I did not already know. It was evident that O'Leary regarded Higgins's death as another piece in the puzzle that confronted him and not as an isolated crime.

Shortly after lunch Lance O'Leary called me into the office.

"Why did you not tell me that the key to the south door disappeared last night?" he began abruptly.

"I forgot it. I ordered a new key to be made for that lock and will have it before night. But of course I had to leave the south door unlocked last night."

"It seems to me you forget rather important things." He spoke sharply.

"I have certain duties to think of," I responded as sharply. "And anyway you didn't ask me."

The tightness around his eyes relaxed somewhat but he did not smile. He rose, went to the door, and after a dissatisfied glance into the main hall he beckoned me into the inner office, shut the door and sat down at the desk. For a moment he sat there silently, his face in his hands.

"Sit down, Miss Keate," he said presently, motioning toward Dr. Balman's cot, and as

I did so he swung around in the swivel chair to face me. "Hope nobody wants to use this room for a few moments," he said wearily. "I've got to think. Look here, was that key gone when you came on duty last night at twelve o'clock?"

"Yes. Olma Flynn, who has first watch, could not find it. She told me of its disappearance as soon as I came on duty."

He nodded slowly.

"Thus providing an easy way into St. Ann's. . . . Into the south wing —" he murmured, and broke off, staring into space, his eyes clouded and far away.

Then all at once he began to talk, leaned back in the chair, and linked his hands together.

"In the first place," he began, "I am convinced that the three crimes are all linked together and that the possession of the radium is the guiding motive. Other motives, such as protection or fear, may enter into the affair but the radium is the main thing. If the radium was actually placed in that loud speaker, it is now in the hands of the person who killed Higgins. To secure the radium was the reason for his entrance into the south wing and into Room 18 last night. We can't know why Higgins was there — unless — unless — You say that he knew where the radium was hidden;

he may have tried to take it himself into his own hands."

He paused as if to consider that possibility; it did not appear to convince him, for he made an impatient gesture.

"Dr. Hajek," he resumed, "has flatly denied that he was out last night; the mud has been brushed off his trousers and off the window sill and it is my word against his. Why is he lying? Then, too, there was someone from the Letheny cottage about the grounds last night. Huldah says that someone left the house about midnight; she heard footsteps on the stairs, and the front door squeaks. She did not know whether it was Gainsay or Miss Letheny, but she is certain that someone went out of that house about midnight and returned probably an hour later."

"Huldah tells the truth always —" I began, but checked myself. If he was willing to talk I was more than willing to listen.

However, I had interrupted him; he looked at me directly and began to speak more briskly and less as if he were thinking aloud.

"You see, Miss Keate, it is all simmering down to the same group, the same circle of those in and about St. Ann's. No one else could have stolen the key to the south door. And as I say, I am inclined to believe that all three crimes had the same motive, if not the same motivating force."

"What do you mean?"

"I mean that in the first two crimes we find several means of death. This leads me to believe that there was a definite plan to steal the radium, possibly on the part of more than one person. In fact, I am quite sure that more than one person had determined to get hold of that radium. But the radium was left in the room. Hidden, but still in Room 18. Why? There is only one possible reason. The thief was interrupted, was forced to hide it there in order to return for it later. But why did the radium remain for so long in the speaker? Why did not the thief return for it earlier in the game? It all points to there being several people interested in that radium, which means, of course, that we may be trying to discover three murderers instead of only one."

"*Three!*"

"There were three murders," he said, laconically cool in the face of my horror. "And Higgins's statement seems to make it sure that the first two murders were not committed by the same man."

"I am positive that the radium was concealed in the loud speaker," he continued after a short pause. "There was no place else for it to be and it must have been in Room 18, for otherwise we would not have had such a series of disturbances in and about that room. Yes, it is evident that several people were convinced that the radium was still in the room and were searching for it. The thing that bothers me is the failure of the — er — original thief to return and remove the radium before anyone else found it."

"Perhaps it was he last night," I suggested.

O'Leary did not appear to hear me.

"There is only one reason and that — if true — is amazing." He reached absently for the shabby little stub of pencil and began twisting it in his fingers, which convinced me that he was on his feet again, so to speak.

Whatever the "amazing" speculation was that had occurred to him, he said nothing more of it.

"I have eliminated certain factors. The first thing to do, you know is to narrow the field of investigation. I find that Mr. Jackson's relatives, who might be supposed to have an interest in his death, have iron-clad alibis."

"Oh." I spoke none too brightly as I had never given a thought to Mr. Jackson's relatives.

"Likewise I am gradually eliminating the unknown factor — I mean by that the possibility of an outsider, a hobo, perhaps, or professional thief acting on the spur of the moment, or following out a planned course of action. It seems more and more certain that those guilty of these crimes are people who are in and about St. Ann's. But since that phase of the matter is so distasteful to you. . . ." His voice trailed away into nothing, he dropped the pencil, adjusted his tie, looked at his watch, ran a hand through his hair and reached for the pencil again.

"There are a few matters of which I've been wanting to talk with you, Miss Keate. This —" he lowered his voice — "this Hajek. Somehow I have got the impression that he and Miss Letheny see a good deal of each other. Different people have mentioned seeing them together. Huldah says he is a frequent caller. What do you think?"

"Why, yes — now that I think of it, it does seem to me that they have a sort of —" At loss for a word I stopped. O'Leary completed the sentence.

"Understanding?"

"Well, yes. And yet I have seen nothing definite. It is just a feeling that I have. And of course, the fact that he has been up at the Letheny cottage a great deal. I've seen him there often."

He twisted the pencil up and down; I wondered that there was any shred of paint remaining on the shabby thing.

"Another thing," he began rather hesitantly. "They say — don't ask me who says, for it is a sort of drifting gossip that we detectives have to encourage — they say that Dr. Letheny admired the pretty nurse."

"The pretty nurse. Who?"

"I thought you'd guess," he said quietly. "I mean Miss Day."

"If he did admire her, I never knew it," I said with vigour.

"You never even surmised it?" he persisted gently.

"No," I said bluntly. "Certainly not." And then recalled certain things. That last dinner — Dr. Letheny's smouldering eyes on Maida — the gesture with which he took her wrap — those burning, restless eyes seeking her in the corridor of the south wing before he turned away through the door and I caught my last glimpse of Dr. Letheny alive. "That is — perhaps — yes," I amended in a smaller voice.

"Did Miss Day return his — interest?"

"No. I'm sure that she did not. Quite the contrary."

"Quite the contrary?"

"I mean that I believe she disliked him particularly. I do not know why."

He lifted his eyes from the pencil. They were clear now and very gray.

"You would likely know," he said casually.

"You possess the strangest aura of — integrity. One feels you are a respecter of confidences. I presume you are the repository of many secrets."

"I'm sure I don't know any secrets," I replied hastily. The man needn't think he could worm things out of me. "I wish," I added, "I wish that you had talked to Higgins."

His expression became serious at once.

"I wish so too," he said soberly. "Though as far as that goes I did talk to Higgins, but couldn't get a thing out of him. He must have been desperately afraid of getting into trouble." He eyed the stub of pencil solicitously. ". . . getting into trouble," he repeated musingly.

"If I had only known the danger he was in," I said regretfully. "But somehow we never know until it is too late."

"About this matter of the lights going out last night. It seems to coincide too strangely with the affair of Thursday night. The lights being out at that time was, of course, an accident, but one is inclined to think that someone profited by that accident to such an extent that he decided to repeat the fortuitous circumstances. But it was actually no accident this time; the switch plug had been purposely pulled out. Now then, the switch box is in the basement, on the wall next to the grade door that leads out just below the main entrance."

I nodded as his keen, serious eyes rose to mine.

"That grade door was locked and the key inside the lock as it should be. Was there time, Miss Keate, between the lights going out and the sound of the shot for someone to come from that grade door around the corner of the hospital, enter the south door in the darkness, go into Eighteen, which is right next to the south door, take the radium from the loud speaker and — and that is as far as we know. We can only surmise, now, how Higgins came into it."

"The intruder might have been Higgins, himself." I was suddenly struck by the thought. "He would have access to the basement, could have stolen the key from the chart desk that would open the south door if it were locked. Perhaps he was taking the radium out of the speaker; he told me, you know, that he knew where it was hidden."

"All the circumstances point to what we call an inside job," admitted O'Leary slowly. "But someone besides Higgins was in Room 18."

"The window?" I suggested.

"No. He could not have come through the window for it was still bolted. How about it,

Miss Keate?" He returned to his inquiry. "How long a time elapsed between the lights going out and the sound of the shot?"

"It seemed a long time," I said hesitantly. "You see, it was so still and dark and I was a little frightened. I waited for a few moments, thinking that the lights would come on again. Yes, I think there was time enough for — for all that you think took place. While I waited I felt current of air on my shoulders."

He looked up quickly.

"That was the door opening, then. You are sure about the length of time? You see it is rather important that we settle that point definitely for if there was not time for all that to go on, it would indicate that there were two people, *besides Higgins,* who were interested in getting into Room 18 last night. And that one of them managed the business of turning off the lights and the other came into Room 18 with the results of which we know. Confound it!" He broke off suddenly. "I wish I needn't have to figure on more than one or two ways of getting in and out of this old hospital. Don't you *ever* have thieves in a hospital! Don't you ever have to safeguard yourselves!"

"Only the third and fourth floor windows," I said absently.

He snorted.

"The third and fourth floor windows! That

does me a lot of good!"

"On account of delirious patients," I said rebukingly. "And as for there being two people trying to get the radium, I think there must be at least that many. I don't believe that one person, alone and unaided, could make so much trouble."

He grinned faintly at that, and then frowned.

"The chief of police wants to arrest the whole outfit at once. He is convinced that you are all in a conspiracy and that Gainsay is the leader. Of course, I don't want to make such a wholesale cleaning. Especially since I — I believe that I'm getting warm. But I don't want any arrests yet. I don't want to put anybody on guard."

"Mr. O'Leary," I said eagerly, emboldened by his half-confidence. "I have heard things of you, of course — what wonderful success you have and all that. What methods do you use?"

He thrust his hands into his pockets, leaned back in the chair and sighed.

"Methods? I don't have any methods. And as to success — wait a few days."

"You don't have any methods?"

"The moment when I'm feeling most useless and most like a failure is not the moment to ask me to tell of my successes. Or my methods.

I don't have methods. I take what the Lord sends and am thankful. Sometimes it is a matter of luck. Mostly it is a matter of drudgery and hard work. Always it is a matter of thinking, thinking, thinking. Of eating, living, sleeping with problems for days and nights. Usually, just about the time you have decided that none of the pieces of the puzzle can possibly fit, all at once something happens and — Click! Things clarify. There is a reason for everything. Nothing just happens. Nothing is an isolated fact. If you have a fact, you know that certain circumstances had to combine to bring it about. It is just logic, reason, the physical, material quality of cause and effect. There isn't anything mysterious about it. It is just the — the arithmetic of analysis. I don't mean that I am infallible. I have to reconsider and revise and correct mistakes, just like anybody else. I'm human — and young. But when you *know* that there is a solution, to the most puzzling problem, all there is to do is worry it out. I suppose the subconscious mind helps."

"That is rather abstract," I said slowly.

"I suppose it sounds that way. Well — here is one definite and concrete trick. As a rule, given enough rope a man can hang himself. Often I find that there will be one little circumstance that only the guilty man knows.

Sooner or later he lets it out. Sometimes I have to trap the man I suspect into such an admission."

I'm sure my eyes were popping out.

"Then that is why you made that extraordinary request of me at the first inquest!" I exclaimed. "I could not understand it. The thing you mentioned seemed so insignificant."

It was remarkable that his eyes could be so clear and so unfathomable at the same time.

"I trust you are discreet," he said evenly.

"Oh, I shan't tell, if that is what you mean," I promised hastily. "I am as interested in solving this mystery as you are. Indeed, I think I may say that I am far more deeply interested."

"Well, keep your eyes and ears open," he said, smiling and rising to open the door for me, and I found myself out in the main hall before I knew it.

It was only a few moments later that I saw him leave; I remember standing at the window beside the main entrance, and watching his long gray roadster swoop silently and swiftly around the curve of the main driveway and into the road. He was seated at the wheel, a slight gray figure, intent only on the muddy highway ahead of him. There was a suggestion of power, of invincibility, in the very repose and economy of motion with which he controlled the long-nosed roadster.

As I turned away I met Maida.

"Such a day!" she murmured with a sigh. "Have you been able to sleep?"

"I haven't tried," I said. "I knew it would be no use."

"Miss Dotty is still upset," went on Maida. "And the training nurses are following their own devices, and everybody is afraid of her own shadow. I wish this business was all settled and forgotten about."

"You don't wish it any more than I do," I agreed fervently. "But do think that O'Leary is doing everything within his power."

"I suppose so," said Maida, without much conviction. She was looking pale and rather ill. "Wasn't that Mr. O'Leary driving away a moment ago?"

"Yes."

"I didn't know that he was here at St. Ann's. He hasn't seen fit to question me yet" — she smiled rather ruefully — "as to poor Higgins. Except, of course, as he did at the inquest and that was so little. I felt he was reserving his inquiry, didn't you? But I thought Mr. O'Leary had gone back to town long ago."

"No. He just left." I paused to yawn. "I'm going to try to get some sleep. Better do likewise." But she shook her head, murmuring something about work, and I went to my room.

Luckily I managed to fall into an uneasy sleep. It was when I had awakened that I found I possessed but one remaining clean uniform and it was of a style that demanded the buttons I had sent to the laundry. Recalling the fact that Maida had an extra set, I went to her room to borrow. She was not there but I went boldly into the room.

And I found the radium!

It was in the pin-cushion, a pretty trifle of mauve taffeta ruffles that I picked up idly to examine more closely. When I felt the shape under the taffeta, when my fingers outlined it, I could not have resisted tearing it apart. The cotton stuffing had been removed and the small box that held the radium was there instead.

I don't know how long I stood as if frozen to the spot. I remember noting that the neat sewing had been torn out as if hastily, and that wide hurried stitches held the seam together. And I remember hearing the voices of several girls passing in the hall outside and thinking that Maida would be coming to her room.

O'Leary had said: "The person who has the radium is the one that killed Higgins."

I could not face Maida with this thing in my hand.

And I could not leave the radium where it was.

In another moment I found myself back in my room, the radium, pin-cushion and all, locked away, the key securely hidden and my mind made up. Painful though it was I should have to tell O'Leary immediately of this thing. I do not hold friendship lightly and the shock of finding the stolen radium in Maida's possession almost unnerved me.

I had forgotten about the buttons and it was something of an anti-climax to catch myself starting down to dinner in a black silk kimono. I had to go to the bottom of my trunk for an old uniform that I had cast aside as being too tight. It was still too tight and very uncomfortable, being made with a Bishop collar which is high and stiff and scratched the lobes of my ears.

There was no need to telephone to O'Leary, for as I neared the general office I caught a glimpse of his smooth brown head bent over some papers on the long table. I entered.

"I have found the radium," I said quietly.

He looked up, jumped to his feet. I did not need to repeat my words.

"Where is it?"

"In my room. Shall I bring it to you?"

He hesitated, his eyes travelling around the office with its several doors and windows.

"This is too public. Someone would be sure to see it. Where did you find it?"

I swallowed.

"In — Miss Day's room."

His gaze narrowed thoughtfully.

"You must tell me about it later. First I must have the radium."

Our voices had dropped to whispers and my heart was pounding.

"Shall we put it in the safe?" I motioned toward the inner office which holds a great steel safe, in a prepared compartment of which the radium is usually kept.

"No." O'Leary shook his head decisively. "No. I must put it in the hands of the chief of police at once. Look here, Miss Keate; in three minutes I shall walk slowly across the main hall with this bundle of newspapers under my arm. At the foot of the stairway I shall pass you just descending. It is rather dark there by the stairs. Hand me the box and keep right on going. Don't stop. Later I shall see you and hear how you found it."

I followed his bidding. As I came slowly down the last flight of stairs he walked carelessly across the hall. There was no one about and I was sure that the transfer was effected without anyone's knowledge.

With a casual nod I went on around the turn and followed the basement stairs down to the dining room. I ate what was set before me and kept my eyes from Maida.

It must have been about twenty minutes later that I ascended the stairs again and paused in the main hall. There was a light in the general office, excited voices, and Dr. Hajek and Dr. Balman were bending over something that lay on the long table.

I entered.

Lance O'Leary was stretched on the table, his face lead-gray, his eyes closed. Dr. Balman had out his stethoscope and was listening intently and Dr. Hajek was forcing aromatic ammonia through O'Leary's pale lips.

There was a rapidly swelling lump back of O'Leary's right ear and the small box that was so precious was not to be seen.

At a glance I understood.

"Is he — alive, Dr. Balman?"

Dr. Balman nodded, detaching the stethoscope with long hands that shook.

"Dr. Hajek and I were starting down to dinner," he explained. His voice sounded hoarse and his anxious eyes were fixed upon O'Leary. "We found him like this. All huddled on the floor there near the stairway."

14

A Matter of Evidence

I must say that I was considerably relieved to see O'Leary's eyelids flutter, the colour return to his face, and to note that his breath began to come more naturally. In a few moments he was sitting upright on the edge of the table, supported by Dr. Balman's arm.

"What on earth happened to you?" inquired Dr. Balman, looking relieved also.

"I don't know," replied O'Leary rather dazedly. "All I remember is something coming down on my head. When did you find me?"

"About fifteen minutes ago. Dr. Hajek and I were just going downstairs. It was not very light in the hallway and you were in the shadow there by the stairs. It — gave us a nasty shock. Do you know why you were attacked?"

O'Leary flicked a warning glance at me and shook his head.

"Haven't the least idea," he said flatly.

Dr. Hajek, who had been standing silently by, stirred at this.

"Then you were not on the point of making

295

a — er — disclosure?" he asked with an air of disappointment. His ruddy face was as unmoved and stolid as ever, but it seemed to me that those dark, knowing eyes were restrained and secretive and did not meet O'Leary's gaze squarely.

"No such luck! By the way, were you men coming up from downstairs when you found me?"

"No," replied Dr. Balman. "No. I had been O.K.-ing some orders in the inner office; Dr. Hajek came out of his room into the general office just as I, too, entered it and we walked together out into the hall and toward the basement stairs."

"You saw nothing unusual?"

"Nothing. We were talking of advertising for a new janitor. It was —" Dr. Balman's kind, distressed eyes roved over O'Leary anxiously as if to be quite sure he was not hurt — "it was, as I said, a shock. For a moment we feared the worst." He drew out a handkerchief and wiped his pale lips nervously, his fingers lingering to pull at his thin beard. "Mr. O'Leary, I know that you are working hard and I don't mean to criticize but really — I —" he hesitated as if put to it to find words. "You see for yourself to what terrible straits this thing has brought us. We don't know what to expect next. Can nothing be done to stop it?"

It was just at this interesting point, of course, that Miss Dotty had to interrupt and summon me away, and it was something after midnight before I saw O'Leary again.

I was on duty at the time, Maida assisting me as usual, and our force augmented again, according to another whim of Miss Dotty's, by two training nurses, both obviously unnerved at their contact with the south wing of such ill repute. Their blue-and-white striped skirts rattled nervously as they trotted here and there about the wing. While I did not feel unduly alarmed myself, still it seemed all too clear that the guilty one was still about, an unknown menace and hence more terrible, and I don't mind admitting that my ears were alert to any alien sounds.

I was sitting at the chart desk when I heard O'Leary's quick, light steps coming along the corridor from the general office. I turned to watch him approach, his gray suit and grave, keen face gradually emerging into the green circle of light that surrounded me.

"Have you found the radium?" I asked at once.

He shook his head.

"Nor who took it from you?"

"Nor who took it — naturally." He dropped into a chair beside me. "Now, Miss Keate, tell me exactly how you came upon it."

Feeling that it was no time to mince matters I complied, much as I disliked the implications the story involved. He listened thoughtfully, drawing a red pencil from his pocket and actually using it to scribble some notes in a small, shabby notebook he brought forth. He did not comment when I had finished, save to ask if Miss Day was on duty. And at the moment Maida herself entered the corridor from some sick room, O'Leary rose and intercepted her at once and the two disappeared into the drug room.

I was left to wait, always a difficult task for one of my temperament and particularly unpleasant that night. It seemed hours but was actually not more than twenty minutes by my watch, before they emerged. Maida's chin was in the air, her cheeks quite scarlet, and her eyes flashing blue fire, but O'Leary was imperturbable. He stopped for a word with me and I suppose noted the anxiety which I was at no pains to hide. He smiled into my gaze a bit ruefully.

"She has a reason for everything," he said quietly. "If I could only be sure that she is telling the truth!"

"She always tells the truth!" I cried indignantly.

"I hope so —" he hesitated. "It is difficult

to explain, but all through her story I had the strangest impression that she had — rehearsed the whole thing."

"What did she say of the radium?"

"Says she found it in a pot of lobelia that was in the hall outside Room 18. She noted that the flowers were withered and needed water, took it to the kitchen to water, noted that it had been disturbed and — found the radium hidden below the plant! She took the radium to her own room until she could get in touch with me. She says she did not know that I was in the hospital after the inquest until she saw me leaving."

"That is true," I said quickly. "And I remember the pot of lobelia, too. Only —" I wrinkled my forehead thoughtfully. "Why, the last I saw it, the thing was still in Room 18! Not in the corridor, at all!"

"When did you see it last?" he asked quickly.

"Last night — about dusk."

He looked at me soberly.

"Then the man in Room 18 last night — if it was a man — must have hidden the radium for fear he would be caught with the incriminating box. He must have thrust it hurriedly into the flower pot and left plant and all in the corridor in the hope of being able to get hold of the radium more easily than if it were left again in Room 18. That is, if we are to believe Miss Day's statement. Positively that lobelia *was not in Room 18* when I examined the room almost immediately after Higgins's death. I did not miss a square inch!"

I was still thinking of Maida.

"Did you ask her about the hypodermic syringe?"

He nodded.

"She says that she found her own needle had disappeared, naturally disliked calling anyone's attention to the fact, in view of the existing circumstances, and simply substituted your tool for the lost one. She says she acted hastily and only from a dislike of being even remotely connected with the tragedies. My own opinion is that someone advised her to do so. Especially since there was a cut-and-dried air about everything she said."

"How did the hypodermic syringe get out there in the shrubbery?"

"Miss Day insists that she knows nothing of that. And I'm more than half inclined to believe her, there."

"The cuff link?" I persisted anxiously.

His clear eyes narrowed.

"The cuff link is the reason that I doubt her whole story. She still declared that she lost the cuff link and that Dr. Letheny must have picked it up. If she would only tell me the truth about that!" He pulled a yellow slip of paper from his notebook, I recognized it immediately. It was the note Jim Gainsay had written and asked me to take to Maida.

"Read it," said O'Leary.

Thinking it more discreet to say nothing of my own connection with the note, I did as he requested. It was headed: "Friday afternoon" and read thus:

Must see you at once. Important. C. knows about last night. Say nothing and let me advise you. Will wait at the bridge. Very anxious since news of this afternoon. Be warned. Cannot urge too emphatically. Please meet me at bridge.

It was signed with a vigorously scrawled "J.G."

I read the thing, read it again and raised my eyes to O'Leary's.

"It was found in Miss Day's room," he explained. "In a pocket of a uniform, in fact; when I asked her to explain it she said at first that it was a message of a personal nature and that she would not explain it. I was forced to urge and she finally admitted exactly three things. First, that the note was written by Jim Gainsay. Second, that 'C' referred to Corole Letheny. And third —" He paused as if to

301

give the coming words more emphasis.

"And third — simply this: That Jim Gainsay was strolling in the orchard about one o'clock on the night Dr. Letheny was killed. He passed the open window of the diet kitchen, saw her within, and stopped for a word or two through the window. Corole Letheny was also in the orchard, heard their conversation, and threatened to start a scandal, knowing that it would not sound well for a nurse to be seen visiting thus when she was on duty and at such an hour. For some reason Corole Letheny has developed a violent dislike for Jim Gainsay. According to Miss Day, then, he wrote to warn her against Corole." O'Leary's clear gray eyes searched my face. "Somehow the reasons Miss Day gave do not seem to warrant the extreme urgency expressed in this note. Do you think so, Miss Keate?"

"I hardly know," I said thoughtfully. "Of course, it takes less than that to start a scandal, particularly if the starter is determined and malicious. And Corole is both. She is naturally rather — feline, you know."

He took the note from my hand.

" 'Since news of this afternoon can only refer to Dr. Letheny's death. No, Miss Keate. What would a little breath of evil comment such as Miss Letheny could start have to do with Dr. Letheny's death? No — there is a deeper reason. I wish I could persuade Miss Day to be frank with me. Well, now to see if Gainsay tells the same story. Probably he will, but we will see." He paused to regard me soberly. "Is there any room here in the wing where Gainsay and I could be undisturbed for a time? This is a case where the very leaves of the shrubbery seem to have ears and I don't want Miss Corole to overhear us — or anyone else."

"Why, yes," I said slowly. "There is the drug room."

The red light above Six gleamed. No other nurse was about, so I interrupted myself to answer and bring Sonny a fresh drink.

"I've been wishing you would come in to see me." said Sonny cheerfully. "I've been alone ever since a man named Gainsay stopped to see me just at supper time. He wanted to know where everyone was and I told him it was just the time when you were all eating. Say, do you know him? I like him. He is a friend of Dr. Letheny's. Say, why doesn't Dr. Letheny come in to see me?"

"Sonny, did you sat that Mr. Gainsay was here in St. Ann's? Here in your room at dinner time?"

"Why, sure, he was here! Just about six o'clock."

"Where did he go when he left your room?"

"I think he went on up the corridor toward the general office. I can't be sure, though, for I was working a new cross-word puzzle and didn't listen for his steps. Say, Miss Keate, want to see my new puzzle?"

I forestalled the thin hand groping on the bedside table.

"Another time, Sonny. You must go to sleep now."

O'Leary's fingers sought the red pencil stub as I told him.

"So," he pondered, "Jim Gainsay was here in St. Ann's."

"Where he had no business to be." I interpolated grimly.

"And he was here at about the time I was knocked out and the radium stolen. This increases my interest in Mr. Gainsay." He thrust his stub of a pencil into his pocket, ran a hand over his already smooth hair, and glanced at his watch. "I think we'll have to disturb Jim Gainsay's rest to-night — if he is asleep. You are sure the drug room will not be in use, Miss Keate?"

"If we need anything I'll get it myself," I promised hastily. There was a sort of repressed smile on his face as he turned away, though I'm sure I don't know why.

Jim Gainsay must not have been asleep, for within five minutes the two men were coming along the corridor from the main entrance. One of the student nurses saw me lead them into the drug room and her eyes would likely have popped out had I not spoken sharply to her. On the theory that every cloud has a silver lining I considered it fortunate that Eleven chose that very time for a rather cataclysmic upheaval which kept Maida thoroughly engrossed for an hour or so, and I don't think she ever knew of the interview that took place there in our wing.

She came very near it once, when she hurried for some soothing drops, but I forestalled her by offering to get the medicine myself. If she thought my hasty offer curious, she said nothing and went back to her patient.

Opening the drug-room door I walked into an electric atmosphere. Jim Gainsay, lounging tall and bronzed against the window sill, was clearly furious; his eyes were narrow and wary, his lean jaw was set, his lips tight and guarded.

I caught the words . . . "entirely a personal matter" in no very pleasant voice from Jim Gainsay.

"I must insist upon an answer, however," said O'Leary. His voice had the keenness of a slender, shining steel blade.

Then both men became aware of my presence, and though I was rather deliberate in measuring the drops, they said nothing further until I left, when the murmur of their voices began again.

The interview prolonged itself and it was a good half hour before I had a chance — that is, needed to go into the drug room again, and it was only for an ice bag.

"And yet you remain a welcome guest in Corole Letheny's house?" said O'Leary.

"Not so darned welcome," replied Jim Gainsay, and I caught the flicker of a smile on O'Leary's face as I closed the door.

In a few moments, however, O'Leary opened the door, peered down the corridor, saw me and beckoned.

His eyes were shining with that peculiarly lucent look as he motioned for me to precede him into the drug room.

"I want you to hear this, Miss Keate," said O'Leary, his voice very quiet but with a tense, alert overtone that caught my ears. "Now, Gainsay, will you repeat that about Higgins?"

Jim Gainsay glanced at me rather sheepishly.

"I was telling O'Leary how it happened that I overheard most of your talk with Higgins the afternoon before his death. It struck me as foolish to let such a mine of information get away, and later in the evening I got hold of Higgins and wormed some more of the story out of him. For the most part he just repeated what he had already told you, Miss Keate. But he did tell me the scrap of conversation that he promised to tell you — remember?"

I nodded.

"It seems that he heard it when he stopped there near the south entrance on his way to see Dr. Letheny. I suppose it was this conversation as much as anything that made him suspicious of what was going on in Room 18. It seems that he knew at once who was on the other side of the bush; it was Corole and Dr. Hajek. Corole said — according to Higgins — 'To follow would be easy, now,' and Hajek said 'Wait till he comes out.' Then Corole said something about it not being difficult and Hajek said 'Leave it to me.' Then Higgins thought he must have made some noise among the leaves, for Corole whispered 'Hush' and he heard them slipping away. Higgins followed but soon lost them in the dark and himself returned to the interesting vicinity of Room 18." He paused.

"Go on," said O'Leary grimly.

"Higgins told you how he came back to the porch and stumbled over a coat. I got him to tell me something about the coat. He said it must have been 'one of them slickers,' for it felt cold and oily. And at the same time he told me a peculiar thing." Again he paused as if what he was about to say was distasteful to him. I glanced at O'Leary; his eyes still wore that strangely luminous expression. Even the glass doors of the cupboards all around us and the shining white tiles seemed to wait expectantly.

"Go on," said O'Leary sharply, his words breaking into the crystal silence.

Jim Gainsay cleared his throat, felt in his pocket for a cigarette, remembered that he was in a hospital and replaced it.

"He said the coat smelled of — ether!"

There was a moment of silence. Then I turned to O'Leary.

"Ether! It was the same slicker! The one that I wore Friday afternoon!"

O'Leary nodded thoughtfully.

"It might be. At any rate we know that no slicker was found on the porch or about the grounds, so it is likely that the murderer of Dr. Letheny carried it away with him. We had a strict guard on St. Ann's the day following the murders. It is barely possible that we can yet trace the coat that you wore, Miss Keate."

"Poor Higgins," said Jim Gainsay gravely. "I had a hard time getting him to tell me that much. He refused to the last to tell me whose face he saw there in Room 18."

"But he failed to raise an alarm even though

he had reason to think that the radium was being removed," murmured O'Leary. "Well, that's all now, thank you, Gainsay."

Jim Gainsay paused for a moment outside the door and I saw him look carefully up and down the dim corridor. No white uniform was in sight, however. Thinking to facilitate his departure I took the key to the south door from its hiding place and let him out that way. When I returned O'Leary was standing under the green light, studying his small notebook. He slipped it into his pocket as I approached.

"Nothing, Miss Keate, but what you heard," he said rather wearily. "His explanation of the note to Miss Day and his activities during the night of the murders are identical with what Miss Day tells us. He sticks to the story of his telegram to his business associates that he told at the inquest. He says he took Dr. Letheny's car and left the grounds of St. Ann's very soon after you met him in the dark. And that he was at a corner about half a mile from St. Ann's' when the storm broke — which does not coincide with what we know. That is, if the lights you saw were the lights of the car he was driving, and it seems reasonable to believe that they were."

"How about his presence here in St. Ann's to-night at the time the radium was taken from you?"

"That got a rise out of him," said O'Leary with an unexpected flash of whimsical satisfaction. "He was angry in a second. Every time Miss Day's name came up he turned savage. If the radium had not disappeared I should be inclined to think that he came to St. Ann's in the hope of seeing Miss Day, but with the radium gone again —" he stopped abruptly, his face becoming grave again and dubious.

The green light cast crawling shadows; the black window pane stared impenetrably at us; far down the corridor a light went on with a subdued click, a glass clinked thinly against something metal, and I heard the soft pad-pad of a nurse's rubber heels.

Presently O'Leary stirred. His eyes, still shining with that very lucent look, met mine intently.

"Corole Letheny is next. Do you want to go to see her with me? Very well, then, suppose we say at eight in the morning. You might just happen into the Letheny cottage and I'll come. I may be a little delayed."

The remaining hours of second watch dragged a little but passed quietly, and promptly at eight o'clock I wrapped myself in my blue, scarlet-lined cape, adjusted the wrinkled folds of the detestable Bishop collar, and let myself out the south door. The path was still wet, the trees and shrubbery were veiled in heavy mist, and the whole world very sombre and desolate.

At the bridge I came upon Jim Gainsay. He was sitting disconsolately on a log a little aside from the path, staring at a toad hopping across his feet and apparently lost in his own morose thoughts. I don't think he had slept for he looked haggard and cold and must have been smoking steadily for hours, for there was a little white circle of cigarette ends around him.

"Young man," I said with some acerbity, "don't you know that cigarettes are coffin nails and you are making yourself subject to indigestion, nervous disorders, tuberculosis and asthma?"

He rose grudgingly and surveyed me without enthusiasm.

"To say nothing of measles and hay fever," he said dourly. "Say, Miss Keate, is there any chance of seeing — her?"

I did not ask whom.

"I don't know. Have you not seen her lately?"

He glanced at me suspiciously, then motioned to a seat on the log and I found myself seated none too comfortably, with the moisture of a tree dripping down and completing the demoralization of my collar, and beside me a man whom I suspected of theft and —

theft, to say the least.

"That was why I was in the hospital last night about dinner time," he said companionably. "I haven't seen her for days and days. She is too damn' devoted to duty."

"Miss Day is a nice girl," I said uncertainly.

"Nice!" He glared at me. "Nice! Is that all you can say for her? Lord! She can have me! The minute I saw her, I thought, 'There she is! There's my girl!' Say!" he drew a long breath — "and after I talked to her alone, there at that kitchen window last Thursday night, I knew Jim Gainsay's time had come! I drove straight into town and wired the company that I should be delayed. And here I stay until she goes with me." He paused and added ruefully: "It may take quite a while to convince her that she wants to go."

"So that was what your message meant?"

He looked at me quickly. No matter what O'Leary said later I do not believe that Gainsay's explanation was anything but spontaneous.

"Why didn't you explain before?" I asked tartly, thinking of the trouble he had caused us.

"Explain!" cried Jim Gainsay in high derision. "The woman says 'Explain'! Explain that I've gone straight off my head about a girl! Please, kind gentlemen, excuse me for hanging around just when murders are being perpetrated and no strangers wanted on the premises. But really, you know, I've just fallen in love. Explain! Hell!"

In some dignity I rose; even justifiable ill-nature can go too far.

"Good-morning, Mr. Gainsay," I said coldly. But as I turned the bend in the path, I looked backward. "I'll ask her to take a walk this afternoon," I promised, being a fool of an old maid. He brightened up at that and the last I saw of him he was casting pebbles at the frog with the liveliest interest on the part of each.

The porch of the Letheny cottage was still unswept and desolate, and though I rang and rang apparently no one heard me. Finally I opened the heavy door and walked into the hall. No one seemed to be about. The door to the study was closed, and thinking to find Corole there if anywhere I approached it. But with my hand actually on the brass knob, I paused, for the door itself swung gently a few inches toward me, I heard a low murmur of voices and realized that some one was on the other side of the door and in the very act of emerging from it.

"You are sure it is safe there?" said someone clearly.

It was Dr. Hajek's voice.

"Quite," said Corole, whose accents were unmistakable.

"Then to-day is as good as any."

"I — suppose so." Corole seemed reluctant.

"Are you backing down?" I had not believed that Fred Hajek's voice could be so ugly.

"No," said Corole. "No."

"Then why not to-day?" The door closed sharply on the last syllable as if propelled by a vigorous motion on the part of the speaker.

In some perplexity I waited. I could still hear the sounds of voices, but the words were unintelligible. All at once, however, the man's voice rose as if in anger, and without pausing to consider my action I simply grasped that brass knob and flung the door open.

I interrupted a strange tableau.

Corole was leaning backward against the table, her lips drawn back in a snarl and her eyes gleaming green fire. Dr. Hajek was no less moved; his face was dark red, his fists clinched, his dark eyes glittering unpleasantly between slitted lids. He was speaking when I opened the door and I caught his last words. They were thick with fury.

". . . and now you refuse. After all I have done — *for you!*"

"Oh, I don't refuse," cried Corole.

Then they both saw me.

Dr. Hajek's dark face flushed a still deeper,

painful red. By an effort, apparently of will, he relaxed his hands, reached for a cap that lay on the table, muttered something under his breath, and wheeled toward the door. Corole recovered her self-possession more easily; she raised her eyebrows and shrugged as if in amusement. She wore an amazing Chinese coat, stiffly embroidered in gold and green, dancing pumps with rhinestone heels and shabby toes, and *no stockings!*

"Good-morning," she said with shameless calm.

I think O'Leary must have met Dr. Hajek in the hall, for I heard his voice before he entered the study. At the door he stopped.

"You, too," said Corole, losing her amused smile.

"May I come in, Miss Letheny?" O'Leary asked. He looked as fresh and well groomed as if he had had a long night's sleep. "I rang the bell but no one answered."

Corole pulled her bizarre coat tighter about her.

"Huldah decided she no longer liked it here," she said. "She left last night — rather abruptly. Yes, do come in, Mr. O'Leary."

There followed an hour I shall not soon forget. I had never seen Lance O'Leary so mercilessly intent. I was both fascinated and awed to note the way he cut through Corole's pretences and poses, her feline evasions and her suave smiles, and by sheer strength of will forced her to give to his inquiries answers that were direct if they were not entirely truthful.

He began with the revolver, but she repeated the denial of all knowledge regarding its presence in Room 18 she had given at the inquest. Also, to further questions as to her visit to Room 18 on the night it had sheltered that irascible patient, Mr. Gastin, she repeated the lame explanation she had given at the time. She admitted coolly enough that she understood the use of a hypodermic outfit, and as coolly, though with an evil glance at me, that she had made a trip through the orchard immediately after hearing of Dr. Letheny's death; she had wished to see Dr. Hajek, she said brazenly, to discuss with him the news of the tragedy.

It was then that O'Leary held before her eyes the small gold sequin.

"Enough of this, Miss Letheny," he said coldly. "It would be better for you to give me your fullest confidence. Why were you at the window of Room 18 last Thursday night? This ornament was found on the window sill. How did it get there?"

Corole stared blankly from the gold sequin to O'Leary, but back of those queer topaz eyes I felt that she was thinking desperately.

"Well," she said finally, "I *was* near Room 18. In fact, I went as far as the window sill. You see, I was walking in the orchard. I was near the porch of the south wing when I heard something — a sort of noise, there at the window of the corner room." She stopped and ran a quick, catlike tongue over her lips. "Room 18, that is. I was rather curious so I crept up nearer the window. A man was opening the screen and crawling into Room 18. He left the screen up and I slipped quietly up to the window. I am rather tall, you know, and as I leaned for a moment on the sill I suppose the sequin got detached from my gown."

"It was very dark that night. Did you see all this?"

She moistened her lips again; they were taking on a bluish tinge.

"I — I see in the dark better than most people." (Which I, for one, did not doubt.) "And anyway I could hear, you know."

"What could you hear? Why should you think that the noise you heard was made by a man crawling in the window of Room 18? That is just a little farfetched, Miss Letheny."

"It is true, anyhow," she said sulkily. "I heard the screen catch as he pulled it up and the sort of — scrambling sound he made, and I could see the patch of light that was his shirt front."

"If all that is true, why did you not rouse St. Ann's at once?"

"Because I knew who the man was."

There was a brief, electric silence.

"Who was the man?" said O'Leary very quietly.

"My cousin, Louis Letheny." She brought the name out with a suggestion of triumph. I do not know whether it was a surprise to O'Leary or not; however, he said nothing for a full moment. His clear gray eyes were studying Corole's face.

"Naturally," went on Corole with a degree of malicious satisfaction, "naturally I could not arouse the hospital to advertise the fact that the head of the institution had just crawled through a window. Who was I to know Dr. Letheny's purpose?"

"You are lying," said O'Leary. "I warned you not to lie. The man you saw crawling through the window of Room 18 was not Dr. Letheny. You and Dr. Hajek were together in the orchard that night and you actually did lean at the window sill, intending to enter Room 18, but Dr. Letheny was already in Room 18. You and Dr. Hajek discussed whether it would be better to wait until Dr. Letheny came out of Room 18, or for Dr. Hajek to follow him into that room."

In the twinkling of an eye Corole had become saffron yellow, the dabs of orange rouge on her cheeks stood out, emphasizing her high cheek-bones with grisly clearness; her eyes were flat and gleaming and her lips had drawn back a little from her teeth and the garish Chinese coat accentuated her ugly pallor.

"Who told you that?" she whispered through those hideous lips.

"Higgins told me," replied O'Leary very distinctly.

"Higgins!" cried Corole hoarsely, flinging up one brown, jewelled hand toward her throat. "Higgins! But he is dead!"

"Higgins told me," repeated O'Leary. "Now then, tell me. What did you and Dr. Hajek do?"

"We — we met at the bridge. We walked together through the orchard." Corole's desperate effort to regain her self-control was not nice to witness.

"Go on."

"Then — as I said — we heard a man in Room 18. And wanted to know what he was doing there. That was natural, I think." She paused.

"Possibly," said O'Leary. "Why did you not wait until this — this man — came out from Eighteen?"

"We did not wait for him. Someone came along. We never knew just who it was, though

319

I thought that it was Jim Gainsay. He was in the orchard that night, too."

"Seems to have been a popular rendezvous," commented O'Leary grimly. "So this approaching person frightened you away?"

"Not at all," denied Corole with a flash of her normal ease. "We just — left."

"Where did you go?"

"Through the apple orchard."

"And having eluded this — er — unknown person, you returned to the intriguing vicinity of Room 18?"

"No," said Corole flatly. "I came immediately home."

"And Dr. Hajek?"

"Returned to his room at St. Ann's."

"Are you sure?"

"Yes."

"How do you know?"

Corole hesitated.

"He told me so, later," she said lamely.

"Why were you intending to intercept Dr. Letheny — or rather, the man whom you thought to be Dr. Letheny?"

Corole leaned forward.

"Look here, I *know* that Louis Letheny was in Room 18 that night!"

"I know that, too," agreed O'Leary quietly.

She leaned back on the cushions, her eyes puzzled and her swinging rhinestone heels catching red and green lights.

"Why did you intend to intercept him?" repeated O'Leary.

"Because — Dr. Hajek felt he should know the reason for Louis's strange actions."

"Dr. Hajek being an interne and Dr. Letheny the head doctor," commented O'Leary skeptically.

Corole's eyes shot a vicious, sidelong look at the detective but she said nothing.

15

Corole is Moved to Candour

A silence fell in the room. O'Leary walked to the window, pulled the heavy, mulberry-coloured drapes aside, and stood there for a moment. The world outside was sodden and cold; the dense green shrubbery strange and unfamiliar with its fallen leaves rotting and its heavy branches dipping. The piano in the alcove opposite me was shrouded with a great black velvet cover, but it seemed to me that ghostly fingers took up the first haunting strains of the C Sharp Minor Prelude. I stirred impatiently and O'Leary turned to face Corole, who sat sullenly still in the davenport, her fingernails digging into an orange pillow.

"Come, Miss Letheny. Give up the radium and tell me the whole truth."

"I have not got the radium. If you don't believe me you can search the house."

"The house has already been searched. Your maid was ordered not to tell you. It was done yesterday while you were — out."

"While I was out yesterday — Tell me, Mr. O'Leary, is anyone else honoured with

322

a — guard? The man from the police department followed me all day yesterday and I suppose is out there now, sitting on the porch railing or somewhere."

"O'Brien, his name is," said O'Leary amiably. "No, you are not the only person thus watched."

"I thought not." Her eyes glinted with malicious satisfaction. "I thought not. What about Jim Gainsay? And Maida Day?"

"Well, what about them?"

"What about them!" To do Corole justice she did hesitate for the barest fraction of a second before she went on: "Is it possible that you do not know that Maida Day was the last person to talk to Louis?"

There was a pause, during which Corole looked in vain for any change of expression in O'Leary's face.

"Are you not surprised!" she cried impatiently. "Goody-goody Maida with her fastidious, touch-me-not ways was in the orchard with Louis after midnight last Thursday night."

"No," said O'Leary. "No. I am not surprised."

"I heard the whole conversation," continued Corole, as if bent on getting some sort of more spirited reaction out of the detective. "I was there in the shadows and heard the whole thing. Louis was wild about Maida — I'm sure I don't know why. Anyway, she did not hesitate to tell him that she didn't return his love." Corole smiled a very cruel little smile. "Poor Louis! They talked for some time. Louis was one of these cold-natured men, as a rule. I was surprised to hear him. It was better than a play."

"Could you see them?" inquired O'Leary drily.

"It was black as tar. But I knew their voices. And anyway I can see in the dark like a cat, so I could tell about where they were — could see the outline of Maida's uniform and Louis's shirt front."

"They could see each other, of course?" asked O'Leary nonchalantly.

"No, I shouldn't think so. I thought I told you that I can see in the dark better than most people. I'm sure they couldn't see each other for I remember that when they met and began to talk, Maida sort of gasped and said 'Who is it?' and Louis answered her."

"How long did they talk?"

"Not long. Perhaps ten or fifteen minutes."

"That was about what time?"

Corole paused before replying, I suppose to be sure that she was admitting nothing as to her own activities on that dark night.

"It must have been just before one o'clock.

I think it was just after Louis had gone to Room 18 with Sarah to visit his patient there."

"Did Miss Day return at once to the hospital?"

"Yes, I think so. She was in a rage. I think poor Louis managed to kiss her and Maida is deplorably high-spirited. She struck him at the last; I was sure of that. They parted on very unfriendly terms." Her eyes slanted maliciously at O'Leary, but he was engrossed in studying the soft figures on the rug at his feet.

"Why do you tell me all this, Miss Letheny?" he asked quietly.

She raised her thin, plucked eyebrows at this, delicately.

"Didn't you ask me to tell you anything that could help you? I should think that it would be of value to know that the last person known to have been with Louis was quarrelling violently with him."

"As a matter of fact, you have done Miss Day a favour," remarked Lance O'Leary. "You have very kindly explained the presence of Miss Day's lapis cuff link in the pocket of Dr. Letheny's dinner jacket."

Corole's eyes flickered.

"I thought you said you were not surprised to hear this — as if you already knew it."

"I suspected some such affair. Miss Day made a point of saying that the last time she *saw* Dr. Letheny was when she left your house Thursday night, and it was perfectly true. She did not *see* him when she talked to him later. But, of course, I knew that she must have had some sort of meeting with him. Indeed," he went on quietly, "I can quite understand Miss Day's reluctance to tell of the matter. Any young woman would shrink from the headlines — can't you see them: 'Beautiful young nurse — Love quarrel with Doctor' — all that sort of thing? Doubtless the cuff link got detached from the cuff and into Dr. Letheny's hand and he thrust it into his pocket thinking to return it — not knowing what was to happen. Thank you for telling me this, Miss Letheny." He walked to the door and paused with his hand on the knob. His face was very stern as he glanced back at Corole. "You are only making things worse for yourself when you refuse to tell the whole truth. Good-morning, Miss Letheny."

Once again on that damp path we said little.

"It was Miss Day's meeting with Dr. Letheny that Corole overheard, then, and threatened to tell of; that is what Gainsay's note to Miss Day meant," said O'Leary musingly as we approached the south door. "Well, that meeting does throw a new light on things — doesn't it? By the way, Miss Keate, I expect to stay in St. Ann's for a night or two. I want

326

no one but you to know of it."

"But where — in what room will you be?"

"Room 18."

I could feel the colour draining from my face.

"That — room is not safe!"

"Nonsense."

"But, Mr. O'Leary — I have not told you what I heard this morning!"

"What's that!"

"Corole — Corole and Dr. Hajek —" He waited in silence while I told him of the singular dialogue that I had interrupted.

"Thank you, Miss Keate," he said quietly when I had finished.

"But — aren't you going to arrest them at once? Before, they do — whatever it is they are planning? We don't want another murder in St. Ann's!"

He shook his head.

"I don't think it will come to that. And anyway, you know — give a man rope enough —" He did not complete his sentence.

I tightened my lips disapprovingly; it seemed to me that handcuffs would be far more efficacious.

"Can you keep a secret, Miss Keate?" said Lance O'Leary suddenly.

I nodded.

"Then, if all goes well, another twenty-four

hours will see the end of this affair." And with that he was gone, leaving me to stand as if frozen on the step and watch that slight gray figure till it vanished around the corner of the hospital.

Another twenty-four hours!

I was still on the step, staring absently into the surrounding greens, when a movement through a lane of trees caught my eyes. There, strolling through the wet orchard, was Jim Gainsay. At his side was Maida, her white cap distinct against that green curtain, her soft black hair waving gently about her lovely face. The navy-blue cape she wore was thrown back so that its scarlet lining gleamed against a fold of her white dress and the scarlet seemed to match her cheeks and lips. As I watched, the two suddenly faced each other. Jim caught at Maida's hands and held them against his face and slowly drew her toward him. She yielded for a moment, then glanced toward St. Ann's windows and pulled away. He relinquished her hands and laughed and after a second she laughed, too. Then they resumed their slow pace, and the white cap and scarlet fold of cape and brown Stetson hat disappeared among the dense green thickets.

He had succeeded in seeing her, then, and I did not need to fulfil my promise.

The rest of the day passed quietly but none

too pleasantly, for the hospital was gloomy and dark and very hushed, the nurses uneasy and nervous, and there was a sort of subdued terror that lurked in the very walls of the great, old place.

I could not sleep, as was my custom, during first watch, and it was fortunate, as it happened, that I could not for I went down to the south wing a little early and thus, I believe, prevented another panic. I am sure that any other nurse seeing Corole as I saw her would have gone completely to pieces.

This is the way it happened.

I found myself in the south wing a good half hour before midnight and strolled casually along the corridor. The south door was locked as it should be, the new key having duly arrived and hanging, very bright and new, on the nail above the chart desk. I remember that I had just decided to find a new and less well-known place for it, and having selected a spot at the right of the door in question was endeavouring to push in a nail with a glass paper weight, and not having much success, when a sort of scratching outside the door caught my ears. I paused to peer through the small squares of glass.

The wind had risen again and the low branches of the trees outside were tossing and moaning. The corridor was not sufficiently light to enable me to see beyond the black panes of glass and they glittered emptily, so that I felt as if eyes were looking in at me. Then, all at once, a face pressed up against the glass. It was a face so haggard, so wild, so fraught with terror that I did not recognize it at once to be Corole's.

As I stared she made an imperative gesture and moved her pale lips in words that I could not hear. The key was in my hand and I unlocked the door. Corole slipped stealthily inside and I closed the door hastily on the wind and rain, locking it before I turned to her.

She was panting, her hair was flying in wet strings about her face and her eyes had great, fiery, black pupils that caught and reflected the light. She was wrapped in a dark silk cloak trimmed with monkey fur that was wet and hung about her neck in long, dank wisps that added to her wild aspect. One hand clutched the cloak across her breast and the other carried a square, leather-covered jewel-case.

I found my voice.

"What are you doing here?" I whispered.

She cast a furtive glance toward the south door.

"Did you lock the door? Come, is there some place where we can talk? Here —" With a swift motion she pushed open the door of Room 18, and pulled me inside.

"Don't turn on the light," she warned me in a tense whisper. And indeed, I had no intention of so doing, for as she spoke I recalled O'Leary's presence in the room. I looked sharply toward the bed and chair but could not tell if either were occupied.

Corole took several deep, shaking breaths before she spoke.

"I've been running," she whispered presently. "I had to get rid of O'Leary's watchdogs." Actually there was an undercurrent of mirth in her whispered accents, though I was sure that she had recently had a bad fright of some kind.

"Did someone follow you?" I asked.

She held her breath for a second; then she released it.

"Yes," she said. "I don't know who it was. Sarah, I had to come here. I — I am afraid to stay in the cottage alone all night. Huldah is gone, you know. I — am afraid. Can't I stay here?"

"Certainly not. Don't be foolish, Corole. St. Ann's is not a hotel."

She gripped my arm and her hand was trembling.

"I tell you I am afraid. Sarah, you must let me stay here. I'll sleep anywhere. I'll sleep right here in this room."

"No. No. You can't do that!"

"I must stay in St. Ann's. You can't put me out bodily. I've got to stay." I felt her shiver violently. "I cannot go through that terrible orchard again. I cannot sleep in Louis Letheny's house to-night. There are ghosts, Sarah, ghosts — oh, you don't know!"

"Ghosts! There are nothing of the kind." I felt my scalp prickle as I spoke.

"Maybe not. Anyway, I must stay here."

"No," I repeated but she must have felt me weakening for she renewed her pleas, even promising to make herself eligible to a room in the hospital by having tonsillitis, if I insisted. She said she felt it coming on owing to her getting so wet and being bareheaded. Which was not only silly, as I assured her, but was not even to be believed, Corole being as sleek and healthy as a young jaguar, and about as even-tempered.

"But you can stay," I relented, "if you will do as I say and keep quiet about it."

"Heavens, yes!" agreed Corole fervently. "All I want to do is keep quiet about it. Shall I just stay right here in Eighteen? I am not afraid." She moved toward the bed.

I grasped her cloak and jerked her back.

"No," I said hastily. "No. You cannot stay in this room." There may have been a note of consternation in my voice and I am quite sure I heard a sort of subdued snicker from

332

the direction of the bed.

Corole heard it, too.

"What was that?" she whispered sharply, starting back against me. I shuddered aside from contact with that dripping monkey fur.

"Probably a cat," I said at random.

"A cat!" I could feel her pull her short skirt tighter around her. "I hate cats. They remind me of — I hate cats."

"Corole, stay right here for a moment or two. *Don't move from the door!* I shall come back and open the door, and you go as fast as you can through the corridor and as far as the general office door. Don't let anyone see you if you can help it and wait there for me."

She murmured something in assent and in less time than it takes to tell, I had manufactured errands to get the nurses into the diet kitchen and drug room, had watched Corole move with the lithe swiftness of an animal through the long shadowy corridor and myself had followed her. My own room was, of course, the only place where I could let her sleep. I even loaned her a night garment; she looked at its long sleeves and high neck dubiously but accepted it.

I gave myself the satisfaction of locking the door and carrying the key away; I did not know whether Corole heard the click of the key or not but I did not intend that Corole Letheny should be allowed to prowl at large through the dark corridors of St. Ann's.

It was a little after twelve when I found myself in the south wing again. Maida was already there and Olma Flynn and the same little, blue-striped student nurse.

I don't mind admitting that I slipped into the diet kitchen at my first opportunity and brewed myself a cup of very strong, black coffee. Corole's advent had shaken my nerves a bit and I did not like the way the wind was murmuring around the corners of the great old building, stirring up forgotten drafts and rattling windows and slapping rain against them.

Second watch, however, passed quite as usual, save for the little air of uncertainty and uneasiness that made itself manifest in our fondness for each other's company, our frequent glances into the shadows, and one or two broken thermometers owing to the sudden crashes of the wind. The light flickered once as if about to go out but mercifully did not do so. I might add that the prevalence of broken thermometers was one of the minor troubles of that week; a thermometer is an easy thing to slip from one's fingers, especially when shaking it, and it is not surprising that Dr. Balman had had to order new thermometers for every wing in St. Ann's.

The hours seemed very long, particularly when it occurred to me that if Corole and Dr. Hajek expected to carry out their scheme that "day" there were only a few hours left in which to do so. Of course, I had Corole safely locked up and if her coming to St. Ann's in well-simulated terror to beg a refuge was actually, as I half suspected, only a part of their plan, why then I had stopped any further activity on her part. But I could not wholly believe that Corole's coming had been prearranged; her panic had been too genuine.

We were not very busy, so I had plenty of time to think. More than once I caught myself eyeing Maida as she went quietly about her business.

Once, when we were both at the desk, engaged in a desultory and half-hearted conversation, footsteps padding softly along the corridor back of us caught our attention and I turned simultaneously with Maida. I noted that her eyes flared black as she whirled and her lips were a quick, set line, and wondered if my own face showed such immediate alarm. However, it was only Olma Flynn, advancing to tell me through chattering teeth that she was sure there was *Something* in Room 18. I was startled for a flash, though at once I realized that it was O'Leary, and Maida went white though she held her shoulders straighter than ever.

I managed to calm Olma, though she clung to her point with a firmness that in my heart I labelled plain mule stubbornness.

"If we are all murdered before morning, Miss Keate, it will be your fault," she said at last.

"Nonsense! If it is a ghost, as you seem to believe, you need not be alarmed. Ghosts can't do anything but moan around the corners." It was unfortunate that just then the wind swept through the draughty old corridor with a most realistic moan, upon which Olma turned green and vanished into the diet kitchen. It was this, I think, that gave rise to a swiftly travelling tale that Room 18 was haunted, a tale that the south wing has never yet been able to live down.

Thinking to warn O'Leary that he must be more circumspect in his behaviour if he wished his presence in that ill-omened room to remain a secret, I watched my chance to slip unobserved into Eighteen. Dawn was creeping into the room by that time and the furniture loomed up dark and black in the cold half-light. The room was quite empty of human presence, though to my tired nerves it seemed that there might be other presences. I shrugged aside the unwelcome thought. A glance at the window showed me that the bolts had been slipped and the screen opened. I had no doubt that O'Leary was making use of that low window as others had done. I resisted a childish impulse to fasten the bolts against his return and returned to the corridor.

With the tinny sound of the breakfast bell away down in the basement, the straggling through the corridors of the day nurses, freshly uniformed if a trifle gray about the eyes, the fragrant smell of coffee floating through the halls, my vigilance relaxed a bit. The night was past and so far as I knew nothing out of the way had occurred. Knowing Corole to be a late sleeper I did not go immediately to my room to release her. Instead I followed Maida and Olma and the student nurse downstairs to the dining room. It was a sorry meal with buckwheat cakes which I despise and which, besides, give me hives, and Miss Dotty relating a very lurid dream and dissolving into tears under Melvina's interpretation. The tears dripped dismally down Miss Dotty's inefficient nose, Melvina enlarged upon the meaning of dreams, and I found that I had sugared my coffee twice. I was glad when the meal was over.

In the intervals of Melvina's sinister monologue I had come to the conclusion that Corole

Letheny under lock and key was not a situation to be lightly relinquished. I sought O'Leary at once, surreptitiously avoiding the day nurses. He was not in Room 18, so I straightened the wrinkled counterpane on the bed and left. As I passed through the corridor of the second charity ward I took a breakfast tray off the dumbwaiter standing there unguarded; the disappearance of the tray caused considerable excitement in the ward, I found later, which was augmented by its reappearance later in the morning in the second-floor linen closet where I had thoughtfully left it, with only the coffee splashed a little, for Corole did not even see that breakfast tray.

When I unlocked the door to my room it required only a glance to see that my bird had flown, so to speak. I set the tray on the dresser and advanced into the room. The bed was tossed and had been slept in, though the night garment I had loaned her was still decorously folded on a chair. The window was open, letting in gusts of rain on my flowered voile curtains which were running in pink and green streaks and later had to be replaced. I crossed to close it and in doing so found the mode of her exit. St. Ann's, as I have said, was an old building with numerous turrets and towers and roof irregularities which included various ledges and wide window casings. From the window beyond mine dropped an old-fashioned, iron fire escape fastened to the old red bricks with rusted bolts. And from my window to the next ran a sort of ledge, narrow, to be sure, and slippery, but there was the ivy to cling to and shrubbery below to break a fall. For a woman of Corole's build and propensities it was not a difficult climb and once on the fire escape the rest was easy. I leaned out the window. Had I still been unconvinced, there was proof of her passage, for caught on an ivy strand there hung a dejected, wet, black wisp of monkey fur.

So Corole was gone! I felt guilty for letting her slip through my fingers but reflected that O'Leary had known of her presence in St. Ann's, and moreover, a woman cannot go far in a drenched coat and no hat.

This comfortable reflection lasted until I went to the wardrobe and found that my best hat was gone. The hat was a very beautiful thing with quantities of artificial violets on it and three yards of looped purple ribbon, and had cost me twenty-five dollars owing to my having it made to order to fit my bobless head. And Corole had brazenly worn it out in the rain, which did not increase my affection for Corole.

I set forth again to find O'Leary, feeling that he should know at once of Corole's flight, pausing only to leave the tray in the second-floor linen closet.

O'Leary turned up at last in the vast old stable, now converted into a garage, that is out back of St. Ann's. He was apparently engaged in sniffing at something that I did not see and that he thrust hurriedly into his pocket at the sound of my approach.

In as few words as possible I told him of Corole's departure.

His face became very sober.

"That's bad," he said. "That's bad. I figured she was safe in your hands. So she got away across that ledge." The place was visible from where we stood, and he surveyed it thoughtfully through the gray streaks of rain.

"Well, it can't be helped now. You say she wore your hat?"

"Yes."

"She would not be apt to return to the Letheny cottage," he mused. "Let me see; it is barely seven o'clock — the stores will not be open for another hour. There is plenty of time."

"The stores?"

"She will go straight to buy a hat," he explained with remarkable lack of tact. "Corole Letheny is not going far in a hat that —" He noted my unsympathetic countenance. "A hat that — er — does not suit her. I mean that

340

she did not choose herself," he amended hastily.

Without saying a word I turned toward the gravelled path that leads back to St. Ann's.

"Wait a minute, Miss Keate," begged O'Leary contritely, seeing perhaps that he had offended me in a matter that no woman can freely forgive. "Please, wait. If you'll forgive me I'll tell you something of interest."

Being exceedingly curious I went back. He drew me into the shadow of a big gray ambulance.

"I want you to keep an eye on Miss Day," he said in a low voice and with an odd glance into the shadows of the place.

"Miss Day!"

"Especially if you see this fellow, Gainsay, hanging around."

"Why, what do you mean? Is Jim Gainsay —"

"Jim Gainsay is the man who was following Corole last night. O'Brien was stationed up at the cottage last night and saw him. It seems that Corole slipped out a side door. She came out so unexpectedly that she was into the orchard before O'Brien was after her. He was going full tilt when he found that someone else was ahead of him, both of them after Corole, who was having the devil's own luck, according to O'Brien, in avoiding tree trunks

341

and shrubbery. O'Brien says she can see in the dark. At the bridge O'Brien caught up with the man and can swear it was Gainsay, but just then a low-hanging branch knocked O'Brien down and senseless for a moment and when he got to his feet Corole and Gainsay were both gone. O'Brien wandered about the orchard hunting them for half the night and I ran into him about five o'clock, soaked to the skin and his face a welt of scratches and his disposition permanently warped."

"So it was Jim Gainsay who gave Corole such a fright," I murmured. "I wonder what he wanted."

"It looks bad for Gainsay," said O'Leary thoughtfully. "Whether he killed Dr. Letheny in a mistaken effort to defend Miss Day, or whether he killed Jackson for the sake of the radium, or whether, thinking that the radium is still at large he is determined to secure it for his own use, in any case it looks bad. I hope your little friend, Miss Day, is not going to be too much hurt."

"You mean if she cares for Gainsay? Maida is not one to wear her heart on her sleeve. If we could only find that radium," I concluded hopelessly.

"Oh, I have the radium," said O'Leary simply.

16

The Red Light Above the Door

"You have the radium!"

He nodded. My mouth open I waited for him to tell me more. In the little silence I heard a sort of rustle and I looked about me in some alarm. O'Leary heard the rustle, too, but his face wore the most peculiar expression of mingled satisfaction and anxiety. He made the barest perceptible gesture against comment, and just at the moment Morgue dropped casually down from an opening above what was formerly a hay loft. I jumped a little at his — I mean, her unexpected advent and O'Leary spoke unconcernedly.

"Yes, I have the radium. Or rather it is in Room 18 which is, I believe, the safest place in the world for it, inasmuch as there is not a soul in St. Ann's who would willingly enter that room — save perhaps your intrepid self."

"How did you find it?"

"Corole brought it to Room 18 last night." O'Leary's voice had lifted to a normal pitch and I recall thinking that he should speak lower. "Corole brought it in her jewel case.

343

The jewel case is there, too; she must have doubted your — er — hospitality."

"Do you mean to say that she had that box of radium in her jewel case!" I cried. "And that she left the whole thing there, in Eighteen?"

"Possibly she agreed with me that it was the safest place in which to leave it. No one would suspect its being back in Room 18. No one would voluntarily enter that room. Oh, she took the precaution to cross to that closet and place the jewel case away back on the shelf. She did that while you were clearing the way for her passage through the halls to your room. She came very near sitting down on the bed to wait," went on O'Leary drily. "And I was endeavouring to give an imitation of a mattress when you opportunely returned."

"Oh," I said brilliantly. "Oh."

"It was the same closet that hid Dr. Letheny's body, added O'Leary meditatively. "I will leave the radium in Room 18 until to-night; it will be under close guard all day, Miss Keate, but I think it safer to wait till to-night, during second watch, when the guards are gone and the wing is quiet, to remove it. I'm not going to run the risk of Gainsay's knocking me senseless again. Of course, we shall have to locate Corole and keep

344

her out when she returns, as she will, for the radium. Then I'll get the stuff away while the hospital is asleep."

"Do you think that is wise?" I asked hesitantly. "Do you think that will be —"

"Ready to go back to the hospital?" interrupted O'Leary, and as we walked along the clean white gravel path he conversed so fluently and determinedly about the effect of the continued moisture upon the crops that I could not get a word in edgewise. At the grade door we paused and O'Leary said a peculiar thing.

"See you later in the day, Miss Keate. Twelve of the twenty-four hours I gave myself are gone, you know. And by the way, you couldn't have done better if you had rehearsed." And with that he was gone, leaving me entirely in the dark as to his meaning and feeling rather irritated. Morgue, who had followed us along the path, brushed against my skirts. She had already lost her air of pride and was taking on a certain harassed appearance besides being very thin. But her yellow eyes raised to mine were still complacent and knowing and so like Corole's that I thrust her impatiently aside with my foot and closed the door sharply.

The rain continued, steadily increasing in fervour as the dreary day passed. All morning I remained in my room, the door locked securely, a chair in front of the window lest Corole should take a notion to return the way she had gone, and myself trying to sleep and succeeding for the most part in staring at the ceiling or at the rain-smeared window.

At noon I rose, dashed ice water on my tired eyes, dressed and started downstairs. The dark day made the vast old place gloomier than ever and lights had had to be turned on all over the building which, however, failed to dispel the lurking shadows. Apparently the nurses were doing their duty as well as might be expected, though I noted that they gathered in groups and that there was a noticeable lack of smothered talk and laughter.

In the north wing of the second floor I caught a glimpse, as I rounded the stairs, of Dr. Hajek, clad in fresh, white duck trousers and coat and certainly not much resembling a thief and a murderer, making his morning rounds, and at the door of the maternity ward I met Dr. Balman, an attendant nurse at his elbow.

It was strange to see the everyday routine going on almost as usual, almost as if we were not held in the cold grip of horror. No, not quite as usual, for there was somehow about the place, emanating from the very, white and expectant walls, an air of suspense, of breathless waiting.

Dr. Balman had noted it, too.

"Even the patients are upset and restless to-day," he said wearily, as I stopped to ask him about Sonny, whose cast did not satisfy me. He rubbed his hand over his high, benevolent forehead, drew it gently over the bruise that still looked red and angry, and sighed.

"It is the weather," I suggested, though it was nothing of the kind.

"Yes. Yes, it must be the weather. A constant succession of cloudy, rainy days such as we have been having is bad for the nerves. I hope this rain sees the end of it." His anxious eyes went past me toward the window at the end of the corridor.

"One wonders where it is all coming from," I commented. "I think, too, that the patients feel the — er — atmosphere of the hospital. The nurses are uneasy and nervous, jump at every sound, and there is a distinct feeling of suspense and — breathlessness in the air."

Dr. Balman nodded; his eyes looked tired and sad under his thin eyebrows.

"I understand what you mean. There is a psychic undercurrent of unrest and alarm that is bound to communicate itself to the sick."

"You aren't looking well, Dr. Balman," I said. "You should have that bruise attended to." And I thought, though I did not say it, that he would profit by some liver pills.

"I haven't had time —" he began; a nurse rattling up to us in her crisp skirts interrupted him with a question and I went on downstairs.

A letter was waiting for me on the rack in the hall I did not recognize the handwriting, which was square and distinct and very painstaking; the signature, however, caught my attention and I ran through the note hastily, read it again more carefully, and with an involuntary glance about me I withdrew into a secluded corner of the hall and read it once more. It was short and to the point.

DEAR MISS:

I think it is my dooty to tell you somthing I heerd. It is about Mr. Gansie I liked him but he is croked. He thinks Miss C whuz name I will not menshun has the radeyum, she said you know more than you will tell about those murders too and he said well what if I do what I want is the radeyum. Then she said youd better get out of here before you land in jail and he said speak for yourself. Then the kitchen door blew shut. You can tell that little man with the gray eyes if you want to.

That Gansie is a bad man he has a revolver in his pocket.

I have left Miss C for good.

Yours respectfully,

HULDAH HANSINGE.

Aside from reading "croked" to be "croaked" and thinking for a wild second that she was announcing Gainsay's death, I had no difficulty in understanding Huldah's amazing epistle. It sounded exactly like her, and Huldah is honest, so I did not even have the dubious satisfaction of doubting her word. It was my duty, too, to turn the thing over to O'Leary, and I should have done so at once had I been able to find him. But he was not to be found and I finally went down to lunch with a heavier heart.

The afternoon passed as slowly as the morning. O'Leary stayed out of sight, I heard no news about Corole or the radium, and the note from Huldah was simply burning a hole in my pocket. I tried telephoning to O'Leary but could not even get an answer from his servant. It was while I was in the general office that someone telephoned for Dr. Hajek. Miss Jones was at the telephone and asked me to call him, saying he was in the south wing.

"It's a woman," she said, winking at me. "She wouldn't give her name or number."

I found Dr. Hajek in Room 17 changing

a dressing. He dropped his forceps and pulled off his rubber gloves so hastily that they split across one palm.

"Pick up those forceps and sterilize them," he directed the attendant nurse. "I'll be back in a moment."

I suppose he noted the disapproval in my face, for as we left he murmured something about having expected an important call and Seventeen being all right until he returned. In the corridor, tipped back against the door of Eighteen, lounged a policeman. Dr. Hajek regarded him speculatively but said nothing concerning his presence, which was, to my mind, an extraordinarily stupid arrangement. It seemed far better, to me, to remove the radium under guard to a place of safekeeping, but O'Leary's business was O'Leary's.

It seemed a singular thing that this man Hajek was at liberty to go about the hospital, his opinions deferred to by the nurses, his duty to administer to the sick, and at the same time he was most certainly involved somehow in the ugly, sordid tragedy that had befallen us. I followed his white coat through the intervening corridors and, recalling a record I had meant to look into, also into the general office. But as I bent over the filing cabinet, though every word of his brief conversation was audible to me, I could make nothing of it. It consisted of three "Yes's," one "No," and finished with "All right." Upon which he hung up the receiver and departed briskly toward the south wing and Seventeen. Miss Jones was no wiser than I, for his eyes had been on her as he talked and she had not dared listen in.

"There's one thing I know, Miss Keate," she said as I was about to leave. "That voice at the other end sounded for all the world like Miss Letheny's."

And some twenty minutes later I was quite sure that I saw Dr. Hajek going unostentatiously out the grade door toward the garage, though when the bell rang for dinner he was sitting in the general office smoking a forbidden cigar and reading the evening papers with the utmost composure.

I spent most of the intervening time wandering about the halls; I was very restless and could not settle down to anything, and altogether the afternoon was a total loss so far as anything interesting was concerned, so I was not in the best of humours at dinner.

Once I caught a fragment of conversation from a little group of nurses down at the end of the table.

". . . and I said. 'What on earth is that man doing out in the elderberry bushes in all this rain?' and she said, 'He is watching Room 18.' "

"Why are they watching Room 18?" asked Miss Ferguson, wide-eyed.

"Don't ask me!" The first girl shrugged her shoulders. "But there have been a couple of men, besides that policeman in the south wing, hanging around all day; I don't think they are police because they don't wear uniforms, but they didn't have their eyes off the windows of Room 18 all day long."

"What do you suppose is the reason?" whispered someone in a tense, shrill whisper that carried.

"I don't know!"

"Mercy, I'm glad I'm not on duty in the south wing," said someone else, and all the eyes at the table immediately focussed on me.

"Well, whatever it is, I wish it would be settled," announced Miss Ferguson vigorously. "I'm getting so nervous I drop everything I touch. And my neck is stiff from twisting it to look back over my shoulder."

Melvina Smith cleared her throat and I left the table at once. I have nothing against Melvina, but if she had been in the south wing during the past week she would have got her fill of horrors.

With the gathering darkness the feeling of impending catastrophe that had hung over us all day intensified itself. By midnight I was as jumpy as a race horse, my heart leaping to my throat at every sound and my hands shaking so that I could scarcely turn off my alarm clock and adjust my cap.

The storm had grown steadily worse and by twelve o'clock was blowing a gale with thunder and lightning making the night hideous. The old building seemed to tremble at each onslaught, and every window casing rattled and every curtain flapped and the whole place seemed to quiver and shudder as if it were alive.

On the way down to the south wing, I don't mind saying that I suffered from something very near to stage fright, at least there was a rock in the pit of my stomach and the backs of my knees felt shaky and not to be depended upon. I very nearly shrieked when I heard footsteps back of me on the stairs, but it was only Maida, going down to duty, and together we walked through those deserted, creaking halls.

I had not been on duty more than twenty minutes when I found a note pinned to the order blank and addressed "Miss Keate"! It was sealed, and across the paper was a single sentence splashed hurriedly:

When the red light shines above 18 answer it.

I wheeled to stare down the length of corridor toward that closed, inscrutable door at its far end. The corridor lost itself in the shadows and the door was itself indistinguishable, but it seemed to me that the faraway panes of glass in the south door caught green glints of light from the shade above my head.

"When the red light shines above 18 answer it."

What was going on in the dark room? What did it mean?

It was fortunate that I had plenty of assistance, for I could not possibly have gone about my duty with this amazing thing in my mind. In fact, I paid very little attention to the demands of the wing and alternated my gaze between my wrist watch and that shadowy end of the south wing corridor.

When the red light shines above 18!

When would it shine — what would I see upon opening that heavy gumwood door?

When the red light shines . . . After what seemed eons of time I strolled casually and with attempted calm in that direction. My heart began to pound violently as I approached that mysterious door. I paused at the south end of the corridor, pretending to scrutinize a thermometer that hung on the wall and listening with all my ears toward that dully gleaming panel of gumwood. Not a sound came from it, and though I lingered for some time in the vicinity, still I heard nothing.

On the way back Olma Flynn stopped me.

"Eleven says he will not take his medicine, Miss Keate. What shall I do?"

I must have answered her rather vaguely and, in fact, barely heard her question. At any rate, she gave me a strange look, whirled to follow my gaze down the corridor south and, seeing nothing, faced me again.

Her eyes were very wide and her mouth hung open.

"What — what did you say, Miss Keate?"

"I'll see about it in the morning," I replied, quite at random. She retreated, eyeing me with trepidation, and later I saw her whispering with the student nurse in the drug room and both of them regarding me distrustfully.

Somehow the seconds dragged along. I took up my post at the chart desk, turning the chair so that it faced the long length of empty, dark corridor, and the dark space above Eighteen was visible to me.

Maida stopped at the desk now and then, and once paused to survey me curiously.

"What on earth is the matter with you, Sarah?" she asked.

"Nothing," I replied, looking for the thousandth time at my watch. It was then a quarter of two.

She studied me oddly for a moment.

"What a night! The wind and rain is getting awfully on my nerves." She unpinned her thermometer, took off the cap and held it closer to her eyes. "I was taking a temperature a moment ago when that loud crack of thunder came and it startled me so that I dropped the thermometer. I don't think" — she paused to squint interestedly along the small glass tube — "I don't think I broke it. For heaven's sake, Sarah!" she broke off in sudden irritation. "Stop staring down the corridor. You make me edgy. What are you looking for? What do you —"

I did not hear the rest of the sentence. I sprang to my feet, peering through the semi-darkness to be sure my eyes had not mistaken me.

They had not!

Gleaming above the door of Eighteen was a single small red light!

17

O'Leary Tells a Story

The next thing I remember is finding myself at the door of Room 18, my fingers on the door knob, my breath coming in gasps and my heart literally in my throat.

What would the opening of that door disclose?

I took a long, shuddering breath, pushed open the door and took a few steps forward.

Intense blackness met my eyes, but through it I heard scraping sounds and heavy breathing and the impact of flesh against flesh, and the indescribable sounds of two bodies struggling together. Instinctively I stepped inside the room, closed the door behind me, and felt along the wall for the electric button.

And at that instant a vivid flash of lightning lit up the room and I caught a glimpse of two men interlocked and swaying and I heard O'Leary's hoarse whisper.

"Don't — turn on — the lights! Don't —" the rest was lost.

I stood there as if frozen to the spot, longing to take a hand in things and not daring to

do so. Then all at once someone said breathlessly:

"O'Leary!"

"Yes."

"Hell."

The men seemed to fall apart.

"All right, then! Here it is!" The words were
whispered in a panting voice that I did not
recognize.

Then I felt rather than saw that the slighter
of the two figures tiptoed to the window next
to the bed, peered through the dashing of rain
outside for a moment, and then tiptoed as cautiously back.

"Into that corner! There, back of the screen!
Miss Keate?"

"Yes."

"Over here, quick!"

I stumbled a little as I passed the foot of the
bed, found a hand outstretched in the darkness
to guide me, and in a flash was in the darkest
corner of the room, behind the burlap screen.

"Be quiet!" warned O'Leary sternly.

Beside me, breathing quickly, was that other
man; as I shrank back a little I came in contact
with something cold, touched it tentatively
with my fingers and drew back, chilled. It
was square and hard and pressing into the
coat of the man at my side. It must be held
in O'Leary's hand.

And I was standing within an inch of the thing. I must have made a sudden movement for O'Leary whispered sharply again: *"Hush!"*

As if petrified, the three of us stood behind that burlap screen. There was not a sound in the room. As my eyes became adjusted to the darkness I found that the window near the bed was faintly visible through the crack in the screen and I glued my gaze to that crack.

Once the man at my side stirred a little and then quieted abruptly, and I had no doubt that that menacing revolver was thrust closer into his ribs.

Just as I felt that my lungs were bursting I became aware that there was a shadow, deeper than the surrounding shadows, there at the window. I blinked and peered closer. Yes, I was sure. Silently, with amazing lack of sound it crept from the window sill into the room, paused for a second and then, so silently that it did not seem to be anything human, it glided across the room and out of my little angle of vision.

Then I was aware that O'Leary was gone and simultaneously I heard a sound like the creaking of a bed spring and O'Leary's voice, cold and hard as that vicious revolver.

"Stand where you are! Hands up! Turn on the light, Miss Keate. Hands up! I've got you!"

Turn on the light!

Cross that room to the door? No, here was the light above the bed! Where was the cord! Ah! My fingers grasped it, pulled convulsively and light flooded the room.

There was a muffled exclamation from the closet door. A man standing there flung his hands over his head. O'Leary was standing on the high, narrow bed, his revolver covering the room. The man behind the screen was still motionless.

"All right, O'Brien," said O'Leary very quietly, without moving his head.

"All right," echoed a voice at the window. There was O'Brien's head at the window and along the sill gleamed the barrel of another revolver, and then another as a stalwart policeman loomed up beside O'Brien.

My head cleared and my eyes stopped blinking in the sudden light.

The man at the closet door was Dr. Fred Hajek. His face was putty-coloured. His small eyes gleamed like a frightened animal's. His raincoat dripped moisture in a little puddle on the floor.

"Got him covered, O'Brien?" said O'Leary cheerfully.

"Right!" said O'Brien.

O'Leary leaped lightly from the bed, strode over to the burlap screen, and pulled it back.

Jim Gainsay stood there, his cap pulled low

over his eyes, his lean jaw set. One hand was thrust into the pocket of his coat, and the other grasped a small, square box. At the sight of the box I gasped something and pointed.

"The — the radium!"

"It's you, is it?" said O'Leary in a strange voice.

Hajek made a sudden movement; O'Leary whirled.

"Stop that!" his voice cracked like a whip. Hajek, with a furious glance at the men in the window, subsided.

O'Leary turned again, walked to the middle of the room and paused, looking from one man to the other with a curious expression in his eyes.

"Well," he said. "I've got you both."

Gainsay started to speak and stopped as the nose of one of the revolvers shifted restlessly.

"Put down your hands if you want to, Hajek," said O'Leary easily. "Or — wait a moment."

He crossed to him, ran his hands quickly over Hajek's pockets, unheeding the fury in those little eyes, extracted a small revolver and tossed it on the bed and smiled.

"There you are, Doctor," he said politely. "You may lower your hands, now."

There was a slight commotion at the window.

"Here's somebody, Mr. O'Leary," said someone. "He was in the shrubbery and you said not to let anybody get away."

O'Leary peered into the little group at the window, then his eyes lightened.

"Oh, it's you, Dr. Balman. You came at just the right time. I think we have bagged our birds. Can you come through the window, Doctor?"

It was Dr. Balman, sure enough, water running off his shoulders and shining in the light as he crawled through the window assisted by the policeman.

Once inside the room Dr. Balman looked slowly about him.

"What is this? What have you found, O'Leary?" His puzzled gaze found the box in Gainsay's hand. He started. "Why — why is that the radium?"

"It may interest you to know, Dr. Balman, that we have caught the murderer and thief."

"What!" cried Dr. Balman. His eyes travelled slowly around the room and his voice broke a little as he cried: "Not — not Fred Hajek?"

O'Leary's keenly exultant eyes softened a little.

"Wait," he said. "There is another in the room."

Taking a key from his pocket, he crossed

lightly to the closed door of the further closet, unlocked it and swung it open. I took a step forward and cried out involuntarily. Instantly I recognized my own purple hat, sodden and drenched, and then, cramped in that small space, a woman's huddled figure. It was Corole!

As we stared she glared back at us for a moment. Then she rose slowly, struggling with cramped muscles. Her eyes, narrow with hate, were fixed on Lance O'Leary.

"I've been there for hours," she said in a strange voice that was hoarse and strained with fury. She stamped her feet to start circulation and flexed her arms slowly. Then she pulled my hat from her head, tossed it contemptuously out of the way and ran her brown hands through her tossed, yellow hair. "You are going to suffer for this," she said. "How dare you force me into that closet, lock the door and leave me!" She took a tigerish step or two toward O'Leary, her nails gleaming suggestively.

"Not so fast, my lady," interposed O'Brien, who had slipped silently through the window. Corole shifted her malignant gaze, regarded O'Brien for a moment, then slowly and malevolently swept the room.

"So you are here, too?" she said to me. "And Dr. Balman. And Jim. Quite a family party."

"You are right," agreed O'Leary smoothly. "Quite a family party. In fact, we need only one more to make our circle complete. Miss Keate, will you please summon Miss Day?"

My heart leaped again as I heard the name, and I heard Jim Gainsay mutter something that was quickly silenced. I opened the door and slid into the corridor; there was no need to call Maida, for there she was, standing opposite the dark door above which still gleamed that ominous red light. She was very white but said nothing as I beckoned her inside the room.

At our entrance O'Leary became active. He motioned to the available chairs.

"Sit down, Miss Day — Miss Keate. Dr. Balman, there is a place on the bed. We may as well make ourselves comfortable for I have a story to tell."

I suppose my eyes went in some anxiety to the precious box in Jim Gainsay's hand that was the cause of it all, for O'Leary smiled a bit grimly.

"Don't be alarmed, Miss Keate. The radium is not in that box; I took it immediately to — a safe place. The box over there was only a bait."

With a disgusted exclamation Jim Gainsay dropped the box and folded his arms. His eyes sought Maida's but she did not return his gaze.

"Well, Dr. Hajek," said O'Leary. "It is too bad it has turned out this way. I thought better of you."

Dr. Hajek lifted his lip in something very like a snarl but said nothing. Corole made a sudden movement which she checked under O'Leary's regard.

"Are you sure it was Dr. Hajek? Tell me about it, O'Leary." The ring of authority was manifest in Dr. Balman's weary tones.

"In my own way," promised O'Leary with an apologetic glance toward Dr. Balman. "In the first place, the superstition which so unpleasantly impressed you, Miss Keate, has been fulfilled again." He paused dramatically, and from somewhere in the room came a sharp sigh of suspense. "The murderer of Jackson *was* near by when you saw blood flowing from that small wound. But he was in — that closet." He pointed. The silence breathed a question that none of us dared speak.

"Yes," said O'Leary, answering the unspoken inquiry. "Yes. It was Dr. Letheny."

"Dr. Letheny!" cried Jim Gainsay.

"Not — not Dr. Letheny," faltered Dr. Balman.

"It was Dr. Letheny," repeated O'Leary quietly.

"I knew it!" cried Corole. "I knew it!"

No one looked at her. Our eyes were without exception fastened upon O'Leary's face.

"How do you know?" I said at last.

O'Leary glanced about the room in indecision, then he shrugged.

"As well here as anywhere," he said. "How did I know that it was Letheny? Why did not Higgins rouse the place? Because he saw the head doctor in this room. Why was there need to hunt for the radium? Because that man who hid the stuff was dead; Dr. Letheny, disturbed about the ugly business, afraid of being caught with it in his possession, hid the thing in the loud speaker, thinking no one saw him. And only Higgins knew where it was, and Higgins, terrified at what he had seen, was afraid to tell for he knew that someone — *someone* had come upon Letheny and killed him and Higgins hoped to escape the same fate. And since there were — others desiring the radium, a hunt was made for it. A search that was finally successful." His clear gray eyes went from Corole to Hajek.

"But just as Dr. Letheny was about to leave the room another man came upon the scene, determined to take the radium for himself. Then — I don't know exactly what happened but the two men struggled and in the struggle Dr. Letheny's head struck with such force that it killed him — *this*" — he crossed the room to the massive, square-cornered lavatory. "I am sure of that," went on O'Leary, "for I examined it before a thing in the room had been touched. The other man, frightened perhaps, knowing that he was in desperate danger of being charged with murder, dragged Dr. Letheny's body into that closet, locked the door and got rid of the key, hoping to postpone the discovery of Dr. Letheny's death for as long as possible and thus cover his own tracks. But first he found that the radium was not to be found and knew that Letheny must have hidden it somewhere in the room. He did not dare search for it then, he would have to return. He retreated by the way he had come, through the window, there, and — and crawled through the window of his own room in the hospital in time to answer Miss Keate who, by that time, was pounding on the door."

His eyes went to Dr. Hajek, whose face was quite ghastly.

O'Leary forestalled the words on Dr. Hajek's lips.

"Not now," he said sternly. "You will have plenty of time to talk — later."

"Then — then you feel sure it was Dr. Letheny who killed Jackson?" asked Dr. Balman incredulously.

"Positive," said O'Leary. "As further proof, the revolver that belongs to Miss Letheny bears Dr. Letheny's finger prints. Why should he bring a revolver to a hospital if his errand was entirely peaceful? He wanted the radium, he needed the money — I honestly believe that the man wanted the money for research." There was a shade of pity in O'Leary's voice. "And as to the mechanics of the situation, Dr. Letheny must have made up his mind quite suddenly to secure the radium for his own use; he came to St. Ann's — I wonder what his feelings were when he examined the patient whom he was soon to rob, I do not think the murder was intentional — then, presumably he left. Outside the hospital he accidentally came upon Miss Day and detained her for some time — er — seizing her sleeve as she attempted to return to the wing, and in so doing detached her cuff-link. Is that right, Miss Day?"

Without a word Maida nodded assent but her deep, blue eyes shot a glance of gratitude toward the young detective.

"Then, determining to carry out his hastily formed plan for stealing the radium, he watched his chance and while Miss Day was busy in the kitchen and Miss Keate was detained for some fifteen minutes in — Room 11?"

"Room 11," I said.

"— he must have slipped along the corridor into the drug room and helped himself

368

to morphine tablets and hypodermic needle and hurried back, unseen, to Room 18. Jackson very likely never knew what happened, but Dr. Letheny was safe because, in the first place, Jackson was not surprised at the presence of his doctor and would have had no occasion to object to a hypodermic injection, and furthermore, on waking from a drugged sleep, impressions immediately preceding that sleep are vague and confused and could scarcely be given as evidence. I do not believe that Dr. Letheny intended to make the dose fatal; I believe he only intended that Jackson should know nothing of the radium being removed, but in his natural excitement Dr. Letheny either misjudged the dose he was giving or the resistive powers of his patient, with the result that we know. Dr. Letheny tossed the needle through the open window, where it was later found. In the main, I believe I am right; there may be slight discrepancies. One can't be absolutely sure when both — er — participants are dead."

There was a moment of tense silence. Then Corole spoke.

"So it was Louis," she said in a tone of ugly satisfaction. "I knew it. I knew it all along for I watched —" She checked herself.

O'Leary turned sharply.

"Just a moment," he said coldly. "Your skirts are not entirely clear. There is Higgins's death yet to explain, and the theft of the radium."

"I knew nothing about Higgins's death," cried Corole.

"Go on, Mr. O'Leary," begged Dr. Balman. Under the light his face looked drawn and aged.

"From that night on the struggle has been for the discovery and possession of the radium. It was thought, by those who knew of Dr. Letheny's participation in the affair, to be still in Room 18. Hajek was determined to find it, even going so far as to steal the key to the south door in order to effect an entrance at any time."

Again Dr. Hajek made an inarticulate murmur which O'Leary silenced.

"Becoming impatient at his continued failure to locate the radium, Miss Letheny herself, who was in — er — in cahoots with Hajek, took a hand in the matter. Knowing what had happened in the room and being by nature extremely superstitious, she was intensely frightened when upon entering Room 18 in the middle of the night in order to make a search for the radium herself, she saw a sheeted figure on the bed. She, too, failed to find the radium."

"You are perfectly right about that," said Corole brazenly. "But you are wrong about —"

"Then one night Hajek grew desperate; he wanted the radium and Corole — that is, Miss Letheny — was reproaching him for his continued failure to find the radium. He recalled the circumstance of the electric-light connection having been damaged by lightning on the night of June seventh, decided that that condition was a valuable help and, repeated, would aid him in making a thorough and prolonged search in Room 18. So he went to the basement, disconnected the electric current, let himself out the grade door, ran around the corner of the hospital, entered the south wing by the unlocked south door, for the windows were bolted, and was into Room 18 in about a minute and a half after he pulled the light switch. Either from reflection or because he had exhausted all the other available hiding places, he went at once to the loud speaker, which by an odd circumstance was the original speaker that was in Room 18 the night of the seventh. But Higgins, in the basement, saw him and followed him. Higgins came upon him in Room 18. As I say, Hajek had at last found the radium and at the knowlege of someone witnessing his theft he shot wildly in the dark, the bullet killing Higgins instantly. Likely

Higgins had said something, indicated in some way that he knew what Hajek was about and what he had taken from that loud speaker. I don't know how it happened that Higgins got up courage enough to follow and threaten Hajek with exposure, but he evidently did. Hajek, frightened at the consequence of his deed, simply acted from primitive impulse; if he were caught on his way from the hospital the possession of the radium would be a distinctly incriminating fact, no matter how he tried to explain it away. He had only a few seconds in which to act, and he followed Dr. Letheny's example, hiding the radium in the first place that came to hand which was — a flower pot. He scooped out the dirt, thrust the box into the aperture and the soil in his pocket and hurried from the wing, around the hospital, in the basement door and to his room — where we found him later. He had barely time to get to his room unobserved."

"I didn't! You are lying! I didn't!" cried Dr. Hajek, his face livid and those glaring eyes going from one to the other of us. "I tell you I didn't!"

At a motion from O'Leary, O'Brien stepped closer to Hajek, thrusting the revolver he held close to Hajek's ribs.

"But — but the mud on the window casing," I began, bewildered. "If he used the grade door and came up by the basement —"

O'Leary interrupted me.

"Miss Day happened on the radium in the pot of lobelias; it was in the corridor where Hajek had placed it in his hurry, knowing that Room 18 would be thoroughly searched. Miss Keate in the meantime — I think we need not go into that. Anyway it came thus to my hands for a moment or two before Hajek knocked me senseless and took the radium. He had managed, from his room off the general office, to hear Miss Keate's announcement and must have watched until she gave it to me —"

"I'll admit to that," cried Dr. Hajek. "But not to that oth—"

"There, there!" O'Brien poked him suggestively and Hajek stopped talking.

"But," began Dr. Balman uncertainly, "I never dreamed it was Dr. Hajek. Why he was right there with me when we found you, O'Leary, there by the stairs. He seemed as astonished as I was." Dr. Balman reached unsteadily for his handkerchief and passed it over his forehead. "This is terrible, O'Leary, terrible." His voice shook. "Do you realize that you are accusing a doctor of St. Ann's of unspeakable crimes? That you are —"

"Truth is truth." There was a queer, icy look in O'Leary's gray eyes. "If a doctor of

St. Ann's is guilty, he is as guilty as any other man would be."

"Oh, yes. Yes, I suppose so," agreed Dr. Balman, reluctantly. "But it is no less — terrible." He shuddered visibly.

I found my tongue.

"Then what part has Mr. Gainsay in all this?"

O'Leary eyed me curiously before replying. Then he turned to Jim Gainsay.

"Gainsay," he said slowly, "is a young man who is going to get into serious trouble sometime through not minding his own business. He is incurably inquisitive and has been quite sure that he and he alone could solve this mystery." There was a gleam of mirth back of those clear, gray eyes.

Jim straightened up, felt absently in his pocket and drew out a pipe, which he held without lighting, the policeman at the window watching him with an impassive countenance.

Jim sighed.

"I *am* a fool," he admitted abruptly. "But, Lord, it didn't seem to me that you were getting anywhere. I had to take a hand in it. I thought the first thing to do was to find the radium."

Corole's slitted eyes flashed green fire.

"You nearly got it, too," she said viciously. "But I got away from you."

"Where did you hide it when Hajek turned it over to you immediately after stealing it from me?" asked O'Leary mildly.

Corole's face was sullen but she replied, taking, I think, a certain pleasure in being the centre of the stage for a moment.

"I dug a hole under one of the trees out there," she motioned with a long, brown hand, on which the topaz shone, toward the orchard. "I left it there all day yesterday — I mean, day before yesterday." She glanced at the window, which was beginning to show a dim, gray light. "And then that night I got away from you," she looked at O'Brien — "and you" — at Jim, this time — "and got it out and brought it here in my jewel case. I thought it would be safe in this room and Sarah was so excited" — she cast a malicious glance toward me — "she never noticed that I came out without my jewel case when she so thoughtfully took me to her room and *locked me in!* How did you find it?"

O'Leary did not reply.

"When Miss Letheny returned for the radium about eleven o'clock to-night I — er — detained her." O'Leary glanced toward the closet from which she had emerged. "I am interested to hear that you admit to having the radium in your possession."

"What can you do about it?" flashed Corole

insolently. "And you are all wrong about Dr. Hajek. I know that he did not shoot Higgins and I know that he did not kill Louis for he was with me both times —"

"That will do, Miss Letheny. Or rather, Mrs. Hajek."

Corole started. Her brown hands clutched at the wall back of her.

"How did you know that?"

O'Brien cleared his throat self-consciously and at the sound Corole whirled to face him.

"I suppose you were following us this afternoon," she said vindictively.

"They were married this afternoon," said O'Leary. "Owing to a conversation overheard by one of us" — I daresay it was my turn to look self-conscious — "we have reason to think that possibly the bride was a bit reluctant, but however that was, they were actually married at the courthouse with Mr. O'Brien — near at hand. Your own desire to perjure yourself, Mrs. Hajek, will not be of any help in the matter, for your husband cannot be cleared."

A strange silence fell; the torrents of rain seemed to be lessening slightly and I heard a roll of thunder away off in the distance.

I was engaged in going over and over to myself O'Leary's explanations; it did not seem to me that he had covered everything, and

I was about to inquire into certain matters when O'Leary spoke again.

"Is everything clear to you, Dr. Balman?" he asked deferentially.

Dr. Balman hesitated.

"I don't know," he said with a puzzled and worried air. "I really don't know. This is" — he paused to pass his hand across his eyes, rubbing the bruise on his cheekbone a little as if it itched — "this is a terrible responsibility, Mr. O'Leary."

O'Leary nodded.

"But you are head of St. Ann's," said O'Leary. "And while the case belongs to the state to prosecute, still I should like to feel that you, as head of the institution of St. Ann's — are satisfied with our findings."

"It doesn't seem — it doesn't seem possible," said Dr. Balman.

O'Leary looked obviously irritated, but said with restrained impatience:

"Is there anything that I have overlooked, Dr. Balman?"

"No. No, I suppose not," Dr. Balman replied uncertainly.

"Perhaps I have not made myself perfectly clear," said O'Leary, still patiently. "Let's begin at the beginning again, Dr. Balman, and piece things out in their logical order. I want to be sure that it is all clear to you."

"No, no! That will not be necessary."

"Yes," insisted O'Leary. "You being head of St. Ann's, Doctor, should be given every scrap of information in my power to give."

"No, no!" said Dr. Balman. "It is very painful to me. And anyway, I think I understand. Dr. Hajek got into Room 18, just after Dr. Letheny had hidden the radium. Isn't that it?"

O'Leary nodded and there was a quickly subdued growl of dissent from Dr. Hajek.

"The two men struggled then, and Dr. Letheny was killed in the struggle?"

Again O'Leary nodded.

"Yes, I think I understand. Still it doesn't seem possible." Dr. Balman regarded Dr. Hajek doubtfully.

"No," said Lance O'Leary slowly. "It does seem strange that Miss Keate should hear nothing of it."

"I believe she did hear something of it," said Dr. Balman, his distressed countenance turning to me. I made some gesture of assent.

"Yes," said O'Leary. "For don't you remember that she came down to the end of the corridor —" He left his sentence hanging in the air, and as he spoke he moved his hand slightly and I was faintly surprised to see little beads of sweat glistening on the back of it, though the night was cool. His face was quiet and composed as usual.

"Oh, yes," said Dr. Balman. "I remember now. Strange she saw or heard nothing of all this when she opened the door of Room 18 and stood there for a moment."

Queer how silent the room was. No one seemed to breathe.

Then Lance O'Leary's voice broke the silence; it was tight and strange and shook a little.

"Only the murderer could know that!" He shot a glance at O'Brien. "Quick!" The last word was like the sharp lash of a whip.

I was never sure just what happened then. There was a scream as Corole flung herself upon Dr. Hajek. There was another struggle going on somewhere else. Figures blurred in rapid motion — there were outcries — I found myself clutching at Maida — Jim Gainsay's tall figure flashed before our eyes.

Then O'Leary's tense voice commanded the situation.

"Right, O'Brien!" he said sharply.

Then the room seemed to clear; things resumed their normal dimensions.

I stared and rubbed my eyes and stared again.

Then my knees weakened under me and I think I screamed.

The handcuffs glittered coldly on Dr. Balman's wrists.

18

O'Leary Revises His Story

It was fitting that the thing should end as it had begun, in Room 18.

I have only a dazed and chaotic memory of them taking Dr. Balman away. Of Corole and Fred Hajek going under guard. Of myself sitting numbly in Room 18, with Maida beside me gripping my hand, until O'Leary returned. Jim accompanied him.

I think it was seeing Jim sit down on the white bed with his coat still wet with rain, and noting the marks of muddy shoes and wet coats on the once white counterpane, that aroused me to a sense of reality.

It was dawn by that time. The electric light was paling and growing sickly under the gray streaks of daybreak at the windows, and I recall a vague little feeling of amazement when the thin rays of washed-out sunlight began to find their way into the room. Sunlight after a week of rain!

O'Leary, entering the room, had closed the door and crossed to the radiator and sunk wearily down upon it. He appeared worn and enormously tired, with no shred of the jubilance I should have expected.

"Well," my voice quavered a little as I spoke. "Well — you have succeeded."

"Yes. I've, got my man."

"You don t seem to be rejoicing about it."

"I am not," said Lance O'Leary flatly. "That is, don't misunderstand me — I am glad that I have done my duty. But I am sorry to see a man, a brilliant scientist, a scholar, a useful surgeon — go wrong. Dr. Balman has actually given his life — mistakenly of course, for his science. He wanted the radium, he needed the money it would bring. For the rest he was, as much as anything, a victim of circumstance. It is a sad thing — yet just."

"Dr. Balman was a wicked man," I said. Odd how we were speaking of him in the past tense.

"Yes," agreed O'Leary. "But Dr. Letheny was equally culpable. Strange how a man can devote his life to a woman or — a career. Well," he broke off, shrugging, "there's no use philosophizing. Don't mind my low spirits. I should feel much lower if I had failed."

"I didn't know what you were doing until Dr. Balman said: 'When she opened the door.' Then I began to have a premonition, for I recalled the request you made at the first inquest."

"What was that?" asked Jim.

"I asked Miss Keate not to mention the fact that when she came down the corridor after hearing the sound that she thought was a door closing and was actually —"

"Don't!" I interrupted with a shudder.

"— was actually something else, she came to the door of Eighteen and opened it and stood there for a few seconds listening."

"Why? Did she hear something? Or see anything?"

"No. But I reasoned that the guilty man must have still been in Room 18. It had not been a moment since the sound of the blow that — the blow that killed Dr. Letheny, and I knew that the man who did it could not have dragged Dr. Letheny's body to the closet, locked the door, and made his escape before Miss Keate got to the door of Eighteen. Hence I knew that only the guilty man *knew what she had done.*"

"Did you plan that far ahead? Did you know you could work him to admit that knowledge?" cried Jim in honest amazement.

O'Leary shook his head, smiling ruefully.

"No. I am but human. But I plan to take every chance. Hoard every possible bit of evidence. That was small but conclusive."

"Is that the only proof you have against Dr. Balman?" asked Jim.

"No. I have others. But I wasn't quite satisfied. You see, I let Balman know that the radium was in this room and would be guarded all day but not at night because I intended to remove it then. Miss Keate helped me there. Dr. Balman was on the other side of the door in the garage this morning — or rather yesterday morning," explained O'Leary to me. "Of course, I had actually removed the radium at once and substituted a dummy box. I expected Balman would try to secure it in the dark of night and hoped to catch him red-handed. But instead — you, Gainsay, nearly spoiled the works for me. You have been a good deal of trouble, one way and another," he interpolated, with a glance that held nothing humorous. "However, I know the reason for your — er — meddling." O'Leary smiled openly at Maida; it was that extraordinary winning smile that he reserved for certain occasions and Maida smiled, too. "I can't say that I blame you for that. Though if you had advised her to tell of the cuff link business in the first place —"

"That cuff link!" murmured Maida with contrition. "I am sorry. I should have explained it immediately. But it — would have meant such publicity. It was so disagreeable." She flushed pinkly and Jim's heart was in his steady eyes fastened upon her.

"But what else do you have against Dr. Balman?" I inquired hastily, for once uninterested in matters of the tender sentiment.

"The story that I told here to-night is, in the main part, true if you simply change the name of Hajek to Balman. For the points against Balman —" he checked off the items on his fingers. "First, finger prints on that revolver of Corole's. Dr. Letheny's and those of Dr. Balman were very clear. It was some time before I could get a good print of Balman's, though I had those of everyone else connected with the case. Then there was the fact that he *asked* to have this low window bolted and the request came simultaneously with the disappearance of the key to the south door; having provided himself with a mode of entrance he was anxious to keep others out of the room that held the radium. Then there was the matter of the ether that you smelled, Miss Keate, the ether that Higgins said was somewhere about the coat that was left there just outside the window of Eighteen, and that you found on a handkerchief in the pocket of that yellow slicker. I found on investigation that the only person seen to leave St. Ann's that Friday evening just at dinner time was Dr. Balman and that he wore a yellow slicker. That was not conclusive, for he might have borrowed it as Miss Keate did. But yesterday morning I found in the side pocket of his car a small empty bottle and a sponge that still had a lingering trace of that very clinging odour."

"But why ether?" said Jim.

"He had evidently intended to anæsthetize Mr. Jackson, steal the radium while the patient was unconscious and get away. But when after waiting about the grounds for some time until he thought the coast was clear he finally got into Room 18, he found another man in the room, the radium gone and his patient dead. The next thing for me to do was to break what appeared to be an alibi. I did so when I found that there was a freight elevator at the back of the apartment house in which Balman lived. He knew how to operate it and must have taken precautions to leave by way of the freight elevator and the basement so that the night man in the front of the house never dreamed that Balman had gone out again. He returned the same way and must have got there just in time to answer the telephone. It was his car that left along the lower road just as the storm broke, Miss Keate."

"He must have driven like mad," I speculated.

"Think what he left behind him," said O'Leary grimly. "He knew, too, that at any moment the alarm might come and his presence would be needed at the hospital. He must be in his rooms when the call came."

"All put together those things are almost — positive proof," said Jim.

"Almost," agreed O'Leary. "But I wanted to trap him into a final admission. To catch him in the act of making off with the radium. And there I failed. When you turned on the light here to-night, Miss Keate, and I saw only Hajek and Gainsay, I was sure that I had failed. But when Dr. Balman came on the scene I began to see my way clear. I caused Hajek considerable anguish of soul but he deserved it. What on earth did you come blundering around for, Gainsay?"

Jim looked uncomfortable.

"Why, you see, O'Leary, I saw Corole come into the south door of St. Ann's last night and watched through the pane of glass. I had nearly caught her and I was convinced that she had the radium in her jewel case. I could barely see in the hospital corridor through that door, but I saw that she left the jewel case in Room 18. So I figured that she likely thought Room 18 a safe place in which to leave the stuff. Thinking it over during the day, I came to the conclusion that it would be a fine thing to recover the radium myself." He laughed rather shamefacedly. "I — didn't think much of you, O'Leary. And I was worried about Miss Day, too. And well — I just made an ass of myself generally."

"You did," said O'Leary. "You did. You had better stick to bridges after this, Mr. Gainsay."

"You are right," said Jim heartily. "But I can't say that I regret having been here. And I still hope that I have not failed — at one thing I have undertaken." His eyes were on Maida and she turned entirely crimson and O'Leary laughed boyishly.

I sighed; time enough for romance when this thing was all clear to me.

"Mr. O'Leary," I said, "can you prove all this?"

He sobered instantly.

"The only thing that is supposition — or rather based solely upon reason, is Dr. Letheny's part in the business, and even there, we know that only certain events could have taken place. As for the rest of it, change Hajek's name to Balman's and — there it is."

And I may as well say here and now that Dr. Balman confessed to the whole thing, and the only point on which O'Leary was mistaken was this: it was Dr. Hajek who took the key from its place above the chart desk on that Sunday night when Maida and I were so frightened. He had slipped out his window with the key, but when he heard us coming he fled from Room 18, around St. Ann's to his room, through the window again, through the corridor from the main part of the hospital to the south wing, tossed the key on the desk and hurried back to his own room.

"Then that arraignment of Hajek was entirely fictitious?" asked Jim.

"Not entirely. He was actually out of the hospital and in the orchard the night Higgins was shot and at the sound of the commotion he hurried back to his room. But he had gone to meet Corole; they were, of course, determined to get the radium and were conspiring together at every opportunity. And on the night of the seventh he and Corole were in the orchard. Their story of seeing a man crawl through the window of Eighteen and waiting to catch him when he emerged is not true, for only Higgins knew of Balman's entrance and he did not know who the man was. But Corole and Hajek knew enough of Dr. Letheny's entrance into St. Ann's to make them sure that, when he was found dead, the radium must still be in the room. For they had listened at the window of Room 18 — don't forget the gold sequin. Oh, yes. Hajek and Corole were determined to get that radium and it *was* Hajek who knocked me senseless there in the hall. That much of my story was true. I saw that the only way to get Balman was to put him off his guard. I was not sure that I could — pull it off; I was afraid my very voice would betray me, that I'd be too eager, too insistent, clumsy, blundering. The least thing would have warned Dr. Balman. I had to get him to talking of it, and he, not yet having descended so low as to want to send someone else to prison for his deed, was willing to temporize, ask questions, attempt to think of something that would clear Dr. Hajek, without at the same time incriminating himself. He was trying to think fast of such possibilities." O'Leary smoothed back his hair and straightened his impeccable tie. "Those few moments were a strain."

"Suppose he had just kept silent, had said nothing at all?" I suggested curiously.

"Oh, I knew he would talk. He had a guilty conscience, you know. It wouldn't have been human to refuse to talk. He knew his own guilt and hence would try to appear innocent. He was bewildered, too, and was never a practical, quick-thinking man. It was a chance but not a risk."

There was a long silence. Away down the hall I heard the faint, muffled sound of the breakfast bell. With that I roused myself and thought for the first time of the wing. I rose, picked up my ruined hat, and at the door stopped to look back on that room.

Room 18! What it had held! What it had witnessed!

O'Leary followed me from the room, Maida and Jim, too. Once in the corridor I found that the small, red signal light was still gleaming dully. I returned to Room 18, pulled the light cord, mechanically straightened the bed, and closed the window.

Maida and Jim had disappeared when I returned to the corridor. O'Leary was standing at the south door, looking through the glass with an amused twinkle in his clear gray eyes. Following his glance I saw Maida's white uniform and Jim's tweed coat vanishing along the once more sunny orchard path.

"Young idiots," I murmured. "And before breakfast, too."

The path recalled to me the Letheny cottage at its other end.

"What about Corole and Hajek?" I asked.

"They were after the radium," said O'Leary hesitantly. "But after all, I think the best thing to do is to get rid of Hajek and let them leave."

"This means reorganization, new doctors, new methods — everything."

O'Leary nodded.

"How true it is," he said thoughtfully, "that even in one of the noblest professions there are scoundrels."

"But the proportion is much smaller," I said loyally. "You'll find a hundred defaulting bankers for one doctor who is untrue to his trust."

He smiled at the warmth of my defence.

"You are recovering yourself, Miss Keate. That last remark was quite in your normal manner."

And at that Olma Flynn tugged my sleeve.

"Will you O. K. the charts, Miss Keate?" Her eyes were round with curiosity and she cast a speculative glance toward Room 18.

Well, that is about all.

The staff doctors met that morning, and the board of directors, and were most generous in their assistance. It was not long before we were fully equipped with resident doctors and reorganized.

Our new head doctor has a wife of Anglo-Saxon ancestry who has filled the cottage with chintz-covered furniture and muslin curtains, and likes to head committees. She has a nosy disposition and we don't get along well. We have two new internes, too; fresh-cheeked boys whom Miss Dotty pets something scandalous.

Dr. Balman developed an infection in the bruise on his cheek and lived only a short while. Corole and Hajek disappeared and have not been heard of since, though lately a report came to me that a woman much resembling Corole and dressed very beautifully had been seen at a European pleasure resort where she made large sums of money gambling. I judged that Corole was falling into soft spots as usual, unhampered by a conscience.

Maida and Jim left for Russia very soon after the events that I have herein recorded took place. I hear from them every so often, long letters full of news and snapshots.

I see Lance O'Leary once in a while, too, and indeed, have given him some slight help on a case or two.

But for the most part I am still at St. Ann's, going about my business as usual, save that I miss a pair of steel-blue eyes.

And I avoid the closed, mysterious door of Room 18.